Daughters OF JARED

Daughters OF JARED

A NOVEL

H.B. MOORE

Covenant Communications, Inc.

Cover image *Woman* © Ekaterina Solovieva, iStockphotography.com

Cover design copyright © 2012 by Covenant Communications, Inc.

Published by Covenant Communications, Inc.
American Fork, Utah

Printed in the United States of America
First Printing: May 2012

18 17 16 15 14 13 12   10 9 8 7 6 5 4 3 2 1

ISBN 13: 978-1-60861-395-3

PRAISE FOR H.B. MOORE'S BOOKS

"[In *Ammon*], Ammon's acts have become even more intriguing through H.B. Moore's creative hands and mind. Ammon is tested and stretched between hate-filled enemies and driving imperatives. As always, Moore leads us into the hearts and minds of heroes, creating a captivating and inspiring tale."

—S. Kent Brown
Emeritus professor of ancient scripture, BYU

"[*Alma the Younger*] is showered with interesting situations and deep betrayals that keep the reader riveted even though he or she may already know the outcome of the tale. Through imaginative conjecture, Moore designs a weighted and foolish life for the young dissenter that eventually thrusts him into a head-to-head battle with the spiritual leaders in a fight for his own soul."

—Melissa DeMoux
Deseret News

"Reading [*Women of the Book of Mormon*], I was edified by my role in the lives of my family. A lot of what I do is background and foundational—but it matters. Both for their growth and mine. I can't wait until my daughters ask why there is so little mention of women in the Book of Mormon. This book is a powerful witness to the fact that life is hard for everyone—that is how we become strong; it is how we learn to carry the yoke of being a daughter of God."

—Josi S. Kilpack
Author of the Sadie Hoffmiller Mystery Series

"*Alma* has it all: vibrant characters, danger, spiritual challenges, and bittersweet joy. Moore has created an epic tale that's simply impossible to put down."

—Jason F. Wright
New York Times Bestselling Author

"[*Alma* is] an exciting and faith-promoting tale—the Book of Mormon in 3D and technicolor."

—Richard H. Cracroft
BYU Magazine

"H. B. Moore takes the reader on an incredible journey of a man who makes the ultimate sacrifice. *Abinadi* is a historically rich, well-researched, poignant account of one of the most influential prophets in the Book of Mormon. Moore's creativity, mixed with the heart of Mesoamerican culture, brings new insights to the influence that the prophet Abinadi had on generations to come."

—Dian Thomas
#1 *New York Times* Bestselling Author

"In the first three volumes of her [Out of Jerusalem] series, H.B. Moore showed that she could create a view of an ancient world that combines the best scholarship with a lively imagination. She does a fine job of walking the tricky line between faithfulness to the scriptures and creative storytelling. She opened up the hearts of her characters in both remarkably touching and authentic ways. In this fourth and final volume, [*Land of Inheritance*], she does all of that, as well as writes one of the most exciting adventure tales I have read in a while."

—Andrew Hall
Association of Mormon Letters

To my daughter, Kara, who, from day one,
has shown an incredible capacity for resiliency.

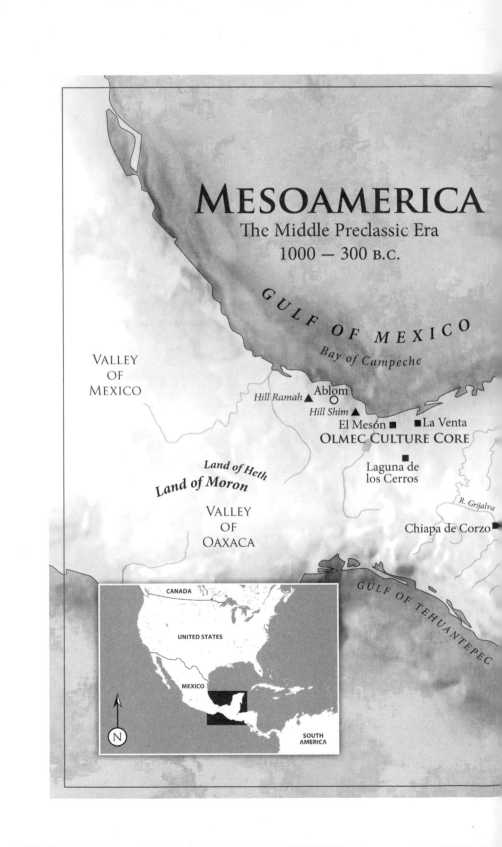

MESOAMERICA
The Middle Preclassic Era
1000 – 300 B.C.

GULF OF MEXICO

Bay of Campeche

VALLEY OF MEXICO

Hill Ramah ▲ Ablom ○

Hill Shim ▲

El Mesón ■   ■La Venta

OLMEC CULTURE CORE

■ Laguna de los Cerros

Land of Heth

Land of Moron

VALLEY OF OAXACA

R. Grijalva

Chiapa de Corzo ■

CANADA

UNITED STATES

MEXICO

SOUTH AMERICA

GULF OF TEHUANTEPEC

N

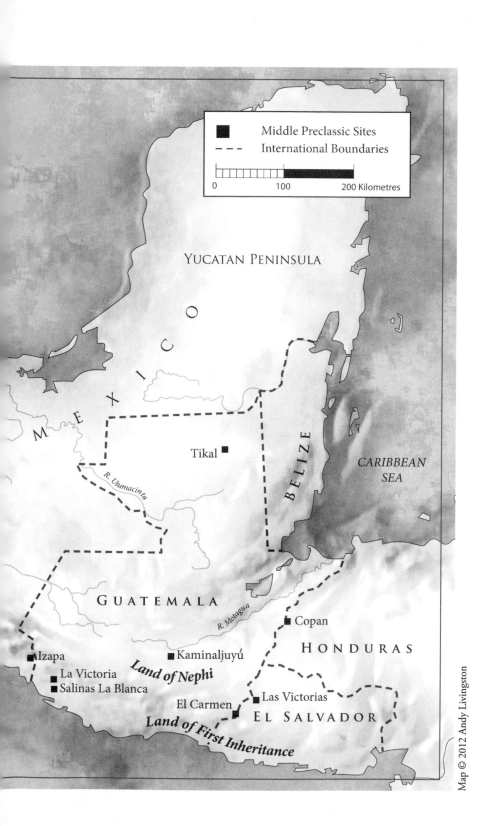

Middle Preclassic Sites
International Boundaries

0   100   200 Kilometres

YUCATAN PENINSULA

M E X I C O

Tikal ■

R. Usumacinta

BELIZE

CARIBBEAN SEA

GUATEMALA

R. Motagua

Copan ■

HONDURAS

Izapa ■
La Victoria ■
Salinas La Blanca ■

Kaminaljuyú ■

Land of Nephi

El Carmen ■   Las Victorias ■

EL SALVADOR

Land of First Inheritance

Map © 2012 Andy Livingston

PREFACE

THE BOOK OF ETHER IS fraught with danger and intrigue. Kingdoms rise and fall; family members are betrayed through secret combinations. Fathers kill sons, brothers fight against brothers, and women plot revenge.

Jared (the second) gained his throne the first time by rebelling against his father, King Omer, and by flattering the people (Ether 8:2). After usurping his father's power, Jared sent him into captivity to quell possibilities of him rising to power again. But Omer continued to have children, and two of his sons, Esrom and Coriantumr, determined to win back the throne for their father. They defeated their older brother, Jared, in battle, and Jared lost his ill-won throne (Ether 8:5–6).

This is where *Daughters of Jared* begins.

When one of the daughters of Jared learns about the ancient conspiracies of secret combinations through the records of her own people, the Jaredites, she decides to instigate a scheme to put her father back on the throne (Ether 8:8–9). Except this scheme calls for the assassination of her grandfather, King Omer.

Daughters of Jared becomes a classic story of evil begetting evil, a tale of both warning and hope. The story is told through the younger daughter's viewpoint as she interacts with her sister, who will stop at nothing to gain power, even sacrificing her integrity in the name of a secret combination, and who will eventually become queen of the Jaredites.

It is no wonder that, centuries later, Moroni refrained from elaborating on the specific oaths, for he rightly feared the downfall of future peoples who might read the records of Ether, though secret combinations have been around since the beginning of time. Cain was the first to fall under Satan's influence and enter into a covenant with Satan (Moses 5:38, 49). This covenant became the beginning of the secret combinations that have withstood the passage of time and societies throughout the last several thousand years. Ether 8:25 still rings true today: "Whoso . . . seeketh to overthrow the freedom of all lands, nations, and countries . . . bringeth to pass the destruction of all people, for it is built up by the devil, who is the father of all lies."

Great and terrible are the consequences of joining a secret combination, as Jared's daughter painfully learns in a very personal manner when she experiences the devastating consequence of Satan's "power upon the hearts of the children of men" (Ether 8:26).

Now the daughter of Jared being exceedingly expert, and seeing the sorrows of her father, thought to devise a plan whereby she could redeem the kingdom unto her father.
—Ether 8:8

CHAPTER 1

Tenth Century bc

"WHAT HAVE I DONE?" MY sister asks me. Her arms are striped with deep claw marks from her own fingernails, fingernails that had once been shaped, stained, and etched with delicate gold designs. They are now broken and tattered—just as my sister's life has become.

I stare at her blood filling the cracks in the stone garden path.

"Naiva," she whispers, her dark eyes capturing mine. "How could I allow them to send my son to the borderland prison? He is everything to me. There's nothing—" Her voice breaks. "There's nothing left of my heart now; it's disappeared into my soul."

"Hush now," I say, though I doubt my sister still has a soul. I look away from her bloody arms as she stretches her hands out, reaching for me. I don't need to see her wild eyes, her unruly long hair soiled with ashes of grief, to know her pain. Nor do I need to see her lips twist with pleas of agony. Her grief and agony are mine too.

No one returns from the borderland—especially no one sent there by the king—even if that person is the king's own son. Rumors have already reached us. My sister's son is being starved.

I pull her into my arms and hold on, trying to soak up her anguish in a small way, something I've done a hundred times over.

He will be fine. He will live, I want to promise her, but I know my words hold no power. If I could command as the Lord does, I would not be crouching next to my sister in the garden, like we're fugitives, on the day we discovered her son is being starved to death by her own husband.

The torchlights begin to flicker out in the small courtyard near the garden we have hidden ourselves away in. The night is thick with darkness, nearly as thick as the silence in our palace of mourning.

To the people in the land of Heth, my sister is known as Queen Asherah. To me, she is simply Ash. My throat tightens as I think of my nephew and what he must feel right now, in a place we cannot reach to comfort him. He is only a child of twelve years. Fresh tears nearly break out when I envision his beautiful face.

Ash trembles inside my arms. Only then do I realize she is whispering again. "I have failed him. What mother lets her own son be tortured and starved by his father?"

I wish for words of solace, yet they will not come. If I can only find a way to save her son, a way to change the king's mind . . . But I know he will not change his mind. He is fear itself. Neither my sister nor I dare approach him since he has banished us from court. There are the other children's lives to consider. There are our own.

Her son, the crown prince, is as good as dead. And Ash has no one to blame but herself. She knew what her husband was when she married him.

The anger and grief inside me build, and desperation rushes in. "I'll find a way to free your son. I'll take him somewhere where Akish can't find him."

"No. He'll catch you both," my sister says, her voice gaining strength. "And then he'll kill you as well." She turns her face, swollen from tears, toward mine. "Don't leave me, Naiva. I couldn't bear this life without you. I have already lost too much." Her voice falters.

We have *all* lost too much, and we are afraid to fight any more.

"Naiva." My sister's voice breaks into my thoughts. "Do you think my son suffers in his last hours? Do you think the gods are there to comfort him?"

I flinch at her plural usage of *god*. Will she ever give up her idols? Each one of them has betrayed her. I cannot answer right away, for I cannot lie to my sister. I have never lied to her, even though I've been beaten, banished, and imprisoned for treason . . . all for telling my sister, the queen, the truth.

"The Lord will comfort him," I whisper. "I have not stopped my prayers for one moment." On any other day, Ash might bristle at my mention of the God I worship, but tonight she accepts my words.

"Do you think your God will allow my black soul into heaven?" she says.

I hesitate, and it's as if Ash knows why I cannot answer. She collapses against me, a wail building in her chest, turning into a high-pitched keening.

The sound of a woman aching for her lost soul and a child whom she will not be reunited with in heaven.

I cling to her as tears finally break free onto my face, for I know the things my sister has done will be impossible for the Lord to forgive.

When we die, my sister and I will spend eternity apart. She, in hell. And when she arrives there, alone and afraid, my already fractured heart will at last break in two.

CHAPTER 2

14 Years Earlier

MY HANDS TREMBLED FROM EXCITEMENT and anticipation as I draped the embroidered shawl over Ash's bare shoulders.

"Hurry, Naiva!" she demanded, impatient as always.

"Nearly finished." As I dabbed orange-blossom oil on her wrists and inner arms, I immediately forgave my sister for her demanding tone. Tonight I was just as excited to attend the reception in honor of the visiting dignitary—Akish, son of Kimnor, from the city of Nehor. Rumors throughout our city said that Akish was very wealthy and very handsome. He was also a friend to our grandfather, King Omer. A new dignitary meant new men, new stories, and new hope.

The sooner my sister was ready, the sooner I could turn to my own preparation. Ash's needs always came before mine. They always had, and as the oldest daughter with the power to choose her husband and future king to the throne, they always would.

I didn't mind. One only had to take a single look at my sister to know she was born to be a queen. The position boasted itself in her mannerisms and very appearance: gold-specked eyes, rich black hair, flawless skin the color of topaz from the high mountains, a long and delicate neck, and a musical voice that stopped merchants in their tracks at the market.

"Come now," Ash said. "We can't be late for the introduction." She turned a critical eye on me. "Are you wearing that?"

I had purposely chosen a plain green tunic with only a single jade necklace for adornment. *I must not outshine my sister. She will be the focus tonight.*

"At least wear the earrings," Ash said, holding out golden rings.

I hesitated. Ash had insisted I get my ears pierced so I could wear the great circles of gold. But my lobes had never healed properly and continued to fester if I wore earrings.

Ash never missed anything, and with a sigh, she said, "Here. Let me do it."

Before I could protest, she'd pricked my ear with one of the gold loops.

"Ow!" I cried out. It pinched then grew hot, and I knew my ear would throb the rest of the evening.

"Hush," she said, pricking my second ear. I bit my lip, trying to stave off the sharp pain.

"All finished." Her voice was triumphant, her pitch higher than normal as she gazed at me with shining eyes. She grabbed my hand and pulled me toward the door. A female servant stepped aside to let us pass.

Music filtered through the hallways, increasing my anticipation. I had only been able to attend evening functions for the past year. At seventeen, I was nearly old enough to be officially introduced at court. Ash had been presented four years before, when she was fifteen, because of her status as heir. Since then, she had spent her evenings in the company of powerful politicians, artists, merchants, and clothiers, unlike my evenings spent painting on vellum.

Tonight was a special exception, and I was allowed to join the banquet— my father had requested my presence. Not even our younger brothers, Shule and Ethem, were allowed to join in.

"Can you feel it?" Ash clamped her hand onto my arm.

"Yes," I said. She didn't have to explain the sense of wonder as we neared the main hall. In my mind I saw the vibrant colors, tasted the exquisite food my father could no longer afford, and felt the heat of the eyes of the men in the room—all looking at my sister. At nineteen, it was unusual that she hadn't married yet. She claimed she was still young.

"I'll choose my own husband in a year or two," she'd told my father more than once. "And he'll eventually rule as king by my side. We'll become the most powerful kingdom in all the land."

Father continued to agree, for what else might he say? No one dared to speak as boldly as my sister. No one dared to point out that there was no longer a kingdom, that our father had lost the war, and that we were at the mercy of our loyals, whose generosity kept food on our table.

Tonight, our misfortunes would be as good as hidden in a corner as we entertained Akish with borrowed money. Like all second-born children, my inheritance was less than half of the firstborn's, which was presently nothing, unless my father could somehow raise a new army and defeat his brothers, Esrom and Coriantumr, and reclaim the kingdom from his father, Omer.

My sister and I stepped into the great hall together, arm in arm. The dancing troupe had already begun its performance, but Akish and his entourage hadn't arrived yet.

"Where are they?" Ash whispered.

I looked around—there were no new faces peering at us. The men of the court watched the young women as they danced together, swirling their full skirts of reds, blues, and greens. None of them compared to Ash's dancing prowess. I was a fair dancer, but like all things between me and my sister, I took a step back to allow her the accolades.

Father sat in his old throne chair, a goblet in hand, dressed in a ratted robe that had seen better days and a tunic already stained with wine. My father was only a faint image of the skilled warrior he had once been, and his stomach protruded from the excess of wine he drank when he was having what he called a "dark day"—which was almost every day. His dark reddish beard needed a trim, but I would not be the one to mention it. Tonight his usually dour face was smiling. My focus went to the object of his pleasure. The storyteller, Tirzah, a woman I'd seen about the market frequently, stood in front of him. Her hair was swept up into an embroidered scarf, and nearly a dozen bracelets lined her arms, likely gifts from her varied audiences. As we walked closer, Tirzah's voice pitched above the music.

"The ancient King Ahah was a hunter among hunters," Tirzah said. "He traveled to the wilderness with a thousand men. They drove the wild beasts forth and formed a circle around the panicked animals, forcing them into an enclosure, where King Ahah could then pick the best game."

By her elaborate gestures, she looked as if she were doing her best to entertain the sullen king—a difficult feat.

It took only a few more seconds before the court became aware of our presence, or more accurately, of Ash's. The women bowed and whispered behind jeweled hands, the men ogled, and our father stood, clapping his hands together for attention.

His smile was faint when his gaze passed over me, but it brightened as he looked at Ash. There had always been a strong bond between them, something that was hard to define and impossible to penetrate. After the death of our mother, I'd felt like the unnoticed child around my father. My sister more than made up for the neglect, but it still brought a pang to my chest as I witnessed the favoritism in such a public setting.

I am the second born, I reminded myself again. *It is to be expected. Why should my life be different than any other second born?*

The court hushed as our father stepped down from his throne. "Behold, my daughters."

Gazes stayed on Ash as she smiled generously and tipped her head in acknowledgment. Nothing was required of me since no one looked at me anyway. The music started up as Ash left my side, mingling with the court guests. Tonight she'd sweet-talk them, and tomorrow our coffers would be full again, and we'd live in elegance for another moon.

I crossed the room and sat on a cushion near my father's throne. He didn't acknowledge me, for his attention was back on the storyteller. I was content being invisible; in fact, I preferred it. There was nothing more interesting than watching the expressions of people as they spoke to my sister. Their faces transformed from the harshness of their labors earned during the day to the absolute pleasure of being in the presence of someone ethereal.

For my sister was just that—a goddess. Her name, Asherah, was the same name for the goddess of heaven. A large statue of the goddess stood at the entrance of the hall, as if presiding over all the events, honoring both the goddess of heaven and the queen-to-be.

The music suddenly faded, and everyone turned toward the entrance.

A tall man entered, flanked by a half dozen other men, all dressed in fine feathered capes. Bands of leather adorned their arms, and thick necklaces of gold lay against their bare chests.

My father immediately rose, and Tirzah stepped aside as the men approached. I stood as well and backed away, a tremor of anticipation spreading through my body. I couldn't take my eyes off the men as they walked toward us, their heads high, their eyes missing nothing, their bodies tanned and taut.

A movement to my left told me my sister was at my side, but I still stared at the men. The tall one stopped and bowed to my father. "Your Highness, King Jared, we are grateful for the invitation," he said in a loud, clear voice.

"Welcome." My father's face glowed with satisfaction. He was rarely addressed as king by anyone outside our loyal circle. Akish had just paid my father the highest honor. "Welcome to my home. I apologize for our humble state."

Akish stepped forward and gripped my father's hand. The man's dark beard was cut short, and it glistened with oil. His brows were thick but well-arched over deep-set eyes, and his hair was cropped close to his head, though curls turned about his ears. I understood the rumors of him being handsome. He had perhaps the longest eyelashes I'd ever seen on a man.

Next to me, my sister let out a sigh, capturing Akish's attention. I wondered if she'd done it on purpose to get him to notice her, though no man would have gone very long without seeing her.

His eyes swept past my sister then stopped on me.

A jolt went through me. I wasn't used to being anyone's focus. Akish stared at me like a man stares at a woman, like I'd seen men stare at my sister. My face certainly flamed red, if not deep scarlet. A touch on my arm from my sister broke my gaze and, thankfully, broke Akish's too, for the next instant he began speaking to my father as if he'd never looked at me.

"He's handsome," my sister whispered in my ear. "And he's a friend of our grandfather's. I'm sure he has incredible stories to tell." She continued to speak, but I hardly heard her. My gaze kept drifting back to Akish. Despite efforts to not stare, I noticed more and more things about him. His long, tapered fingers, the jade ring on his right hand, the way his gold necklace reflected against his muscled chest . . .

My throat went dry, and my heart pounded as if I'd just run to the hills and back. What was wrong with me? I blinked and tore my gaze from Akish, looking at the other men. Unlike Akish, they watched my sister. They hadn't made the mistake of wasting their time looking at me. These men were normal, like the men we encountered every day, like the men who would give their right arms to please my sister.

Then my father spoke again, his deep voice cutting through my thoughts as he introduced us. "Naiva is a fine artist. Since she is the second daughter, her skills in art might provide her a living one day," he said with a chuckle.

In truth, I should have been pleased at the backward, yet rare, compliment from my father, but I was mortified. Akish looked at me again, and for some reason, I wanted him to think I was an accomplished woman—skilled in all the things my sister had been taught—and that I would never stoop to earning a living selling paintings in the market.

"Of course, you've heard of Asherah, my eldest daughter." The pride oozed from my father's lips.

Ash stepped forward boldly, though none of the men seemed taken aback.

Akish's lips formed a smile that was more than polite, but still, his gaze flickered back to me, and I was again on fire with the attention.

I was stunned. A man who wasn't instantly besotted with my sister was a rarity—an impossibility if I hadn't seen it for myself. I prayed that my sister didn't notice. Her temper was worse than most methods of execution a king might dream up.

Akish stepped forward and took my sister's hand, bringing it to his full lips. She smiled up at him and let her hand linger. Behind her gaze was a challenge, a game Ash liked to play. But instead of becoming cowed and besotted, Akish returned her stare, strength in his gaze. When he released her and straightened, his eyes went to me again, and before I could move, his hand grasped mine.

I practically felt my father's and sister's astonishment mirroring my own as Akish kissed my hand, that of a second daughter, a daughter who held no significance in the family except to serve the eldest. His lips were warm, and his beard brushed against my skin ever so softly. He smelled of earth and spices. Until this moment, I had never noticed one man's scent from another.

His fingers tightened on mine for an instant before he released me, or maybe I imagined it. I wasn't sure. No man had ever kissed my hand like I was a queen before.

CHAPTER 3

My sister didn't speak to me for two days after Akish and his men left. She had noticed the special attention Akish had shown me, but even worse, the whole court had noticed. My father had tried to make light of it, though he, too, watched me closely now.

On the third day, Ash came into my chamber with a smile on her face and acted as if she had never been upset with me. I knew she was up to something.

"Eat with me," Ash begged. She was usually cross in the mornings and preferred to take the first meal by herself. She tugged my hand, pulling me onto the veranda that overlooked the gardens. Two male servants quickly disappeared when we arrived. Both of the servants were borrowed, coming in the mornings to work then returning to their masters' homes to finish out the rest of the day. The meal was already laid out for one, but my sister insisted I sit.

We lounged on the cushions and bit into the juicy guava. I watched her carefully. "Is Father well?"

"He is sad again," Ash said, almost to herself. She looked out over the garden, her face glowing in the morning light as the sun warmed the eastern sky.

"Father's been sad for many years," I said in my matter-of-fact way. "His two loves are gone. Our mother is dead, and his kingdom is lost. We, his daughters, are his only solace now."

Her dark eyes turned to me. "We can't bring our mother back. Yet . . ." Her gaze was far away again.

"Ash? What are you thinking?"

She stood and stepped down from the veranda. I followed as she moved aimlessly through the garden. When I reached Ash, she stopped and faced me. I recoiled at the determination I saw in her eyes. My stomach tightened, and I regretted the fruit I'd eaten.

"Sorcery won't bring our mother back, no matter what the oracle says," I said. "And it's too dangerous to try."

"I'm not thinking about Mother." Her eyes narrowed. "We must help our father get his kingdom back."

"How?" I said. "By raising a militia? Going against Grandfather again? We've already discussed this. Grandfather is more powerful than ever. Our loyals will be killed on the first day of battle, and then we'll have nothing and nowhere to live."

Ash grabbed my arm and leaned close enough that I smelled the cinnamon in her hair. "I've been reading records from many generations ago and have studied their ancient conspiracies. If my plan works, we'll each have our *own* palace." Her words came out in a rush as her voice rose in pitch. "Every person in the land will bow down to us. And I will be queen. Father will be restored to his former glory. There will be no war, no loyals killed."

"How can that be? Who will you marry that is powerful enough to win the kingdom back?" I pulled away from her, afraid of her frenzied speech, afraid of what I might hear. War meant loss of life, grieving in the roads, and danger for the royal family.

She straightened, her gaze exultant. "Come with me, dear sister. Listen to what I have to tell Father." She hurried away, and it was all I could do to keep up with her. She passed the supper table without a glance and entered our home. It was not difficult to locate Father in the mornings, for he usually stayed in bed until midday. He preferred to stay up late at night, surrounding himself with entertainment.

A single guard was stationed outside his room. At the sight of us, the guard squared his shoulders and bowed deeply.

"I must speak with the king," Ash said.

The guard knew better than to dissuade my sister, no matter what the hour. He opened the door and called into the room. "Her Highness seeks an audience."

Father did not respond, so Ash pushed past the guard. We found my father just waking in his large platform bed, bleary eyed. He smiled as Ash poured a generous amount of wine into a goblet by his bedside.

"Here, Father, it will help you wake." She handed the goblet to him and waited for him to take his first swallow.

"Why is the king still in bed on such a beautiful morning?" Ash said.

If anyone but my sister had spoken those words, our father would have been furious. For his favorite daughter, he simply chuckled. "The nights have been very long lately, as you know, my dear."

"I'll tell you why," she said in a sweet but careful voice. "Because my father has been wrongfully forced to give up his throne. My father, who won the kingdom because of the love of the people, has been enslaved in his homeland by his own brothers, treated as a mere pauper when he should be revered by all. You should be wearing furs and feathered capes, not thin robes. You should have a vast selection of jewelry and headdresses to choose from for every meal."

My father sat up straighter in his bed, his attention purely focused on his beloved daughter. The determination in her eyes was plain, and it demanded his attention.

"The people have not changed." Ash took my father's hand in hers. "They want you as their king, but they are afraid to go against Grandfather. We must give them what they truly want." She kissed his hand. "And what they want is *you*."

Father's eyes were bright with pleasure. "How do you know they want me?"

"It's whispered in every corner, by every set of lips." She kissed his other hand. "I have heard their pleas more than a thousand times. The people must have their wish."

"How will we gain back the throne?" Father said in a reverent voice.

"Do you not remember how King Shule obtained his kingdom more than once?"

I stared at my sister. Although I'd spent fewer hours in learning than her, I knew the old accounts well. Shule had battled his brother Corihor and had given the kingdom back to their father, Kib. When Kib bestowed the kingship to Shule, his nephew Noah rose up and battled for the kingdom. Later, a son of Shule crept into the house of Noah and killed him.

I exhaled, my heart thumping. Every story that included the kingdom of Shule involved battles or secret murders.

My father released Ash's hand and threw off his covers. He swung his legs over the bed and stood, drawing himself up to his full height. "What are you saying?"

Ash drew back, a twisted smile on her face. "The kings of old obtained their kingdoms through secret strategies. And I have just that—" She lowered her voice conspiratorially—"*a secret plan.*" She knelt before my father and took his hand. "Soon, Father—soon every citizen will kneel before you as I do now."

Father gripped her fingers, his eyes burning with excitement. "Tell me your idea."

"First," Ash said, "we must invite Akish back to our home. I have made some inquiries and discovered he will be the ideal man to fulfill my plan."

My head snapped in Ash's direction. How could she involve Akish in her plan to restore my father's throne? My heart pounded, both with fear and exhilaration. I couldn't wait to see Akish again, but what did my sister want with *him*? She'd always had her way in everything. I was afraid. Afraid of what she might do.

What would it be now?

* * *

The week passed in a flurry as preparations were made for the arrival of Akish's party once again. Ash kept our few house servants busy from dawn till the darkest hours of the night, scouring the floors, painting the chipped wooden walls, repairing the rugs, and preparing food. My father seemed almost jovial, and his laughter frequently rang throughout the halls. It was almost as if Mother were still alive and my father had his kingdom back.

On the afternoon that Akish was to arrive, my sister came to my bed-chamber.

I quickly hid the painting I was working on by turning over the vellum on the table. The paint would smear, but I didn't want my sister to see it in case she recognized the man in the picture.

Through all of the preparations, I had not questioned my sister, for every time I thought of Akish, my face heated, and I didn't want her to notice. To speak of him would surely bring a bright blush to my cheeks. But thoughts of him wouldn't leave my mind, and I had to dispel them somehow. That's why I had tried to paint him, unsuccessfully, many times. Charred remains of various images of Akish's face lay in the cooking room's fire pit.

Ash didn't seem to notice my haste and only smiled when I looked up. "We must go to the ponds and wash ourselves."

We collected perfumes and oil vials and carried them in a satchel to the ponds. Our home was secluded from the rest of the city, surrounded by trees and paths that twisted their way to the hills. We set out on the path leading to our favorite pond.

The brilliant sky and warm sun lightened my mood, and it matched my sister's as we walked, arms linked.

"You and Father will love my idea," Ash said.

"Will you not tell me yet?" I peered over at her. Ash's hair had come undone and now trailed down her back, reaching her waist.

"Soon." She laughed. "I can't wait to see the look on your face."

We reached the clearing. The pond was brilliant green in the afternoon sun, a backdrop to the lazing insects above it. She let go of my arm, stripped off her tunic, and jumped into the water.

"Ash!" I cried out. "Someone might come along."

She dove under the water then came up, her hair wet, her smile victorious.

"Come on," she said. "No one will see."

I waded in more slowly, still wearing my under-tunic.

"Oh, Naiva, you must learn to have some fun." She splashed me, but I ignored her.

I lowered myself into the water until I was soaked up to my neck. In one giant movement, Ash flew at me and dunked me.

I came up sputtering. The battle was on. I dove and locked onto her legs, dragging her down until we were both submerged. We wrestled in the silent underworld—everything seemed to move in slow motion. Our hair billowed out, our limbs graceful, our eyes wide.

Then I burst to the surface, gasping for air, Ash right behind me. Our energy spent, we floated until Ash said, "Fetch the oils for our hair."

I stole out of the pond, on alert—I'd never trusted that we might be completely alone. The paths to the ponds were well traveled in the evenings but not so much during the day. Ash seemed to have no such concern. I removed an oil vial from the satchel and joined Ash in the water again. We rubbed the oil into each other's hair then rinsed it out. The residue remained, which would make our hair soft and shiny when it dried.

I climbed onto the shore and rubbed oil on my arms and legs then lay down in the grass. As I closed my eyes, the sun warmed me and dried my clothes. I was drowsy with relaxation when Ash came to sit beside me.

I peeked at her. She had pulled on her under-tunic and was rifling through the satchel. "This one," she said, handing over pomegranate oil. "Rub it into my back."

I complied, and after her shoulders and neck glistened, she rubbed her own arms and legs. I lay back down and breathed in the sweet scent of pomegranate and listened to the buzzing insects and the gentle breeze that swayed the bordering trees.

I sensed the movement before I actually heard any change in sound. Alert, I sat up abruptly, looking toward the path that led uphill, parallel with the river. No one. Then I saw movement in the trees straight across from us. "Ash," I whispered, reaching out to her. She bolted upright next to me, clutching at her damp tunic.

A man in a faded kilt stepped out of the trees. His beard was long and scraggly, his body filthy. His eyes were wide, his mouth open, as if he was just as surprised to see us. Perhaps he was only looking for a place to bathe. At least that's what I thought until I saw the curved dagger gripped in his hand.

CHAPTER 4

Ash screamed.

I scrambled to my feet, pulling her with me. A thousand thoughts went through my mind, all laced with panic. The man stepped forward, holding his dagger out in front of him, his eyes shining wildly. Ash cowered behind me and screamed again.

We stepped back together, almost stumbling. My throat had tightened, making it impossible to speak or to scream.

He looked from me to my sister then smiled, revealing stumps for teeth. Perspiration broke out on my neck.

"Go away!" Ash cried out.

Something broke inside me, and my voice came back. "Leave us alone." I stooped and picked up a rock as big as my fist. "Stay back!"

"Our brothers are just down the path." Ash gripped my arm with a trembling hand.

The man tilted his head, his leering eyes sending another jolt of panic through me. "The sons of Jared are no more than boys."

I felt as if I'd already been pierced through with the man's dagger. He knew who we were.

"Our guards are within earshot," Ash said.

"We'll have to make haste then." He lunged forward.

I threw the rock at him, but it fell short. Ash tugged me, and we turned and ran toward the downhill path. She stumbled in front of me, and we collided, both of us tumbling to the ground.

"Hurry," Ash yelled as we climbed to our feet and started running again. But the man had reached us, and he leapt on me as Ash continued running.

He pulled me down, his hands clawing at my flailing arms and legs. The metal of the dagger, hot and sharp, touched my neck.

I stopped fighting and nearly stopped breathing as his other hand clamped around my neck, pressing me against the rocky ground.

Ash screamed again.

Hit him with something, I wanted to shout at her, but I was mute as I stared into the man's wild eyes. His beard brushed my face, and the blade of the dagger pressed deeper against my skin until I feared it would penetrate.

Darkness pushed against the edges of my mind and threatened to overcome me completely. My vision blurred as his impossibly strong grip tightened around my neck. Just as the scene around me faded to gray, something exploded above me. Blackness claimed my mind, encompassing me in absolute silence, and my body felt heavy, as if a great weight pressed upon it, literally pushing me into the earth.

Then the weight lifted, and the black dissipated into gray again. When the gray cleared to blue, I realized my eyes were open and staring at the sky. The sounds rushed back with full force. Ash was crying and yelling, but there were other sounds too—men shouting, commanding.

Was there a whole band of them? Would they carry us off into the hills or leave us for dead? Were they enemies of my father? Did they work for my grandfather?

"She's awake." Ash's voice.

I opened my mouth, but when I tried to speak, my throat felt as if it had been set aflame.

Someone lifted me, and I almost fainted again with the motion. I blinked, forcing myself to stay conscious. There was Ash, peering anxiously at me. Then another pair of eyes—blacker than the night.

Akish.

Where had he come from? He must have heard our screams and come to our aid. But how had he been near the ponds? They were in the opposite direction of Nehor. My neck throbbed fiercely, and the questions continued to dart through my mind, but I suddenly felt tired— so exhausted that I closed my eyes, and as Akish carried me in his capable arms, I dreamed of him kissing my hand again.

* * *

Akish held out his hand to me, never taking his eyes from mine. I reached for him and shivered as our hands touched. Then we were dancing together. I fit into his arms easily and he into mine. Somewhere in the background sat my sister and my father. They were angry, but I didn't care. For tonight, all I saw was Akish. And all he saw was me.

The warmth of Akish's touch faded as I became aware of my burning throat, both inside and out. My thirst was fiercer than I'd ever felt before, and I almost couldn't catch a breath. I opened my eyes as the image of Akish faded, my heart rate increasing as I thought of him watching over my bedside. But the eyes that now watched me weren't black like Akish's. They were the most extraordinary color I'd ever seen—the color of leaves in the deepest of forests. Green and brown intermingling, as if they battled for space.

The eyes belonged to a man, a complete stranger. The burning in my throat spread to my chest as it constricted in panic. The man seemed to understand my confusion and fear, and he reached out to touch my shoulder.

"I'm a healer," he said. "Your father asked me to watch over you and let him know when you awaken."

The healers I knew were elderly, thin, and pale from sitting hunched over in their huts, studying herbs and making poultices. This man was built like a warrior, with thick arms, broad shoulders, and a short beard. His dark hair was long but tied back with a leather band. Something about the shape of his face was familiar, but I knew I had never seen him before.

"My sister . . ." I croaked.

His hand was still on my shoulder. "She's well. Frightened, but no injuries." His gaze searched mine. "You were fortunate that my brother heard the screams. We tease him that he has ears like a dog, and this once, it paid off."

"Brother?" I whispered.

"Akish," the man said, his eyes assessing me.

The warmth returned to my body, and if I hadn't been in so much pain, I might have smiled. It *had* been Akish. It hadn't been a dream. He had really carried me to safety.

"How—" I winced, my throat searing.

The man fetched a cup of wine. He gently lifted my head and put the cup to my lips. I took a sip, trying not to wince. I leaned back again, closing my eyes briefly, if only to cut off the intense gaze of this man who was Akish's brother. He hadn't been with Akish on the previous visit. I would have remembered. His physique would be hard to miss.

"Rest, Naiva," the man said. "Your neck and throat will take some time to heal. You shouldn't try to speak unless necessary." He paused, and I opened my eyes, captured again in the unusual color that reminded me of the forest, and again wondered how this man was a gentle healer when he looked as if he could command an army.

"I must go now to tell your father you've awakened. Your sister and Akish will want to know as well." He stood and left the room. I felt an unexplained pang of emptiness when he left. I couldn't understand it.

Maybe it was because he'd mentioned my sister and Akish in the same phrase, as if it were natural to mention them together.

CHAPTER 5

ASH ABSOLUTELY GLOWED WHEN SHE entered my chamber. Even through my exhaustion, I noticed something had changed, something had happened to her in the time I'd been in bed. She rushed to my side and clasped my hand.

"You're awake." Her voice was breathless. "When Levi told me, I hardly dared to hope. But here you are!"

Levi. I hadn't even asked his name.

My sister turned to someone standing in the doorway. "You were right. Your brother is an excellent healer."

It was too painful to turn my head to see the man in the doorway. Akish stepped into the room as my sister gushed over me.

His eyes held mine, and I felt as if I were about to burst. There was the same intensity, the same power I'd felt in his gaze the first time I'd met him. I wondered if he felt it as well or if I was just ignorant of relationships between men and women.

Ash took his hand, leading him to the bed. My eyes went to their intertwined fingers, and my stomach formed into a knot. My sister had spent most of her young adult life flirting with men, teasing them, asking favors, but never had she been so casually affectionate. Why did she have to be so toward Akish?

"Thank you," I said, though it hurt to speak.

He released my sister's hand and knelt by my bed, totally oblivious to her surprised stare. He caressed my palms. I had the sudden urge to wrap my arms about his neck. "How are you feeling?" His voice carried thick concern.

Ash cut in. "I was terrified for you. When that man started strangling you, I was about ready to rip the dagger out of his hand, when who should come? Akish!" She knelt next to him, her face beaming as she clutched his arm. "He arrived just in time. He and his men—they are truly heroes. There will be a big feast tomorrow in celebration."

One side of Akish's mouth lifted into a smile, but his eyes were still on me. He released my hands and touched my neck. A mixture of pain and pleasure coursed through me at his touch. I didn't want him to know the pain, since I didn't want him to move away. I wished that my sister, for once, would leave the room.

"I know the man who hurt you," Akish said in a low voice, his fingers moving from my neck to my shoulder then lifting, taking the heat with him. "He was in prison for stealing. Was probably released recently or had escaped." His eyes narrowed. "He won't touch you again."

"Is he in prison again?" I whispered.

"He's dead."

Akish's expression told me I didn't want to know the details. My father entered the room, his entourage with him. Akish rose and stepped back, allowing my father to peer down on me. "We owe Akish a great deal of gratitude. He has preserved my daughter's honor." He turned to my sister. "It's not fitting for a queen-to-be to travel without escorts."

"Yes, Father," Ash murmured.

Then he turned away—my father, who always held the well-being of my sister with utmost importance. My neck would heal, my voice would return to strength, but my heart sustained a new crack in it as I watched my father leave.

Ash looked at Akish, her gaze open and admiring. "We should let her rest." She linked her arm through his, and they left together. At their retreat, I sensed that I had just lost something—something I may have never held in the first place.

* * *

The next day my voice sounded hoarse. If I whispered, the pain was manageable. I heard the clatter and hum of preparation for the celebration feast coming from various parts of the house. I was stuck in bed for the most part, at least confined to my room. No one wanted to see the ugly bruising that had appeared. Besides, the swelling became more uncomfortable when I walked around.

The door opened in the early afternoon. I wasn't surprised to see Levi, the healer, again. He poured me a drink. "Here, you must be thirsty."

I took a sip, grimacing at the pain of swallowing.

"How does your neck feel?" he asked.

"Better," I whispered. I glanced at him, wondering again about him. Now that I knew he was brother to Akish, I saw the resemblance, though Akish was thinner, taller, and more elegant looking.

He nodded. "Keep whispering. It will allow your voice to heal faster." He uncovered a bowl on a table by my bed. "This is a poultice you should apply three times a day. In about a week, the soreness will be gone."

He leaned forward and gingerly touched my neck. "The swelling has increased, but that's normal. Tonight it'll be at its worst." He pulled a small vial from a satchel slung across his shoulder. "This will help you sleep if the pain is too much. Pour half of it into a drink." He set the vial on the table and stood. "I must leave. I trust your father will find a local healer to check in on you."

"You're not staying?" I asked.

Hesitation flickered across his face. "My brother and I . . . we don't mix in the same society. I was only traveling with him because I had another matter to attend to in your city."

I wanted to ask him questions about who he really was, what matters he had to attend to, how they happened to be near the ponds when my sister and I were attacked, but my throat burned hot. I reached for the cup and took another sip. I winced again as I swallowed.

Levi picked up the bowl. "I'll do the first treatment before I go."

I closed my eyes as his fingers spread the poultice on my neck. It was cool and soothing to the touch. When he finished, he replaced the bowl and covered it with a cloth.

"How well do you know Akish?" he asked.

His question surprised me. Surely he knew this was only Akish's second visit to our home. "Very little," I whispered.

Levi looked at me for a moment, his brows furrowed, as if he were trying to determine whether or not I was speaking the truth. I didn't understand how I'd given him any cause for suspicion.

"Your sister has been very . . . friendly . . . toward him. I thought perhaps he'd spent a great deal of time here."

"No," I said. "We've only met him once before."

Something like relief crossed Levi's face. He nodded and started to move away again.

I don't know what possessed me, but I reached out and touched his arm. He looked down, equally surprised. "What has my sister said?" I asked.

"Nothing." Levi crouched so our faces were level. "But my brother is not the hero he appears to be. There are things he has done—"

Voices in the hallway stopped his speech. He rose. "I must go." He suddenly leaned over me, his face close to mine. "Be careful. My brother is used to getting his way." He touched the hair that curled about my shoulders. "He has spoken of you—"

The door to my chamber opened. Levi jerked back just as my sister entered the room with Akish. They walked into my chamber, arm in arm.

Immediately I thought of my appearance, my bedraggled hair, my unwashed body, the ugly bruising along my neck, all things I had not considered in Levi's presence. Akish crossed the room, his presence striking, as if he were a member of the royal family—a family who hadn't lost its kingdom.

Levi faced the pair, and the gazes of the two brothers met.

"You're leaving?" Akish asked, his words short and clipped.

"Yes," Levi said. It was not hard to read the tenseness in each man's posture.

Akish was the first to break gazes, his eyes traveling to mine. The way he looked at me made me feel as if we were the only ones in the room. But all too soon, my sister was speaking, infiltrating our space.

With a backward glance, Levi left, his expression drawn and tight. I didn't have time to dwell on his words about his brother because when Akish was in the room, nothing else seemed to matter. He pulled the stool closer to my bed and sat down. "What did the healer say?"

It was strange that he referred to his brother that way, but I answered. "The swelling will be at its worst tonight."

He folded his hands on top of my bed, only a short distance from me. He was close enough that if I moved just slightly, we'd be touching. My sister reached for my hand, grasping it. She brushed by Akish with a smile as she did so.

"We must sit with you tonight then and distract you from the pain," Akish said, as if it were a perfectly natural thing to do.

"Oh," my sister said, "we'll make sure she is well taken care of, but we must attend my father's feast."

"Of course." Akish's eyes stayed on me. My sister seemed mollified, but I knew she didn't like the attention off of her. My chamber had become positively stifling with the three of us.

"She should rest," she said in a honeyed voice.

My sister effectively escorted Akish out of the room; then she was back in my chamber, standing next to my bed, her arms folded. "You're not going to ruin tonight's feast."

I wished I could sit up, or stand, to face her. I felt helpless in my condition.

She continued. "If Akish, or any of his men, try to spend time with you, you'll send them away. You will *not* visit with them." She leaned toward me, fire in her eyes. "I have a plan—do you understand? Drawing Akish into your room and making him feel sorry for you isn't going to help me."

"I'm not—"

"Hush!" Her eyes darted away as voices sounded outside my chamber, but the disturbance soon passed. "Akish told me a very interesting story about our ancestors today. A story of how kingdoms were won and lost." Her eyes shone with excitement. I could only imagine what it took to win a kingdom. Bloodshed, loss, and betrayal.

"Ash, you must be careful," I said.

"I will be most careful." She gripped my hand. "But it's imperative that you stay in your chamber until Akish and his men leave."

I tried to sit up, but my neck jolted with pain. "Why?"

Her grip tightened as she lowered her voice to a hiss. "Because, my dear sister, Akish is part of my plan, and I can't have him salivating over my little sister."

The words both repulsed and excited me. Was it possible Akish truly held interest in me? If my sister had noticed, perhaps it wasn't in my imagination. Levi's warning came to my mind, but I pushed it defiantly away.

"Ash—"

"I don't want to hear it," she said. "I've seen the way he looks at you. Everyone has. He's made no secret of his opinion of your beauty." She paused. "Don't look so startled. We're practically twins, and you know how my beauty is heralded. With the right amount of paint on your face and fine clothing, men's heads will turn and look at the *second* daughter of Jared."

She released my hand and turned away, but I knew she was far from finished. Her next words were filled with venom. "But the second daughter is nothing. She has no rights, no inheritance, and would be fortunate to make a decent match some day." Ash faced me, her expression dark. "But as the first daughter, *I* will be the queen. Father has acknowledged that I'll have the kingdom to share with my husband when I marry."

I sank farther into the bed, wishing I had been born into a family of blacksmiths.

"You'll have every privilege afforded a queen's sister if you but follow my plans now. Those who are loyal to me will gain their reward in the future." She knelt by my bed, her eyes boring into mine. "You're my sister and my first loyalty. You'll have the best that I can offer. But I need your pledge, Naiva, that you'll be loyal to *me*."

There was no use asking what Father would say because I already knew he supported her, whatever her grand plot might be. In my hesitation, she grew agitated. She'd expected me to immediately comply, like always. But I wasn't so sure now. What if her plan backfired? What if there was a future for Akish and me? I'd be free of my home, become the mistress of his, and start a new life where I was the one casting the shadows, not living in them.

"Naiva," her voice was sharp, "say no, or try to thwart my plans, and you will be sent to the temples."

This time I did sit up. The pain in my neck nearly caused me to faint, but I held out with sheer determination. "You have no power to send me there."

"You know Father always listens to me."

I did know. I stared into her golden brown eyes, eyelids painted with precision and highlighted in greens and blues. Then I saw her as Akish must see her—as every man must see her. A beautiful goddess. I might share some of the same physical appearances as my sister, but everything about her was superior.

"Has Akish agreed to become part of your arrangement, then?" I whispered.

Her mouth softened into a smile. "Yes, his part is integral. He has great influence in our grandfather's court, a man trusted in the highest circles, but I believe he sympathizes with Father." She rubbed her hands together. "And he is so very handsome."

"What are you scheming?" I asked, dread flooding through me. I couldn't believe my sister truly cared for Akish, but if he were an important part of her plan to restore our father's throne, she would stop at nothing.

"All will be revealed soon," Ash said. "Will you promise to obey me?"

No, I wanted to say, but I couldn't face the temple. I couldn't live a life as a priestess, confined to religious rituals day and night. "Yes," I whispered.

My sister patted my arm. "Rest now, my dear sister."

When she left the room, instead of relief at her absence, agitation took its place. Levi's words ran through my mind. *My brother is used to getting his way.* He had tried to warn me about his brother. What if Akish already knew about my sister's plot? What if instead of playing into her hands, he was actually guiding them?

I leaned back, wondering if there was any way out of the impending storm. When my eyes finally closed, I imagined only death, destruction, and deep sorrow on the horizon.

CHAPTER 6

SOMETHING TICKLED MY FINGERS, AND I awoke with a start. The bedchamber was dark, except for a few burning oil lamps. My eyes widened as I saw the source of the tickling sensation. Akish sat next to the bed, his fingers brushing against mine. I gasped, and my voice caught in my throat.

His hand closed over mine. "Don't be afraid."

"Where is—"

"Asherah is preparing for the feast." He tilted his head, his gaze intense, unnerving. "I wanted to see how you were doing."

Akish had come to see me. *Me.* What would my sister think? She'd specifically told me to send Akish away should he attempt to visit. I then wondered how she'd known he might.

"You shouldn't be here," I whispered, wishing desperately I could speak in a normal voice and that I could wear something beautiful and attend the feast tonight. Perhaps sit at the same table as he.

"I know I shouldn't be." His black eyes grew blacker. "But when I first saw you, I knew there was something different about you. I can't stop thinking about our first meeting."

My pulse thudded in my ears.

He leaned toward me, his hand sliding up my arm. Perspiration broke out on my forehead.

"I'm only a second daughter." As soon as I said it, I chastised myself. I sounded like a child.

His lips parted into a smile. "I don't think we should let that deter us."

My heart pounded. What was he saying? I hardly dared to believe, to hope. I imagined my sister's fury, but Akish was a powerful man. Would he let my sister stand in his way?

"Whatever happens," he began, "I want you to remember there is something powerful between us. Something that can never be taken away, no matter what happens." His hand went to my shoulder, and he leaned closer until his beard brushed against my chin, his eyes absorbing me. Just as his breath puffed against my lips, the door to my chamber cracked open.

Akish drew back slowly, much too slowly and much too calmly to face the woman who stood there, her mouth agape.

My sister closed her mouth, her eyes going from me to Akish. She blinked, as if she couldn't believe we were together, alone, when she'd forbidden this very thing.

Akish merely squeezed my hand and smiled at Ash.

She flushed red and stepped into the room, her hands twisting together. "Father is ready for us. You need to accompany your men to the feast."

Akish released my hand, giving me a lingering look, then stood. "Very well. I'll see you there."

He swept out, his exit leaving me bereft.

I took my time in turning my gaze to my sister. "I told him he shouldn't have come." As I said it, I knew the words wouldn't satisfy her.

Her hands clenched into fists at her side. "Tonight, after the feast, I'll dance for him." Her eyes glittered with hatred, and a lifeless smile stretched her lips. "Do you hear me, Naiva? I'll dance for him, and he'll choose me. I am the *elder* sister. He wants to be king just as much as I want to be queen. I didn't want to tell you this yet, but marrying Akish is part of the plan to get Father's kingdom back."

I wanted to scream. I wanted to slap her. Instead, I just stared in horror at the villain my sister had become. She raised a shaking finger. "*No one* will stop this. Not you, not him. This is your only warning."

She turned and left the room without waiting for my reply.

I pulled the coverlet over my head. My entire body shook with revulsion. My sister wouldn't only dance for Akish, I knew; she'd seduce him. That was the only way. She'd put her honor on the line and force Akish into marriage. Then he'd be under her control and at her mercy. Just like I already was.

Warn Akish. The words pierced my mind, but I hesitated. How might I warn him? Steal into his chamber after the feast and the dancing? If Akish truly cared for me, he'd find a way to keep his distance from my sister. If . . .

Doubts flooded my mind. Was I willing to risk defying my sister for a man I hardly knew? A man who plainly knew how to flatter a woman? A man who happened to light the sun within me?

Two agonizing hours later, I was on my feet, unsteady but walking. By the time I'd crossed my room to the door, I felt stronger, maybe not physically but I felt more determined. I pulled a shawl over my head, concealing my hair, along with my bruised neck. I didn't want to be recognized immediately.

The great hall was filled with more guests than I'd seen in years. From the shadowed entrance, I scanned the room for Akish. It wasn't hard to find him. He sat at the banquet table—surrounded by his men, as usual— with my father. Across the table sat Ash, looking radiant and beautiful, her gaze set openly, without apology, on Akish. Anyone in the room would know of her interest in him.

Scraps of meat and half-eaten fruit littered the table, and I cringed at the waste—something we could ill afford. After tonight, my father would have many favors to repay, if and when he regained his throne.

Oh, Ash, I wanted to wail. *What is your plot? And why does it have to include Akish?*

He was dressed in finery more elaborate than I'd seen about our home in a long time. Rings flashed on his fingers, and his lean figure was accentuated with a narrow-fitting tunic. The scarlet cape he wore brought out the black in his eyes. His posture was casual, his eyes too bright, as if he'd been plied with plenty of wine. Of course. Wine mixed in with my sister's beautiful dancing figure could disarm any man.

As if in response to my thoughts, the musicians at the far side of the room began to play. Servants rushed around, their heads lowered as they cleared the empty platters and half-eaten food.

I remained in the shadows as four dancers stationed themselves in front of my father. With his nod, they began to dance. I'd seen them before—a traveling group of women numbering anywhere from four to ten at a time.

The dancers moved to the rhythm in unison, their fitted bodices stopping above bare torsos. Their colorful skirts swirled against their elegant legs. Everyone in the hall became mesmerized by their performance. I leaned against the wall, exhaustion starting to creep in. When would my sister command the attention? Her eyes moved back and forth between the dancers and Akish, as if to assess his approval. It seemed every male in the room approved, their feet tapping to the rhythm, their eyes wide with appreciation.

The music slowed and changed its rhythm. The dancers left the floor, as if on cue, and Ash gracefully took their place. I slumped against the wall as she danced surefooted and with one focus in mind. Even on my most graceful days, I couldn't dance so well.

Every eye in the room focused on her. Every man wishing she danced for him. But there was only one she danced for tonight. Her movements were slow and measured, in perfect time with the throbbing music.

It pained me to do so, but I dragged my gaze to Akish. The soft words he'd spoken to me just hours before faded like thin smoke. Tonight, his eyes were on my sister and her only.

The mesmerized look he'd given the previous dancers was nothing compared to the trance my sister had put him in. His position was clear. She had won. I had lost.

* * *

The next days passed in a haze. I still suffered from pain and swelling, while Ash practically floated instead of walked about our home. She spent every moment with Akish.

I was in the garden when Ash came to tell me the news. Squealing like a young girl, she threw her arms around my neck.

I knew why she was excited, but I didn't want to hear. I snapped at her instead. "You're hurting me." My voice was a blend between a whisper and the sound of a hoarse elderly woman.

"Sorry, my dear Naiva." She pulled back, her eyes larger than ever, her lips redder, her skin more brilliant—the look of a woman whose plans were working to perfection. "Akish asked me to be his wife!"

Inside, my heart shrank, but on the outside, I smiled. "Are you sure you want to be a married woman? Remember you told me you wanted to wait and that nineteen was too young for you?"

"Naiva—always so practical." She patted me on the cheek like one of her pet goats. "Don't worry. We'll find a husband for you."

I couldn't imagine anyone replacing Akish in my heart. How would I spend time with him and my sister and pretend? Pretend I wasn't upset . . . Pretend I didn't care for him? I still felt Akish's gaze absorbing me, heard his quiet words when he sat on my bed. I blinked against the burning in my eyes.

Ash continued, ignoring my silence. "Our children will grow up together, the best of friends. They'll learn from the masters, eat delicacies, and dress in the finest clothing in the land. People will bow to the ground when we walk the streets. They'll bring us gifts, so many we won't be able to store them all. We'll have adjoining palaces with an underground passageway connecting them." She laughed and twirled, her face turned toward heaven.

"What's next in your plan?" I asked.

She stopped, her mouth pulling into a frown. "This is the happiest day of my life, and I'll not have you put a damper on it." She spread out her arms and shouted to the sky. "Thank you, *Asherah*, goddess of heaven! I owe my good fortune to you."

"Has Father given his permission?" I pressed.

Ash lowered her hands. "Come with me." She tugged my arm until we stood in a secluded part of the garden, surrounded by thick trees. Her voice was breathless when she spoke. "Father told Akish he will grant the marriage when Akish brings him the head of Omer, the king."

Revulsion swept through me, covering me like a thick rug. It was I who felt breathless now. My mouth fell open, and I couldn't speak for a moment. Looking into my sister's shining eyes, I realized she was not repulsed or even surprised at Father's demand. Horror pulsed through me as I realized the truth of it. "This was *your* plan, wasn't it?"

Her lips parted into a smile, and she squeezed my hands so hard it hurt. "Akish is the man to do this. I saw it in him from the moment we met. He has the power and the influence. Our grandfather would never suspect Akish of leading a plot against him."

"So Akish's desire for you is so great he is willing to kill the king?" It was hard to believe. I had seen Akish's open desire for *me*. How could he trade that to marry my sister? Did he care enough about her to kill for her? To tarnish his soul forever? She certainly didn't love him but saw him as a means to redeem my father's throne. Did Akish love her?

My sister touched my jaw. "I'm sorry if this news surprises you. You must know that Akish is in love with me."

"Because you tricked him?" My voice trembled with anger. "And now he's forced to keep your honor?"

Her lips curved into a secretive smile. "He'll always be mine. He may have given you fleeting attention, but he's fiercely devoted to me now."

I turned from her. I couldn't bear to see her triumphant gaze. She had seduced him. And she had won. She always won whatever prize there was to have. "And . . . your betrothed . . . has agreed to Father's demands?" I refused to say his name. My heart twisted to even think of it.

"Yes."

The word pressed like heavy clay over my body, closing around my heart. My sister left the garden, a hum on her lips. I sank to the ground, clutching my hands in front of me, wishing I had a god or goddess to pray to who didn't also hear my sister. I had never felt so alone. I was nothing but a pawn. And now Akish was as well.

What would be the price of this treachery? Would riches or the throne make up for the burden of our grandfather's death upon her soul? How could my own sister let such evilness grow in her heart? And now she'd entangled both Akish and me in her web.

CHAPTER 7

AKISH AND MY FATHER SPENT many hours together, working by torchlight well into the night. As each night crept by, the sense of dread increased inside me. As each morning dawned, I felt as if I couldn't quite catch my breath. I was always listening, always waiting and wondering when the news of the foul deed would be delivered.

I thought of my grandfather more than I had ever previously done. Each moment I lived, I wondered if it would be the last moment he lived. Would my grandfather know in the moments before his death that he had been betrayed by his own son and granddaughter?

Our home became the meeting place. Although we'd heard Akish's home was larger and more lavish, the chance was too great that the secret meetings would be discovered by the king. I stayed away from Akish and those of his household who had traveled to join in my father's quest. It proved more difficult to stay away from my sister. She'd sworn me to secrecy, with the threat of banning me to the temple, of course, and I had complied.

What else should I do? Live with a villager? Marry a widower and care for a brood of children? I would be marked wherever I went. No one would risk taking me in.

I watched from my windows, watched from the gardens, for signs of people coming and going. I half expected Levi to arrive, but he never did. I guessed that the brothers not mixing in social circles included plotting the death of a king. And when I wasn't watching the others, I painted furiously, often washing the paint from the animal skins before it dried and starting over.

I had painted Akish a dozen different ways. His eyes filled with love; his eyes filled with hatred; his face blank, only concentrating on his long fingers. I painted my sister, never close up but always at a distance—dancing through the garden. Dancing for Akish. Arguing with my father. I even painted Levi once but couldn't get the color of his eyes right. I washed away the green and brown tones of the painting in a basin full of water.

When I tired of painting, I found an excuse to leave the house. Ash was under protective guard at all times, but I had a bit more freedom. No one cared as much about what I was doing or was concerned with my safety. I stole into the marketplace on occasion. I relished watching the women doing absolutely normal things, with their children running about their legs as they haggled over the price of cloth or painted water jugs. The merchants knew who I was but didn't bother calling my attention since they also knew I had no spending money. I contented myself with looking at the merchandise, delaying the time that I must return to my home and the darkness that had descended upon it.

I had only seen my grandfather once, and that was from afar. As I watched the mothers with their children, I wondered how it might be that a child turned on a parent. At what moment did the relationship change from nurturing to dangerous? Was it there from birth, or was it something brought on by circumstance? And most of all, I wondered why I'd been born into the family of Jared. Even through the hardship and the embarrassment of my father losing his throne, I had never imagined he'd plot his own father's death. As I passed a meat merchant, he bowed to me, his eyes following my direction. A loyal, I guessed.

When I left the marketplace, I sensed someone watching me. I turned, but everyone seemed to be going about their business, effectively ignoring me. I detoured so I'd pass by the main temple, the temple of the sun. I left a meager offering of a painted figurine. I carried the wooden carvings with me, handing them out to small children sometimes. They delighted in wrapping scraps of cloth on the figures or putting strands of hair or grass on the heads.

The small statues were all I could really part with and represented bits of myself and my talents, which were required in each offering. I climbed several steps until I reached the first statue of the sun god. I knelt before it and chanted a short prayer. Then I paused and asked for protection from the acts that my sister and Akish were planning. What if they were discovered? What if our own grandfather threw us in prison? As I straightened, a priest stepped out of the temple above me. His robes were deep brown; his head was shaved and glistened in the sunlight. Two other priests stepped out, one holding a young fawn. The first sacrifice of the day. At the close of the market, the villagers would line up with their offerings of quail and small animals to be sacrificed on the altars of the temple.

I decided to take a shorter path home than through the heart of the city. I veered onto a lane that led alongside the temple then cut back toward my father's home. The air was cool beneath the trees, and I relished being completely alone, surrounded by only the birds and the trees.

Then I heard footsteps behind me, and I realized I wasn't really alone—and perhaps had never been. I left the path and concealed myself behind some trees. A moment later, a man stepped into view. My heart lurched. I recognized him as one of Akish's servants who I'd seen about our home. He slowed, looking from side to side, confirming my suspicion that he'd been following me.

I was tempted to let him pass but had questions only he could answer. Emerging from behind the trees, I faced him. Before he spoke, I said, "Who sent you?"

He stared at me but said nothing.

"My sister?"

Still nothing.

"My father? Akish?"

The man took a step back and motioned me onto the path.

"Very well," I said, moving ahead of him. "I'll find out for myself."

Once back home, I went directly to my sister's chamber. Her servant stopped me at the door. "She's sleeping."

I wasn't surprised; Ash spent her nights in conference with my father and Akish now.

So with my heart pounding, I made my way to the other side of the house. I didn't know if Akish was even around. He seemed to come and go during the day, making me wonder when he slept. I stopped outside his chamber, but everything was silent and dark. Perhaps he was asleep as well. Holding my breath, I pushed open the door. Still quiet. No one was in the bed, and just as I stepped back into the hall, someone said, "Hello."

I turned and nearly bumped into Akish. He steered me into his chamber and shut the door. I was too dumbstruck to react, other than to stare up at him.

His expression was nonchalant, but his gaze held curiosity.

"Did you send your man to follow me?" I blurted out.

"I did."

It took me a second to realize he'd admitted to it—which I wasn't prepared for. Nor was I prepared to be standing in his chamber, alone with him.

My breath grew short. "Why?"

"I want you protected. Your father and sister don't see to it, but *I* want you safe."

"Why?" It came out as a whisper.

"Because you're important to me."

I stared at him, lost in his black eyes. He held my gaze, his mouth turning up at the sides. There was so much I wanted to ask him, but the only thing I managed was, "I don't understand."

"You don't understand why you need protection or why I sent my man to follow you?"

"Both."

"You need protection because you're the daughter of a king who has been exiled and will soon rise to full power."

I flinched at his allusion to the deed it would take to restore that power.

"And," he took a step toward me, "I sent my man to follow you so he could protect you and report back to me."

My face heated. "You are spying, then."

"No." He moved even closer. "You must know—you must know that I care for you."

I moved near the door, my throat tight. "You're betrothed to my sister. You shouldn't say such things. You'll be my brother-in-law."

Akish moved closer again, trapping me against the door. He wasn't touching me, yet if I moved even slightly, he would be. "My relationship with your sister has nothing to do with us," he said.

I gasped. "You—"

His hands went to my face, trailing down my neck then moving to the back of my head and through my hair. "Naiva, we can find our own happiness together." His low voice sent vibrations through my body. "We don't need to let convention dictate to us. You and I will exist in our own world."

His breath was cool and sweet on my face, his lips ever so close that I almost felt them on mine. I ached for his touch, but my heart screamed *fool!*

"No." I shoved him away. He didn't resist, didn't try to stop me, but simply watched me fling open his door and flee down the hall.

* * *

I spent the rest of the evening in my room, alternating between staring in numbness at the walls and crying. Akish had admitted he cared for me, that he wanted to be with me, but he wasn't willing to give up my sister. He didn't choose her over me like I had at first believed. He wanted us both.

My stomach roiled with nausea as I turned face down on my bed. Why were the gods so against me? How could they be so cruel as to play this game?

Akish thought of me as no more than a harlot. My sister would never put up with him having a second wife or a concubine, so if I wanted to be loved by Akish, I'd have to resort to being the secret woman in his life.

Never, I promised myself. Akish would never touch me again.

Tears burned my eyes as I wept for the injustice of it all. The first man—the only man—to express a deep interest in me was just like my father. Putting power and the wealth of the kingdom first, before any child or friend, not caring who the quest for power hurt along the way.

My sister and Akish would make a formidable pair. But once the freshness of their courtship wore off, what would be left? Would their relationship amount to dregs in a wine skin? And then who would he go looking for? *Not me—I won't allow it.*

I climbed off my bed and took a shuddering breath. Night had fallen during my wallowing, and my room was filled with shadows as deep as Akish's eyes. I changed out of my tunic and pulled on a clean one. Akish had touched what I was wearing, and I would burn it, cleanse myself of him once and for all. He was plotting to murder my grandfather, and he would be marrying my sister soon after the foul deed was done. There could be nothing in my heart or in my possession that belonged to him.

I lit an oil lamp and stared at my reflection in the metal square on my wall. Then I tugged a comb through my hair and twisted it into a knot. I opened the vials of paint that I usually reserved for my sister and began to delicately paint my eyes and lips. I filled in my lips with scarlet, and my eyes looked twice as large outlined with smoky gray. I rubbed plumeria oil onto my skin until it shone soft and dewy. I stood back, assessing myself. I did indeed look like my sister, though I was more angular and she more voluptuous.

I stole along the hallway and escaped into the garden without encountering anyone. There, I lit my used tunic on fire and watched the black smoke climb into the night sky. It obscured the glittering stars, as my sister's evil plan involving Akish had obscured my hopes.

A couple of servants came running into the garden then stopped short when they saw it was only me burning a small article. They watched for a moment with me then turned and left me to my ashes.

When my tunic had disappeared into the smoldering flames, I watched the breeze dissipate the smoke then turned back to the house. Tonight I'd sit in on the council with my father. I would learn everything possible about the plan so I could warn my grandfather. I had no idea how to send a warning, or if I really had the courage to do it, but just thinking of rebelling made me feel a little better.

I walked into the council room. My sister and father were there but no Akish. My father sat with his hands gripped together, staring straight ahead. My sister paced circles. When she saw me, she ran toward me and grasped my hands. "You must pray with us."

"For what?" I looked from her to my father.

"For Akish. He's left to bring your grandfather's head."

All warmth drained from my body. I hadn't expected the deed to be done tonight. I had thought I might discover more and find out a way to prevent it. Not that I was sure I *could* prevent it, but now all hope was gone. It was far too late. I wanted to collapse. My sister tugged at my arm, leading me to the statue of the goddess Asherah in the corner of the room. Copal incense simmered on a platter in front of the idol, permeating the air with a strong, spicy aroma.

We fell on our knees next to each other, she in prayer and I in weak failure. We leaned forward then bowed our heads to the floor. My sister chanted, and I followed with her, praising goddess Asherah and asking for her blessings.

My body heated, thinking of how we were asking for the wrong blessing. We were asking to be protected from the evil deed of murder. So what if the outcome reinstated my father's throne, one he had rightfully won? A man's life would be taken tonight, and not just the life of any man—the life of our grandfather, the king. And out of the three of us— me, my sister, and my father—I would be the only one having nightmares.

With our pleadings and prayers finished, I turned to my sister. "How long has he been gone?"

"An hour. We don't expect his return until very late."

One hour. I had missed Akish's departure by one hour. But what could I really have done? Set out before him? Shown up at my grandfather's palace to warn him? He barely knew who I was and would most likely have thrown me into prison. But still, I couldn't stomach the thought of someone trying to murder my grandfather.

The next hours crawled by, each minute seeming longer than the previous one. I stayed in the same room with my father and sister so I might hear the morbid news with them. I didn't know if I could stomach seeing the severed head of my grandfather, but I wanted to witness the moment my entire fate would change.

Soon after midnight, Ash stood from where she reclined on a set of cushions. Her back went ramrod straight, her eyes wide. "Someone's coming."

CHAPTER 8

AKISH SWEPT INTO THE HOUSE the instant my sister opened the front door. Perspiration shone on his face, his cloak was torn and muddy, and his hands were empty.

My father stepped forward, the question on his lips.

Akish held up his hands and took a deep breath. "King Omer has escaped," he said in a hoarse voice.

We stood there, stunned.

Akish touched his throat, and I immediately understood. I fetched him a cup of wine and handed it over. After a long swallow, he said, "Bring him forward."

Behind Akish, his men shoved a thin boy forward who looked to be eleven or twelve years old. He was dressed as a servant and trembled like a dog. "This boy told us that Omer was warned in a dream about a plot to take his life. Tell them." He gave a push, and the boy stumbled toward us.

His voice was high pitched and frightened. "King Omer gathered his family together and told them of a vision he had from the Lord."

My father scoffed.

The boy looked even more frightened. "The Lord told King Omer that there were those who sought his destruction and would try to overthrow his kingdom. He commanded the king to take his family and flee the land."

"The *Lord* commanded him?" Ash broke in. "Do you mean the God Omer worships?"

Fear streaked the boy's face, but he nodded.

"I don't believe it," Father said. "Omer's God is not real. I think someone gave away our plot." My father's eyes focused on the young servant. "Boy, have you seen any of these men at court in the past few weeks?"

The boy inhaled sharply and turned to look at Akish's men. After a trembling moment, he replied that he had not.

My father crossed to the boy and took him by both shoulders. "Look again very carefully."

The boy's face paled, but he looked at each man in turn. Then he raised a thin finger and pointed at Akish. "Him."

Akish only nodded. "Of course. I've spent time each day in Omer's court to keep our friendship thriving. But I had heard nothing about the meeting with his family." He narrowed his eyes at the boy. "When was the meeting?"

"Two days ago," the boy said, pulling away from my father and Akish. "It was late at night. No servants or court members were present. The only reason I knew was I had fallen asleep in the corner of the throne room by accident. No one knew I was there."

My father watched him carefully, and I did as well. I searched for any flicker of the eyes, any indication that this boy was lying. Could it be possible that there was a God who warned a king of danger? It was fantastic to consider. But this boy didn't appear to be lying. He just looked frightened.

"When did Omer leave?" my father asked.

"This morning," the boy said.

"Who else knows what happened?" my sister asked.

The boy's eyes went to her. "Most of the servants left with the family. A few returned to their homes."

"So the rumors have been spreading all day that Omer has left his kingdom?" Ash continued.

The boy licked his lips. "I suppose."

She turned to my father. "We must take immediate action. We must claim the palace and send out an edict that declares you as king."

Akish stepped forward, bowing to my father. "Your Highness, I've not completed my task. I will follow Omer until I have his head."

My father studied Akish for a moment. "No, son. You've restored my power, just not in the exact method planned. I need the new husband of my daughter to be at my side, safe, and ready to build up my kingdom." He reached for Ash's hand and put her hand in Akish's. "Before these witnesses, I give Akish, son of Kimnor, permission to marry my Asherah, daughter of Jared the Second."

As Akish gripped my sister's hand fiercely and smiled at her, I felt a pang in my heart. I pushed it away as soon as it surfaced though. Akish didn't deserve any more time in my thoughts.

My father stepped back and said in a loud voice, "Lock this boy up until we decide what to do with him. Then notify the rest of the household that we leave tonight. When the sun rises in the morning, there will be a new king in the palace!"

As the boy was led away, Ash spoke up. "Father, the boy knows of our plot now. He must be executed."

Blood rushed to my head at my sister's callousness. But I needed to tread carefully. "We can force him to take an oath of loyalty. The boy knows those at court who follow Omer. He can warn us of danger."

Ash narrowed her eyes at me, but my father nodded. "We'll give the boy the option. He'll pledge loyalty to me, or he'll die."

* * *

The servant boy's name was Lib.

As we traveled through the night toward our new home, I followed the servant who had tied himself to Lib so the boy wouldn't run away.

"Tell me of Omer's God," I whispered to Lib. We were spread out enough that neither my father nor sister could overhear our conversation.

Lib cast me a furtive glance, but I smiled broadly to prove I was friendly. To prove it further, I said, "I'm Naiva. You'll like my younger brothers, Shule and Ethem. Perhaps you can be their playmate."

The thin features of his face seemed to soften. "Thank you for sparing my life."

"You're welcome," I said so he would believe I had some influence after all. I knew if Ash or my father had truly been set on executing Lib, nothing I could have said would have swayed them. It was good for Lib to think he had an ally, someone here to protect him. In time, he'd find out I was as much a pawn as he was. But until then, I was determined to learn as much about my grandfather's family as possible.

"What is the name of Omer's God?"

"The king calls him *Lord*," Lib said.

"Don't let my father hear you call Omer *king*," I said. Lib looked duly chastised.

"Is there a great statue of the Lord in the palace?" I asked.

"No." A smile touched his thin face. The first I'd seen. It looked so out of place on him that I wondered how much the boy had ever smiled. Sleeping in the corner of a throne room couldn't be much of a life. "The king—Omer—doesn't believe in statues or idols of his God. He says his God is the only God and doesn't need a statue. He says his God is in everything, everywhere."

"Do you believe that?" I couldn't help asking.

The boy nodded. I thought about the arrogance of a god who claimed to be the only one. We prayed to many gods and goddesses, depending on what our needs were. How could one god handle all the requests? I peered at Lib, but his expression was placid, as if he believed in the possibility of only one god.

"Where are your parents?" I asked.

"They are dead." Lib's tone didn't sound sad, just matter-of-fact, as if he'd been asked many times about his parents. "They were servants to Omer. They died when I was four. The royal family took me in, knowing I was too young to be much use, but there was nowhere else for me to go."

"So you lived with Omer during the great battle," I mused. "What do you remember?"

"I was only six or seven," Lib said, his voice suddenly sounding very grown-up. He may be young still, but he'd seen a lot. "I remember fetching water for the men building the new palace."

My father had set the old one on fire after being ousted from the kingdom. His last jab of revenge. Now his revenge had come full circle.

We fell into silence as we neared the palace. Even in the moonlight, it was a majestic sight. There were several parts to the building and two levels that rose to the sky. It spread across a low hill, the white color of the building shaded lavender beneath the moon.

Approaching the palace without guards to stop us, or servants to gather and watch, was a surreal experience. "Why has no one come to ransack the place?" I whispered to Lib.

"They are afraid."

"Of Omer?"

"No. Of the Lord."

What power this God must have over the people to even frighten them in my grandfather's desertion. There were no torches to light our way or warm food to welcome us. I was one of the last to step inside the grand entryway. The desertion felt even more complete and final inside. I looked upward at the immense ceiling. It was three times higher than that of our small house.

My father instructed Lib to lead him to the king's chamber, where he would establish himself. Ash was preoccupied with Akish, so I found myself exploring on my own. I carried a torch our servants had located and lit, and I walked through the eerily empty halls, in and out of rooms.

I found the cooking rooms toward the back of the palace. Stopping in the entryway, I noticed the baskets of fruit, vegetables, and roots, the jars filled with grain, the herbs hanging on the wall—all left as if only abandoned overnight, not permanently. I imagined the bustle that took place here when Omer and his family occupied the palace. With such a large family of children and grandchildren, the cooking room was probably in use from dawn to dusk.

I continued through the palace until I arrived at my father's new chamber. I halted at the doorway, peering in past the open door. He was in the middle of a conversation with a servant, so he didn't acknowledge me. His favorite rug had already been placed on the bed, and his collection of swords sat propped against the wall. The rest of our belongings would be sent for over the next few days. My sister came up behind me.

"What do you think?" Her eyes glowed with excitement.

"This place is beautiful."

She clasped her hands and squealed. "It is. Come, I'll show you to your chamber."

Together we left my father's room, and though I should have felt elation to have a palace to live in, the darkness of the hallways seemed to predate the darkness that was to come. No, we didn't have to shed blood to gain the kingdom back; for that I was grateful. But we had plotted Omer's death. Would the people accept my father? Would they rebel? Would Omer's other sons return to again claim what was theirs?

Ash stopped in front of a large room that already contained several burning oil lamps. Shadows danced merrily along the walls—light and dark alternating, illuminating murals that had been painted there. A collection of vials, with brushes and perfumes, sat on a low table, as if the room were waiting for the owner's return.

My sister stepped inside and spun around, her arms out. "This is all yours, Naiva! What do you think?"

"Amazing," I said in a quiet voice. This room was as large as my father's chamber in our previous house. Stepping inside, I felt as if I were intruding on another person's private life. The soft blues and purples of the room told me a woman had lived here. Perhaps my cousin or aunt. I picked up a vial of perfume and inhaled. Pomegranate. I set the perfume down. "Where is your room?" I asked, looking around.

"I'll sleep with you tonight . . . and with Akish tomorrow night."

I snapped my head around to gape at her. She laughed at my shock.

"Father says we can marry tomorrow evening. I wanted to wait a few weeks to plan everything and invite the whole city, but Father insisted. When Akish also insisted, I gave in." She wrapped her arms around herself. "Can you believe that tomorrow night I'll be in Akish's bed?"

I turned away and walked toward the high windows. Tomorrow night my sister would be a married woman. Tomorrow night Akish would sever all hope of us ever being together. I swallowed against the hard lump in my throat. "Let us sleep," I managed to say, concealing the trembling of my voice. "Dawn is very close."

We climbed into the great bed, and as my sister's body warmed my back, I thought of the princess who'd left her things behind that day. Where was she sleeping now?

CHAPTER 9

By MIDAFTERNOON THE NEXT DAY, my father's edict had been sent to all of the aristocracy's households. Our new royal heralds, formerly plain servants, spread the message far and wide, announcing the rise of the new king along every main road, in every gathering place, and in the market center.

By fleeing the land, Omer had made it clear that he was giving up the throne. And with his son Jared, former king and heir to the throne, taking his place, no disputes could be heard. It seemed the people didn't want another war like the one that had secured Omer's throne. My father essentially walked into the palace with no resistance.

He discovered Omer's royal headdress in the throne room.

I came into the throne room as he was trying on the headdress. He turned with a rare smile on his face—rare because it was directed at me.

"What do you think, Naiva?" He raised his chin, nearly setting the headdress off balance. It was a thick gold band encased with jewels. The headdress extended two handspans high and was made of a combination of quetzal feathers and pieces of jaguar fur.

"It looks very foreboding," I said.

"I shall be known as a foreboding king, then." He chuckled. "Are your sister's wedding clothes ready?"

"Nearly," Ash said, coming in behind me. "Oh, Father, the headdress is marvelous." She rushed past me to examine it. "We must have the coronation tonight right after the wedding. All of our guests will be witnesses to your ascension to the throne."

My father beamed with pleasure but said, "It won't take the attention from your wedding?"

"I won't mind." She kissed my father's cheek. "The guards will all be in place, protecting us. And Akish says the sooner you are seen taking command of the city, the less chance of a rebellion."

I quietly slipped out of the room; they didn't even notice my escape.

The worry inside me deepened. We'd have many guests tonight, though the marriage announcement had just been made. I wondered how many in the crowd would be supporters of Omer and if our lives might be in true danger.

I detoured through the gardens. They were magnificent, with climbing vines, flowers in various stages of bloom, thick bushes, and elegant trees. I looked forward to days spent among the flowers.

Soon I heard two male voices—arguing. I slowed and changed direction. Then I hesitated. One was familiar. Akish.

Deciding that I didn't want to run into an angry Akish, I continued away from them, taking a side path that led deeper into the garden. Although it would take me longer to get back to my chamber, it would ensure I wasn't seen or heard.

I left the sound of arguing behind, and by the time I reached my chamber, I was ready for the day to be over. I had hardly slept, and now we'd be celebrating—or at least I'd be pretending to—my father's rise to power and my sister's marriage into the early hours.

I splashed water on my face from my chamber basin. One thing had certainly changed—fresh water in our rooms. I quickly readied for the evening, knowing once Ash called me for help, I wouldn't have time for myself.

I chose an indigo tunic that fell to just below my knees. The dark color would keep my presence subdued and in the background compared to the bride. I also pulled my hair away from my face and plaited it so it fell down my back in a single tress. I would wear no headdress but only a jade necklace for adornment.

It wasn't long before a servant knocked on my door. When I opened it, a woman I'd never seen before stood there with her head bowed and her arms clasped. I wondered if she was from Omer's household or a new recruit.

"Your sister is waiting," was all she said. I followed her along the hall, though I knew perfectly well where my sister's new bedchamber was. When I stepped into the room she was to share with Akish, I first saw a barrage of clothing scattered about, half of which I didn't recognize. I wondered if my sister had sent for all of this cloth from the market or if she had raided the previous owner's things.

"Naiva! You must help me." Ash flung herself at me, and her arms tightened in a brief embrace. "I simply can't decide what colors to wear."

"What about our mother's wedding clothes?" My heart tightened—we'd always talked about wearing our mother's things. I drew away from her needy embrace. "I thought you always wanted to wear them."

"That was a young girl's wish. I have to forge my own way now, establish my own traditions. The people need to see me as their future queen."

I nodded, feeling numb. Everything my sister did had a motive, even choosing her wedding clothes.

We spent the next hour draping cloth over her shoulders until she was finally satisfied with a deep scarlet hue. I oiled her arms and legs then inserted large gold circles in her earlobes. When we finished, she was radiant from head to foot. Her black hair hung like a curtain down her back, shining in the late afternoon light that streamed through the windows.

"Do you think Akish will be pleased?" she asked.

Looking at my sister, there was no question that any man would consider himself fortunate to possess such a beautiful woman. "Of course," I said. "Every man's eyes will be locked on you."

She moved close, nearly touching me. "I meant, do you think *Akish* will be pleased with me?"

"How could he not?"

She lowered her gaze for a moment, and then she looked up, her eyes moist. "He sees me as a prize to gain in order to become more powerful."

I swallowed, trying to think of something to say. She might be right. In fact, I had suspected for some time that Akish was using my sister. Yet, wasn't she using him? Regardless, he was using me too, and my instincts propelled me to protect my sister. "A man wouldn't be a man if he didn't understand all that marrying you would entail. You'd never be happy with a man less ambitious than Akish. He's handsome and well spoken, and he obviously adores you."

Her face softened into a smile, and the tears remained at bay. "He seems to adore me, doesn't he?"

I nodded, fighting my own tears. Here I was trying to reassure my sister of a man's affections, a man whom I had once hoped might hold true affection for me. I had wondered about his feelings for me, and now I wondered about his feelings for my sister. It seemed he cared nothing for integrity or honesty. He'd gone to great lengths and would probably continue to do so in order to gain more power.

"I hope to please him in everything." My sister grasped my arm. Her eyes held half fear, half excitement. "Tonight I'll share a bed with my husband as a married woman." She inhaled and released her grip.

Turning away, I busied myself with folding the discarded pieces of cloth. I didn't want to think of Akish and my sister as they crossed the threshold into a married life.

"My slippers," she said.

I fetched the beaded slippers she'd made the week before. They fit snugly on her feet, covering the dye on her toenails.

"Now go see if the guests have arrived yet," she said.

I rose to my feet, wanting to escape my sister's room, then hurried along the corridor toward the great hall. Everywhere, the sounds of preparations were prevalent. Turning the last corner, I collided with someone and nearly fell, but a hand reached out to steady me. Looking up, I found myself gazing into those forest-colored eyes.

"Levi?" I said, more of a question than a statement.

"Are you all right?" His hand remained on my arm.

"Yes. What are you doing here?" As soon as I said it, I felt foolish. Of course he'd come for the wedding.

His face darkened slightly. "I'm here to oversee the guards."

"For the wedding celebrations?"

He gave a brief nod. "My brother wants me to be a permanent fixture here at the palace as head of the guards." His expression turned into a scowl.

"Oh. I'm surprised you weren't asked to be our healer."

Levi's mouth softened into a smile. "I'm not exactly a full healer. Those skills are something I picked up in my travels."

"Travels?"

He didn't answer but stared at my neck. His hand brushed just below my chin. "I see you've healed nicely. How does your throat feel?"

I didn't flinch at his touch like I'd expected. In fact, I didn't feel nervous being alone with him at all, not like I was with his brother. "I'm much better. Thank you for all your help." I was surprised at how easy it was to talk to him, like a friend. Much different from being around Akish—when one word or touch set my mind spinning.

"You're welcome," Levi said, his voice suddenly soft. He dropped his hand. "I'd better get back to my orders."

He stepped past me, and I wished I could find a way to ask him to stay. Instead, I said, "Perhaps you can tell me about your travels another time."

He stopped and turned his head. "I'm leaving right after the celebration. I'm not taking the post." His eyes locked onto mine again. "I hope my brother hasn't been too cruel."

"No," I said, the answer automatic, but I wondered exactly what he meant.

"Remember what I told you before." His voice fell. "If you ever need anything or need someplace to go—"

"There you are," a voice boomed out. Akish strode down the hallway, dressed in all his wedding finery. It took my breath away. His height seemed magnified by the narrow kilt he wore. The wide belt that encircled his waist carried a long, curved dagger, its hilt polished silver. His cape was made of jaguar fur. His beard had been clipped short, emphasizing his long, elegant neck.

Akish's eyes flickered to me and settled for a moment. "I see you've been spending your time more wisely than I," he said to his brother.

"What do you need?" Levi asked him.

Akish passed his brother and stopped right in front of me. His eyes soaked in my clothing, my hair, my simple adornment. "You look lovely, Naiva. Perhaps more lovely than my bride." He chuckled, his eyes bright. Then he leaned forward and whispered, "But don't tell her that."

My face felt as if it had touched fire, and I stepped back, afraid that he'd touch me in front of his brother. What did Levi think? What did *I* think?

I took another step back, my heart pounding. "I must go," I mumbled then turned and tried not to run, keeping my steps evenly paced as I walked around the corner.

I slumped against the wall, trying to catch my breath. The wall felt cool, and pressing through my tunic, it chilled my skin. I knew I had to keep moving, but I might collapse if I didn't calm my breathing first.

Akish and Levi were still around the corner, speaking in low, urgent voices.

"Leave her alone," Levi said. "She's an innocent."

"She's delightful. A sweet girl, to be sure," Akish said. "I'd never hurt her."

My face flushed at Akish's praise. I placed my hand over my heart, trying to will the beating to slow.

"Akish—" Levi's tone held warning.

"Who do you think I am?" Akish said. "I'll be an exemplary citizen of this family. The adoring husband. The brilliant son-in-law. And the *attentive* brother-in-law."

The pounding in my heart increased at Levi's next words. "That's what I'm afraid of."

"What were you doing just now? Warning her?" Akish's voice grew louder, angry. "Telling her to stay away from your older, villainous brother?"

"Do I need to tell her that?" Levi asked.

A scoff. Then Akish said, "She can take care of herself. I have every confidence in that. You, on the other hand, are no longer welcome here. I don't need a self-righteous brother watching my every move day and night. I don't need someone who complains about idols in the palace, who is sympathetic to Omer's God. And how Jared has regained his power too conveniently, how I'm marrying Asherah only for the throne, or what I think about her sister."

"Then I'll be gone before the hour is up," Levi said in a tight voice.

My chest tightened at the thought of Levi leaving. But I didn't take time to analyze why I suddenly hoped Levi would stay at the palace. I slipped away, deathly afraid that one of them might come around the corner and see me. I found an empty room, which appeared to contain rolled up rugs and other storage items. I sat among the dust and cobwebs, trying to make sense of Levi and Akish. Who to believe? Who to trust? Akish was marrying my sister—shouldn't I be able to trust my brother-in-law? It seemed both my sister and father trusted him. He said he wouldn't harm me, and I wondered why Levi thought he might.

My heart couldn't be relied on—I *was* innocent. Inexperienced. At least Levi was right about that. I wished he weren't leaving. Something about his presence calmed me, made me feel secure—like someone cared. And I wanted to find out what Akish meant by Levi being sympathetic to Omer's God. The only thing I knew for certain was that my life would never be the same from this moment forward.

CHAPTER 10

AKISH AND ASH'S WEDDING COULD only be described as dazzling. Fit for royalty in every detail. Every influential person in the city seemed to want the favor of the new king and were generously donating money and other items for the celebration.

In just a single day, my father's rise to the throne had turned out an entire city in celebration. Yes, I had my doubts. Perhaps the people were simply trying to please my father by spending the night drinking wine and dancing in celebration, or perhaps they truly loved him. Perhaps it was a little of both. Despite my feelings about my father on a personal level, I wanted him to be happy, to be revered, to be a successful and happy monarch. My home life could only be the better for it. And I didn't know how my relationship with my sister might change now that she was a married woman.

I watched Akish gently take my sister's arms and lead her to the feast table. His attention was on her—and her only. No other woman in the room could compare to my sister's beauty, and all of us were content to sit back and let her be the center of attention. That night, every man fell in love with Ash, and every woman wished she were in the arms of Akish. I wondered what it would feel like to be in my sister's place—if only for an evening.

The feast was beyond anything I could remember decorating our table. There was everything from quail eggs to platters of steaming meats, baskets of fruits and nuts, and thick agave juice. I took my seat with my brothers, Shule and Ethem, who gobbled down the food. Shule, at twelve, was the older of the two. He resembled my sister and me the most—dark hair, dark eyes, naturally thin. Ethem, at ten, had fairer skin and pale brown eyes. They both had tremendous appetites. I tried to keep my gaze from my sister and her new husband as much as possible but couldn't help peeking when Akish fed her honey delicacies and she offered him slow sips of a cacao drink.

After the feast, Akish and Ash moved among the guests, greeting them and paying compliments. After all, the people's taxes would now pay for our luxuries. A little goodwill tonight would go a long way. When Akish walked past my end of the table, his fingers brushed my shoulder. I looked at him, startled, and he smiled at me then immediately directed his attention to my brothers.

"Are you looking forward to your apprenticeships?" he asked them.

I straightened. "What apprenticeships?"

Akish's gaze enveloped me, his eyes humorous. "Shule and Ethem, as sons of the great King Jared, will be trained in the art of military strategy. As the king's sons, they will live in the prestigious home of the nobleman Hearthom, who led your father to victory during his first reign."

I looked at my younger brothers. Ethem nodded to me, a smile on his face.

"We can still visit the palace," Shule said, "if we aren't too busy."

"I hope you'll never be too busy to visit your family," I said. My brothers were growing up, and I wasn't happy about it.

"Don't worry, boys," Akish said. "I'll watch over both of your sisters."

Shule nodded solemnly, as if it were what he'd wished for. Akish continued to linger at our end of the table, his gaze on me, and I focused desperately on my platter. His hand rested on my shoulder again. I stiffened at his touch, hoping my sister wouldn't notice. She was at the other end of the room though. Finally, he moved on. Finally, I was able to exhale.

The heralds blew their shell trumpets, announcing a change in the event's direction. My father stood in front of his new throne, flanked by my sister and Akish. The head priest of the Sun Temple came forward, carrying the royal headdress. On top of his customary dark brown robe was a deep yellow-colored cape, representing the color of the sun. His shaved head and wrinkled face made him look likewise, commanding even more respect.

"We are assembled today in celebration of the union between Akish, son of Kimnor, and Asherah, daughter of King Jared," the priest said. His voice was low yet powerful, infiltrating every corner of the room. "We now thank the almighty sun god who has blessed our land once again with our returning monarch. A monarch who was wrongfully ousted from his title. Tonight I reinstate him as king, sovereign, and supreme ruler over the land of Heth and all surrounding provinces."

"Amen," Akish said in a loud voice, followed by the rest of the assembly. The priest stepped forward as my father sank to one knee, head bowed. After placing the royal headdress on my father, the priest turned to the crowd. "Praise the sun god. And praise King Jared. Our true king has returned." The people repeated the words, and I was caught up in the revelry as they cheered and clapped.

A long line formed as everyone took turns congratulating my father and then the married couple. Servants scuttled about, collecting the food and platters, refilling wine goblets. The music resumed, though louder this time. There would be plenty of entertainment tonight, culminating in a special dance my sister would perform for her new husband.

I slipped out of the room, the music wafting behind me. I hoped Ash wouldn't notice my absence, but I didn't have the heart, or stomach, to watch her dance for her husband. Everything had changed. My sister was married, my father was crowned, and now my brothers were leaving.

I was left alone—again.

* * *

My brothers left the next morning, their faces awash with excitement. I held back my concerns because I knew they were primarily about missing my brothers. "Come home often," I said, kissing both Shule and Ethem. They squirmed beneath my embrace. It felt strange to call this new palace "home" so soon, but I would have to grow used to it.

I didn't see Ash after my brothers left, nor did I see her the next day. On the third morning after her wedding, she appeared in my room. She ran to me and threw her arms around my neck.

"Oh, Naiva!"

And then she burst into tears.

"What's happened?" I cried out, confusion balling into a knot in my stomach.

She pulled away and wiped at her face. "I don't know. One moment I'm deliriously happy; the next I'm crying like a child."

"Has he . . . been kind to you?"

"He's been wonderful, but I've become fiercely envious. If anything captures his attention and takes his focus away from me, even for a single moment, I become upset," she said, her lips trembling again.

This was not my sister. This was not what I expected. She was always the one with the power—even over her own emotions.

"This morning," she continued, "he was gone when I awakened. I had no idea where. I searched the palace in my bed clothes; I even opened your door to check inside."

"Mine?"

Her hand went to my arm. "I know he'd never come here—never be unfaithful. And I'm ashamed to say it even crossed my mind." She took a deep breath. "But I was wild with worry, and I came up with the most horrifying possibilities to explain his actions."

"Where was he?" I asked.

"In the cooking room, fetching me a bowl of fruit for the morning meal. He didn't want to wake me," she said, wiping her eyes again.

"That's good, right?"

She nodded. "Yes, of course. He told me I was being foolish. And then I started to cry in front of him."

I couldn't imagine how Akish might deal with a crying wife. But I didn't need to. Ash wasn't finished with her story.

"He was so sweet," she said, sniffling again. "Absolutely charming." Her voice took on an edge. "But I still worry. What if he becomes bored with me? What if he wants a concubine?"

"This is our home," I said. "Father won't allow it."

"Father had concubines," she said.

I stared at her, disbelieving. "No, he didn't."

"Perhaps you were too young to understand. It was before he lost the throne." Her face paled, and she turned away.

I wasn't too young to understand now, but the horror of it slammed into my stomach. How could my father do that to my mother? What had she thought? I felt ill. My heart ached for her and hardened further against my father. How could he? Yes, he was king; yes, it was considered a symbol of power and wealth—but . . . I looked at Ash. Her shoulders shook with silent sobs.

I took a deep breath, knowing I needed to comfort my sister. "You shouldn't worry. You're the most beautiful woman in the city," I said, but it came out more of a whisper, so it wasn't entirely convincing. My mother had been beautiful, had given my father four children, but apparently that hadn't been enough. Then I thought of the things Akish had said to me, and a shiver passed over me.

Ash crossed the chamber and stood in front of the narrow window, looking out as she wrapped her arms around herself. "*You* are beautiful."

My breath caught in my throat, and I stumbled through the next words. "No one compares to you. You should have seen everyone watching you at your wedding. Any man in that room would have traded places with Akish."

"Akish said he thinks you're beautiful." Her voice sounded dead, dull. She turned from the window, regarding me with narrowed eyes.

My face heated, and my stomach felt as if I'd swallowed a rock. The compliment from Akish was almost unbearable—now that it was too late. My sister must not know the pleasure and pain that collided in my breast at those words. "I'm your *sister*, Ash. A compliment to me is one to you as well." I hoped to change the direction of the conversation. What was Akish's purpose in telling my sister he thought I was beautiful? "We should go to the market today and see if there are any new treasures to be found."

She continued to stare at me.

"Come on." The brightness in my voice was false. "The fresh air will lift your spirits." I extended my hand, hoping she'd take it. We could be young girls again, giggling through the streets, commenting on the people we passed, and talking about our dreams of the future.

Ash didn't move, her expression as hard as limestone. "Tell me, Naiva. Tell me if my husband has kissed you."

"No! Never," I nearly shouted. "How can you even ask that?"

She blinked but said nothing.

"Don't you know me?"

She closed her eyes for a second then opened them again. "I'm sorry. I told you I was going mad."

"Come." I crossed to her and tucked my hand in hers. "We'll go out for a while and let Akish be the one to worry."

She smiled at that.

CHAPTER 11

THE DAYS AND WEEKS PASSED swiftly, and Ash practically floated through the palace, laughing and taking delight in everything. Yet no matter how happy she seemed, I often caught her giving me a hard stare, eyes narrow, expression distrustful.

My sister's marriage had put a wedge between us—one that others may not have noticed, but one I felt deep within my heart. The pain came from the fact that Ash had touched on the truth of Akish noticing me. His previous words and actions had confirmed it, and at one time, I'd desired it. My whispered prayers at night were to forget any thoughts or feelings I'd had for the man who was now my brother-in-law and to see him as whom he ought to be to me.

About three weeks after the marriage, I was finally set free. Although not in the manner I'd expected.

Ash became ill, and the first rumors were that perhaps she was with child.

"It's much too early for signs of a child to make me ill," Ash told me.

I was in her chamber, sitting by her bed. I had spent most of the past two days by her side, keeping her skin cool from its burning. "How do you know for certain?"

"I sent for the healer this morning. He told me that even if I had conceived on my wedding night, the symptoms wouldn't be so strong yet."

"So you are not with child?"

"I may still be. It's very early to tell," she said with a smile on her pale face. She closed her eyes as I placed a wet cloth on her forehead.

It was moments like these, when Ash needed me, that I felt close to my sister again. But I couldn't rely on her being ill forever. Once she was better and full of energy, I would again become afraid of her silent accusations.

Her eyes opened, and she lifted a lethargic hand. "Have you seen Akish yet today?"

"Not yet," I said. "He may be training the guard." Since Levi had refused to accept the position as head guard, Akish had taken over until he could find someone trustworthy.

Ash dropped her hand and turned her head away.

"What is it? Should I call the healer back?"

"No," Ash whispered. "Find out where my husband is. He's been gone a lot since I've been ill."

That was exactly why I was spending so much time with my sister. It would have been impossible if her husband were hovering over her as well.

I left Ash to rest and walked along the hallway, asking various servants where Akish might be. One told me he'd seen him last in the gardens. Another said he was at the training field behind the palace. I found him at neither.

That night, just as I was about to fall asleep, I thought I heard a woman's laughter. Was my sister finally recovered? I hadn't heard her laugh for days. I rose from my bed, hoping a servant would know how Ash was doing. I certainly didn't want to interrupt if she was with Akish. In the hallway, everything was silent, so I stepped back into my room. The laughter came again, but it wasn't from the hallway, as I first thought. I opened the window and peered out into the garden.

The moon hung heavy and full, casting its pale light over the gardens. The laughter started then stifled quickly. Curiosity burned in my chest, and I turned away from the window and grabbed a cloak. Perhaps it was one of the servants, but the unease in my stomach wouldn't go away. I crept through the halls and exited the palace. A sleepy-looking guard looked a bit surprised when I exited, but he didn't try to stop me. In the gardens, I kept to the shadows as much as possible, pulling the hood on my cape over my head.

Then I slowed to a dead stop.

On a bench my sister and I frequently sat on was the storyteller Tirzah— the woman my father had invited to our banquets. She was sitting next to Akish, her arms wrapped around his neck. His hands were at her waist, and he was smiling. When he leaned down and pressed his lips against her neck, her laughter bubbled up again.

Horrified, I stepped back, bumping into a branch. The branch cracked, and before I could decide if Akish had heard me, I turned and ran.

Back in my room, I shut my window as quietly as possible and blew out the oil lamp. Then I huddled on my bed, hoping and praying that Akish hadn't seen me. But I prayed even harder for my sister. Her suspicions had proved correct. I suppose a wife would suspect that type of thing. The image of Akish kissing Tirzah sent shooting pain through my head and heart. For my sister. For me. For my family. We had a traitor in our midst.

How would I tell her? The struggle for me wasn't *if* I'd tell her but how. And when.

I hugged my torso as I started to shake. The tears were unavoidable now, and they wet my cheeks, trailing into my hair. I had once allowed myself to be flattered by this man, and now as I remembered Levi's words about his brother, I realized they had been a true warning.

The laughter from the gardens had long since stopped, and I assumed they'd heard me and moved to a more private place or broken things off for the night.

A light knock sounded on my door, and I froze. I didn't move, hardly daring to breathe, hoping whoever it was would go away. I couldn't face my sister. If it was a servant telling me she was ill again, I couldn't look her in the eyes and not have her notice something was wrong.

But the voice that whispered through the door was not a woman's.

"Naiva, I know you're awake," Akish said. "Open the door."

I couldn't move, even if I wanted to. Fear trapped me. He had seen me in the garden. My heart skipped a beat when I heard a scraping sound. The door slowly opened.

When Akish stepped into my chamber, I bit back a scream of fright. He was at my side in seconds, his hands on my shoulders, gripping them hard.

"It was you, wasn't it?" he demanded.

I nodded, the fear too thick to let me speak.

"You won't say anything to your sister; she is too frail." His hands dug into my shoulder and would leave dark bruises. If I were to use any word to describe my sister, in sickness or health, it would never be *frail*.

"She deserves to know the man she married," I managed to choke out.

Akish leaned forward, his face so close to mine that I smelled the flowers of the garden on him—most likely from Tirzah. I shuddered, and his nose lifted in a sneer. "I'm not asking you to keep quiet. It's a *command*."

I pulled away, but his hands stayed on my shoulders, pressing me against the bed. "Promise me," he said.

"No." I couldn't lie to my sister. I couldn't live with this secret between us.

His face darkened in anger. "You will obey me, or you'll pay severe consequences."

"I already have," I spat out.

His hand shot out and slapped me across the cheek.

I gasped, the tears instantly burning in my eyes. I curled away from him, but he yanked me back around to face him.

His lips nearly touched my ear as he growled, "If you tell your sister, I'll be back, and you'll wish you never crossed me."

* * *

My sister fully recovered a few days after I caught Akish in the garden with Tirzah. I was careful to avoid being alone in her company, since the temptation to tell her was too great. If she asked me about her husband or where he spent his extra time, I would be forced to reveal what I knew. I wondered if she'd be more upset at her husband if she found out or at me for not telling her the moment I knew. Every time I was about to slip into my sister's room or pull her aside, I remembered Akish's angry face, his rough hands pushing me down on the bed, his whispered threats in my ear.

Akish acted as if nothing had happened.

The storyteller was at every evening meal in our household. I watched her spend time with my father, smile at Akish, and entertain our ever-growing court with her tales. Was her attention more so on Akish than the other men? If I hadn't been looking, I wouldn't have noticed. But a brighter flush came to her cheeks when she spoke to him.

I watched my sister too. I wondered if she noticed the attention from Tirzah. Perhaps she suspected already, relieving me of the duty of telling her. But while I watched my sister closely night after night, I realized something. She was in love with her husband.

I was quite certain she hadn't been truly in love with Akish when they had married and definitely not when she had first danced for him. She had been entranced, perhaps, but more interested in using him to win my father's kingdom back. But now . . . I noticed the small things. The tilt of her head when he spoke to her, the way she touched him each time he was near, and her intense gaze as she watched his every movement.

If she was in love with her husband, I could understand her jealousy.

The last thing I wanted to do was break my sister's heart—which meant the last thing I could do was tell her of Akish's infidelity.

"The oracle has arrived," someone called out.

We were in the middle of our evening supper, surrounded by the usual guests of the high court.

My father clapped his hands together, commanding everyone's attention. I looked toward the door and saw an elderly woman standing there. She gazed at us openly, as if she could see into all of us at once.

A tiny shiver passed through me, but I couldn't understand it. I'd heard oracles speak before. My father had called upon them in the past.

I had never seen this woman. Her graying hair hung loose about her shoulders in soft waves. Her skin was wrinkled with age, but her hands appeared to be as smooth as a child's. Everyone settled on their cushions as she walked into the room.

"Welcome," my father said. "Are you the one Akish sent for?"

"I am." Her voice carried clear and distinct to all those in the room.

"Would you like food or drink?" my father said.

"I am ready to deliver my message."

A smile flashed across my father's face. "Then please begin." He sat back down, his expression eager.

Oracles came and went, making declarations of weather, the harvest, and the health of the children and offered blessings upon the king. I assumed Akish had brought the oracle in so the court might hear her blessings upon our family.

But as the oracle spoke, her words came out as a warning.

"Jared, son of Omer, you are in grave danger," the oracle said. "Hold close only those you trust the most. Forces are against you in all corners of the kingdom. You must not eat or drink, for surely you will die."

Akish jumped to his feet, his face dark red. "Guards, take her away! How dare you threaten the king?"

As the guards rushed forward, my father stood as well, looking deathly pale. Ash ran to his side then turned to face the oracle.

The woman simply stood in one place, her expression passive as if she'd just foretold the rainy season, not paying attention to the guards as they ran up to seize her. She made no movement to struggle, to deny or clarify what she'd said, but simply allowed herself to be led out of the room.

"Who is that woman?" Ash cried out as the oracle was taken away. She wrapped her arms about my father, who looked visibly shaken.

Akish declared, "She is mad. She is not who I thought she was. Her reputation was misquoted." He turned to face the stunned court. "The person who misled me will be punished. Guards, bring me Kib, son of Corom."

"What did she mean?" Ash wailed. "How can my father not eat or drink? He will surely starve."

Akish put his arm around her and pressed his lips against her hair, murmuring words I could not hear.

After a few moments, the people of the court started to whisper to each other, and conversation eventually returned to normal. But my heart didn't stop pounding. The woman had looked far from mad to me. What had she truly seen about my father's future? Was it something that every king had to fear? Traitors? A rebellion? That was nothing new. Kings could trust few people around them. My sister's concern was the same as mine, no matter how Akish tried to explain the oracle's words away.

I left the room before Kib could be brought to face Akish and my father. I did not care to hear any explanations or witness the fullness of Akish's wrath.

When I reached the cooking rooms, everyone was talking about the oracle's message. The servants were used to seeing me in the cooking rooms, looking through the vegetables, fruits, and herbs to make dyes for my paints. But when I entered this time, the buzz quieted, and all eyes turned to me.

"Does anyone know if the oracle's predictions have come true before?" I asked.

Several servants looked away or down at the ground. One boy stepped forward. Lib. "King Omer didn't consult the oracles."

Sara, a heavy-set woman, hushed him.

But Lib met my gaze openly.

"Why not?" I asked.

"King Omer listened only to the one true God," Lib said.

Sara put a hand on Lib's shoulder. "That's enough, boy."

"It's all right, Sara," I said. "I'm not going to report anything back to my father." I looked at Lib again. "Omer's God knew more than the oracles?"

Lib glanced at Sara then to me. "Many people might have spiritual powers. But King Omer only needed to rely on the Lord."

"What do you think the oracle meant?" I felt strange asking a boy to interpret a spiritual leader.

Lib swallowed audibly. "You won't report this to your father?"

"No, I swear on my life."

"King Jared did not obtain this kingdom in righteousness, not the first time and not the second time. How can anyone who hasn't lived honestly expect honesty in return?" His face reddened. "Not to say that we aren't very loyal and would never wish any harm—"

"I know you're all loyal." I raised my hand to stop his fumbled explanation. I looked into the eyes of the servants in the cooking room. "Whether or not we believe in the oracle, we must be vigilant. Every bit of food or drink that is prepared for the king will be tasted in his presence. He must eat and drink to live. But we must prevent any tainting of his food or drink."

All eyes were on me.

"Agreed?"

Lib stepped forward. "I will be the king's taster." A few of the servants gasped.

I smiled. "Excellent. Come with me. We'll share our plan with my father."

He glanced nervously at Sara, but he followed me out into the hall.

"I want you to tell me more about the Lord," I said in a quiet voice as we walked.

Lib looked at me, wariness in his eyes.

I stopped and met his gaze. "I truly want to learn. I am no spy for my father, though protecting his life is my greatest wish."

"Tonight, then. We'll meet in the garden."

I strode into the throne room and found my father and Akish sitting with my sister. Many of the court guests had left. I approached and told them of my command to the cooking servants. My father's eyes studied me, and it was the first time I saw them glow with appreciation for *me*.

My sister clasped her hands together. "Brilliant, Naiva. The oracle must have meant someone might try to poison Father."

"Lib has agreed to be the taster," I said.

Akish narrowed his eyes. I wondered if he was surprised that I had come up with a taster. "He will do," Akish said, as if we needed his approval on the matter.

CHAPTER 12

"GOD IS ALL-KNOWING," LIB SAID in a hushed voice. We'd been meeting in the garden late at night for the past week so I could learn about the God of King Omer.

Lib's eyes were bright in the moonlight. The more I learned about the Lord, the more I wanted to know. "He sees everything. He knows each of us," he continued.

"Does He know our names, or does He see us as a mass of people?" I asked.

"He knows our names." Lib paused as the breeze stirred about us. "He knows your name, Naiva."

His words made me shiver, not with cold but with warmth. The pleasant feeling of comfort was still new to me. It had permeated my body on the first night Lib had told me about his God. And it had returned when I'd pondered what I had learned.

"You're feeling His presence again?" Lib asked, bringing me back from my revelry.

"Yes," I said in a soft voice. I was on the verge of trembling, but I didn't want Lib to know how much this warm feeling affected me. What would he think? Would he laugh?

"I feel it too," he whispered, putting his thin hand on my arm.

I looked at him, surprised to see tears shining in his eyes. So it wasn't shameful to feel as if I were about to cry and laugh at the same time.

"He brings us joy and love and peace. That is what King Omer taught." When he said Omer's name, he lowered his voice and glanced around. We had been careful, very careful, but we still feared being discovered.

"Do you think Omer and his people are faring well?"

"The Lord is still with them," Lib said. "I've heard rumors that he has settled in the land of Ablom."

"By the seashore?" I asked.

"You've heard of the place?"

I thought of the education I'd received as a member of the royal family. "I've heard of many places," I said quietly. I wondered what it would be like to live someplace away from idols, someplace among family members who weren't cunning and controlling. It was times like this that I missed my mother. "My mother used to come into my chamber and ask me about my paintings. It was the only time I felt that someone really cared for me, perhaps even loved me." I shook my head, unsure why I'd told Lib that.

"I barely remember my parents, but at least I know they loved me," Lib said.

Tears stung my eyes. This boy had lost his parents, but he always had their love. I still had my father—but not his love. I used to think my sister loved me, but over the past months, I understood she only loved me when I was doing her bidding—conditional love.

"We make a fine pair," I said with a tremulous smile.

"A fine pair of *traitors*," a voice spoke behind us.

I flinched, and Lib scrambled to his feet.

"Akish?" I turned, peering through the darkness at his silhouette.

"Come with me, Naiva." His voice was tense, warning me not to cross him.

I slowly stood and touched Lib's shoulder. He shook with fear. "We were just talking."

"Of course you were." Akish stepped into the full light of the moon. His features were sharp and angled as the shadows planed his face. "Only talking about King Omer, who has been a traitor to us. And only talking about Omer's false God, the one the servants still pine for."

His black eyes flashed, anger flaring from them. "How can you be so foolish, woman? Any encouragement from you, the king's daughter, and these sniveling servants will start a revolt. Is that what you want? Your friends soaking in their own blood?"

I took a step away, horrified at Akish's threat. "Choosing a god to worship is no cause for bloodshed."

"You know it is," Akish hissed. "It's the very cause for bloodshed. And I will not shy away from doing whatever it takes to protect my king." His eyes flickered over Lib. "Leave the boy. I'll deal with him later. But you, Naiva, are coming with me."

The dread in my stomach intensified. I didn't want to face him alone. Suddenly, I was the one shaking. As if Lib could read my thoughts, he stepped in front of me, bravely holding his head high. "We're not going to revolt. We were only talking about religious beliefs."

Akish lashed out at Lib, striking him across the cheek. "Away with you, boy!"

Lib stumbled back, and I grabbed his arm to stop him from falling.

"How dare you," I spat out.

"If you want to live to see the next sunrise," Akish's voice was filled with barely controlled fury, "leave this garden now."

"Go," I whispered to Lib, my voice shaking now. "I'll be all right."

Lib hesitated, but finally, he scurried away, casting several fearful glances over his shoulder. I hated to see him go, but a twelve-year-old boy was no match for Akish.

Akish's hand gripped my arm.

I wrenched away. "Don't touch me."

He chuckled softly and grabbed my arm again, tighter. He pulled me along the winding path, deeper into the garden.

"Where are we going?"

"Where we can't be overheard," Akish said, his voice a deceptive, pleasant hum. "You and the boy should have thought of that."

"Don't hurt the boy."

"Why are you so concerned about a servant?"

"He's a child. He was only answering my questions."

Akish stopped, forcing me to turn and look at him. "And why do you have so many questions, my dearest Naiva?"

I cringed at the familiarity in his words and answered vaguely. "I have questions that haven't been answered."

A smile twisted the corners of his mouth up. "Because you're tired of worshipping your sister since you know she's no goddess like she fools the people into believing?"

I looked away, the truth too harsh to acknowledge. How could Akish cut to the depths of my soul so easily?

"I want you to trust me," Akish said in a surprisingly gentle voice.

I looked up at him, startled. The anger had melted into something I didn't quite recognize. Kindness?

His grip relaxed, and his hand moved up my arm. My stomach hardened again as the fear immediately returned full force.

"Relax, Naiva. I'm not going to hurt you." He was close, so close. "I'm not going to hurt the boy either." His voice practically purred. "I want you to understand that what you're doing is very dangerous. Remember the oracle's warning?"

I nodded, too numb to speak.

"Her words were harsh and threatening. But they also served as a warning for us to be ever watchful. Do you know what I did to that man who recommended the oracle?"

"What?" I whispered, my heart pounding in my ears, making it difficult to concentrate.

"Nothing."

My gaze met his. He was watching for my reaction, and when he saw my surprise, his hand moved higher until it was on my shoulder.

"I thanked him. Do you know why?" he continued.

I shook my head, too aware of his nearness. I wanted to push him away, scream, but I didn't dare. He could restrain me as easily as a helpless bird.

"The oracle was right," Akish said. "Yes, the oracle upset your sister and father, but a warning should never go unheeded."

When his fingers stroked my jaw, I came to my senses and pulled away. Akish made no move to stop me. I finally regained my voice. "What do my questions for Lib have to do with the oracle?"

"Lib used to work for Omer, as did many of the people in this city. We must purge *everything* that reflects the old king, even his God." Akish studied me, then he extended his hand. "I want your oath that you'll not pursue this anymore."

I looked at his outstretched hand. It would be so easy to take it. Commit to a truce with my brother-in-law. Live in harmony as a family. But I knew that meant always obeying. Always doing what he wanted. What my sister wanted. What my father wanted.

And what if they were *all* wrong?

I took a deep breath then turned and fled.

* * *

I shouldn't have been surprised when the summons came at the crack of dawn. I hadn't slept, and now it was confirmed that Akish hadn't slept either.

When I entered the throne room, there sat my father and sister, both looking as if they were statues of stone. Gone was the affectionate greeting of my sister. This morning was nothing but formalities.

Akish wasted no time stating his case and recommending that I be sent to the temple.

I was communicating with the servants.

I was encouraging a rebellion.

I was sympathetic to my grandfather.

I was a traitor to the king.

There was no vote, no court, no other opinions heard. My sister stood and walked out of the room, her face immobile, her eyes vacant. My father's voice was cold when he said, "Send her to the temple."

The words floated over me like a dream—I'd heard them, but I couldn't quite believe they had been spoken about me. My entire body felt numb, and I wanted desperately to wake from the nightmare. *This is a dream,* I tried to convince myself as two guards escorted me to my room. Guards! Escorting *me.*

But it was no dream as I gathered a few paint vials and scrolls of animal vellum. It was no dream as I packed my mother's seashell comb. And it was no dream as I carried a satchel full of my belongings through the arid hallways of the palace and out the front entrance.

I passed the cook, Sara, in the corridor. Her eyes were soulful, and her lips pinched tightly together as she watched me.

I tried to tell myself I'd now be living in a holy place, where I might find refuge after all. Where my father and sister and brother-in-law could no longer hurt me, no longer control me. But even I could not convince myself as I walked out of the palace.

Akish's tall form dwarfed the courtyard, where he waited, his hands clasped behind his back. When he saw me, he dismissed the guards by announcing, "I will escort her myself."

The guards scurried away, as if relieved to be out of my presence or Akish's or both.

I stood still, waiting for my brother-in-law's command. My sister and father were nowhere to be seen, though that didn't mean my sister wasn't watching from some secluded window. I hoped she was, and I hoped she'd lie awake all night and wonder why she hadn't protected me from her own husband.

"After you," Akish said with a wide sweep of his hand. Anyone observing us might think we were on a morning errand, perhaps to select a fine gift for my sister's upcoming birthday—sister and brother-in-law seeking to please the next queen. But the satchel I carried was an indicator that this was anything but a morning stroll. I drew up my shawl and pulled it over my head, partially concealing my face from the sun and partially from curious gazes.

The market was in full bloom as we walked through it. Merchants called out to us before turning to another customer when they realized we were not there for purchasing or even browsing. I pulled my shawl down across my forehead, feeling a measure of security in the added privacy.

As we approached the Sun Temple, a dull ache tempered my usual awe at the magnificent edifice. Surely I wouldn't be here long. Surely my sister, or even my father, would reconsider soon and send for me. I licked my lips as we started up the temple steps. Smoke wafted from the two altars, indicating recent sacrifices. The head priest, wearing a dark brown robe, came out of the entrance as we ascended. His wrinkled face looked familiar—not too long ago he'd ordained my father as the new king.

I met his gaze then glanced away quickly, not pleased with what I saw there. Anticipation. Expectancy. He knew we why we had come. Akish must have sent a servant to alert him.

The priest barely contained a smile as we arrived on the first plateau.

"Naiva," the priest said, "welcome to the temple of the sun. We are most honored to have your patronage. And the sun god is pleased as well." As he spoke, two women seemed to materialize behind him. They wore long, filmy robes the color of new maize.

I'd seen priestesses from a distance at festivals but never this close up. One of them, who looked a year or two older than me, smiled encouragingly. The taller priestess stared at me openly, but there was no hint of a smile or any sort of welcome. The hair tumbling over her shoulders was threaded with silver strands, though her face still looked young.

"Nelise and Raynelle, this is your new sister," the priest continued. He looked again at me. "They'll show you to the women's chambers. Prayers begin at the sun's zenith."

My eyes pricked with tears. I had only one sister, and these women were not her. Nelise, the petite woman, held out her hand. It was then I noticed the intricate designs that wrapped around her wrist and scaled along her arm. A quick glance told me her other arm was equally decorated.

Nelise grabbed hold of my hand, and in an instant, Raynelle was at my side, taking my satchel from me. They propelled me into the temple's cool interior. I barely had time to notice the beams of sunlight coming in from near the ceiling, illuminating the polished stone floor, before they whisked me through a door. We immediately fell into darkness, but the priestesses continued to press forward, guiding me along a narrow passage.

Before my eyes had time to adjust to the dim light, we stepped into a large, brightly lit chamber, again by sunlight streaming in from above. If I hadn't known better, I'd have thought I was standing inside the sun from the brilliance of the room. Everything shone, from the gleaming floor to the bright yellow cloth hanging from the walls and the soft orange woven blankets on the cots.

A sleeping chamber, obviously.

"Here's your place," Nelise said, speaking for the first time. Her voice sounded like a musical hum. Quiet, yet melodic.

Her hand patted the bed, and I blinked, trying to adjust to the glow of the room.

Nelise giggled. "You'll grow used to it."

Raynelle set my satchel on the bed and opened it. Before I could protest, she emptied the contents onto the bed. Nelise immediately joined her, combing through my things. Raynelle said nothing, but Nelise exclaimed over each article, as if she'd never held the likes of any of them in her hands before, let alone possessed them.

"Paint for your cheeks?" Nelise said, holding up a vial of red dye.

"No, it's for the paintings I do of people."

"People?" Nelise's eyes widened. "Are you a tomb artist?"

I hid a smile. "No, I paint on the scrolls." I pointed to the rolled vellum.

"Oh, we have an artist for a sister," Nelise said, reaching for them. "Can you paint me?"

"Sister!" Raynelle chastened Nelise. "Leisure time is at the end of the week."

Nelise's face went bright red. "That's what I meant . . . during the next leisure time."

"Now, let's prepare our new sister for the prayers," Raynelle said.

CHAPTER 13

WEEKS PASSED . . . WEEKS OF NOT knowing what was happening at the palace, not knowing how my sister was, how my father was adjusting to his new crown, or what had become of Lib. Was he still a servant? Had he been punished?

The knot in my stomach never really left. It wasn't so much that I longed to be in my beautiful room at the palace, but I missed Ash. As much as I felt betrayed by her and her husband, I had expected her to at least visit or send a servant to inquire about my well-being.

But there had been nothing.

I followed along with my new duties, hoping for the day to come that I'd be returned home.

Nelise became my ever-present shadow. She told me of her simple life in the small village of Isla. Although she seemed in awe of me and the life I had come from, I envied her. To live in a place where you weren't watched and every move you made weighed against possible treason. Even though Nelise was older than I and more familiar with the temple routine, I seemed to be guiding *her*.

Raynelle continued to observe from the background and didn't hesitate to correct or reprimand either one of us. The other priestesses were pleasant women, and I immediately sensed their strong bond of sisterhood, though it made me miss my true sister all the more.

Our prayer ritual began with a prayer at sunrise each morning then resumed midday at the sun's zenith. The final round of prayers took place as the sun hovered at the horizon. I memorized the prayers and chanted them with the priests and priestesses, but I felt nothing in my heart. Not even devotion or gratitude. The only gratitude I felt was to know that I was too young to be a full priestess.

Though Nelise's decorated arms fascinated me and were beautiful in their own way, I couldn't imagine the pain that came from such a ritual.

"When you turn eighteen, you'll be initiated into the full priesthood," Nelise whispered to me one morning as we walked through the dim halls to our chamber. Her small hand tugged on my arm, and I slowed my step, allowing the other women to move ahead. Once they were out of sight, Nelise said, "Come, I'll show you the ritual room."

My heart pounded as we turned a corner I'd never been around and descended a set of steps leading beneath the temple. "Are you sure I'm allowed to see it?"

She giggled. "No, but we'll not tell a soul." We arrived at a low door, barely illuminated by a torch farther down the corridor. Nelise unlatched the door and pushed it inward. The room was almost pitch black. We walked forward, clinging to each other, until our legs hit a table of sorts. I gasped.

"That's the altar," Nelise whispered. "Wait here; I'll bring a torch."

She scurried away before I had a chance to stop her. So I waited in the cold, dark room, surrounded by unseen nothingness until she returned.

The glow of the torch cast garish shadows, and I was surprised to see that the room was rounded. Along the circular walls were several sconces, waiting for their own torches. I stood by a low altar, longer than any I'd ever seen—the length of a man. I noticed the ropes hanging from the sides, and I wondered what they might be for. Then horror pierced my heart.

I turned to meet Nelise's ethereal gaze.

She seemed to read my horror-filled expression and quickly explained. "This is where the skin designs are done. Don't worry, the priestess is given a special tonic to help her sleep during the entire procedure. I didn't feel anything." She moved to the end of the altar, holding the torch high. She pointed to a dark metal box. "Open it."

My stomach twisted in alarm, and I shook my head.

"All right, I will." Nelise handed me the torch. She lifted the top of the box and pulled out a long, sharp needle.

"That's what they use?" I choked out.

"It looks worse than it really is." She lightly traced over a twisting vine on her arm. "It makes us beautiful in the eyes of the sun god. It lets him know we are truly his."

My throat felt too tight to swallow. I stepped back, putting distance between me and Nelise and the long needle. In the wavering light, she looked mad. Perhaps she was. How could someone *enjoy* having her skin carved and dyed?

I took another step. Nelise didn't seem to notice. Not for the first time, I wondered why she'd come to the temple. Was it a betrothal gone wrong? Were her parents unable to care for her? Had she been unfaithful with a married man? All of these were reasons for a young woman to be sent into service at the temple.

"Don't you want to know what else happens in this room?" Nelise said in a loud whisper. "Don't you want to know the final ritual?" Her usually warm eyes shone like black daggers, flashing perilously.

"Let's go," I said, trying to keep my voice steady. "We'll be missed."

Nelise took a step toward me. "After we are marked, we become true partners of the sun god through the fertility ritual."

That stopped me, and I hesitated near the door. "Fertility ritual?"

"We give ourselves to the priests in the name of the sun god." She spread her arms out, the needle still in one hand. "Our virtue becomes the sacrifice upon the altar."

The words took a moment to sink in. And when they did, the blood drained from my face. The altar blurred before me, and I grew dizzy. I reached for the door to steady myself. "This fertility ritual is the final initiation to be a full priestess?"

"Yes. It's wonderful to make a true sacrifice for the sun god."

I inhaled sharply, trying to get more air, but the room was stifling, and the heat of the torch didn't help. I straightened to my full height, which was not much taller than Nelise. "Put the needle back," I said in an authoritative voice. "We must return to the other women before we are discovered." *And I must find a way to escape the temple. Where I'll go, I don't know, but I'd rather be a beggar than a priestess.*

Nelise's smile faded, and she seemed to comprehend the urgency in my tone. With relief on my part, she replaced the needle and left the room with me, pulling the door shut with a thud. Her eyes still had a faraway look in them, but at least she followed me back up the stairs and into the familiar corridors beyond.

In the privacy of my bed that night, with darkness at last separating me from the other women, I curled into a tight ball, wishing I could disappear. I had no idea the priestesses were expected to perform fertility reenactments with the priests. I'd thought the temple was a sacred and holy place, a place where an unfortunate woman might find refuge and live out her days in noble service. A place a woman could remain virtuous.

I wanted to speak to Lib, ask him my questions. But I knew a twelve-year-old boy had less chance of knowing about fertility rituals than I, a seventeen-year-old woman. Surely I'd be gone before my eighteenth birthday. Surely I'd not be forced to go through the initiation.

When morning dawned, I was a different Naiva. I had grown up. Whatever I'd believed until now had all changed. There had been no word from my family for more than a moon. They had as good as forgotten me. It would be up to me to get out of this place.

I went through the motions of the day, chanting the prayers, weaving shawls for the poor, polishing the floors to a shine, all the while planning my escape. It would have to be at night, when my absence wouldn't be noticed right away. Surely the head priest would contact my family, and whether or not they sent out a search for me, I wanted to be someplace where I couldn't be forced to return to any temple.

* * *

Weeks passed while I planned my escape, waiting for the right opportunity. Each day was a day closer to leaving.

When a head priest stopped me in the hall one day, I was surprised when he said, "You have a visitor."

I walked, anticipation pounding in my breast as I followed the priest into the grand hall of the temple. There on a bench sat a veiled woman. She didn't stand to greet me but simply extended her slim hand.

I knew instantly that it was Ash.

I ran, not caring that my feet slapped unceremoniously against the stone floor, and sank onto the bench next to her. "Ash?" I breathed.

She fell into my arms, her body trembling, and I naturally slipped into my role as comforter once again.

"What's happened?" I demanded, pulling back.

Her eyes shone wet through the dark veil she wore.

"Father's dead." Her hands went to her face and sobs wracked her body.

I couldn't move, couldn't breathe, couldn't think. "How—what?" I gasped.

Her hands gripped my arms, and the sobs halted, her tone turning fierce. "Murdered. By my husband!"

The dread that had started as a seed when I had first seen Ash in the temple sprouted into full horror, spreading like black dye through my limbs until I couldn't hold myself upright.

I slipped to the floor, clutching at my middle, rocking back and forth, as I tried to purge my sister's words from my head.

CHAPTER 14

It was Raynelle who led two grieving sisters into a small chamber to give us a place to mourn. It was Raynelle who mopped our brows with cool, wet cloths. She prayed over us, she held us, and then she told us to dry our tears.

Raynelle's sharp, narrow face hovered near my own. She peered into my eyes until I was forced to meet her gaze. "You must be strong for your sister. She needs you now more than ever."

I struggled to sit up on the bed, where I'd been instructed to lie down. The room probably belonged to one of the priests. It contained a single bed, a stool, and a jug of water. There were no things of comfort, only absolute necessities.

I looked toward Ash, who sat against the wall in the corner of the room, her knees drawn up to her chest. Her veil was off, but her swollen red eyes stared straight ahead, vacant.

Raynelle stepped quietly out of the room. I suspected she hovered outside the door, should one of us call for her.

Swallowing against the lump in my throat, I stood on shaky legs, expecting them to give out at any moment. I crossed to Ash and knelt before her. Taking her hands in mine, I said, "You must tell me what happened. Everything."

Ash met my gaze, and when she finally spoke, her words chilled me to my very soul.

"You can't imagine the hell I've lived through since Father banished you to the temple." Her hands tightened against mine until it was painful. "I've made the most horrible mistake."

"What have you done?" I asked, assuming she meant sending me to the temple.

"I married Akish."

I blew out a breath. I had been there when she'd chosen him, when she planned to seduce him, when she'd married him—all for our father. All for the kingdom that was no longer his.

This must be a mistake, I thought. *This can't be happening. Akish didn't kill our father. He's my sister's husband. A man I might have married if I had been the eldest.*

"What did . . . Akish do?" My throat felt dry, the words sour in my mouth.

"He commissioned men to attack Father during one of the audience sessions in the throne room. The guards always search everyone, but somehow, three men slipped through with swords." Ash's voice dropped, and her gaze slid from mine. "Akish claims he doesn't know any of the men. But I know better. Akish swore them to the oath of the ancients."

Just like you swore Akish in when plotting Grandfather's death, I thought. But I did not say it. Not now. My mind raced as I imagined my father trying to defend himself against three men. He'd been a proficient soldier many years ago but was in no such shape now.

Although my stomach was tight with horror, I asked, "Did Father fight them off? Did he have a chance at least?"

"No," Ash whispered. Tears dripped down her cheeks. "The men attacked ferociously. Father's head was severed before anyone had time to react."

A violent shudder passed through me, and I doubled over. My father—no matter the disappointments and pain he had brought me—didn't deserve to die this way. I straightened, anger fueling my strength, and paced the room, walking from one blank wall to the other. "What did Akish say exactly?"

"Does it matter? He's a master with words." Ash's voice sounded bitter. "He came to me soon after and told me Father had been attacked in his own throne room by sympathizers to Omer." She paused, taking deep breaths. "But I saw the truth in Akish's eyes. What should have been sorrow for the death of his father-in-law was only triumph."

My stomach roiled. I had seen that same look in my sister's eyes many times.

"I couldn't believe it at first," she continued. "I ran to Father's chamber. He was covered with a rug, but I was desperate and pulled it off to see for myself." Her voice choked, and she brought her trembling hands to her mouth. "They hadn't even cleaned up the blood yet."

I hurried over and wrapped her in my arms as she sobbed.

After several moments, she drew in a shaky breath then said, "No one dares question Akish." She looked at me with wide, sorrow-filled eyes. "It's been three days, Naiva, since Father was murdered."

"Three days?" I cried out.

Ash's face grew even paler. "Akish locked me in our chamber and forced me to keep quiet. The servants who were present were sworn to secrecy. He says it's to give him more time to find the guilty men. But I think it's to give the men more time to get away."

My stomach wrenched, and I turned away and gripped the edge of the bed, fighting to keep my stomach still. The image of my father's lifeless body decaying in his own chamber was unbearable. No matter how he treated me, how little love existed between us, I knew he deserved a king's burial. Not to rot away, hidden from his own people.

I lifted my head to study my sister's swollen face. "Why did Akish let you come now?"

"It was part of our bargain. I lie about the way Father died, and you get to return to the palace." She gripped her hands together. "And . . . there is a child growing within me. I insisted that only you can care for me in my condition."

The breath left me. That morning I would have welcomed any excuse to leave the temple and had planned to escape somehow. But not this way. Not home to a man who'd most likely killed my father. If he could kill a king, what else might he do?

Ash reached her arms out to me, and I was in them within seconds. We crouched on the cold floor, holding each other, two sisters united in a terrible cause.

"Please," she whispered. "Please come home with me. I can't bear it without you. I'm sorry for letting him send you away. My child will need his aunt to love him." Her arms tightened as she buried her face in my shoulder. "Look at the mess I've made. Can you help me?"

I stroked her hair, my tears blending with hers.

"You are all I have left," she said. "No one understands me like you. Akish has promised that if you'll worship as we do, you'll always be protected in our home."

I had two choices, three perhaps. I could stay at the temple and never see my brother-in-law or my father's body again, but then I wouldn't see my sister or her child. In fewer than six months, I would go through the initiation and become a full priestess and devote myself to the sun god, but I dreaded the fertility ritual more than death itself. Or I could continue to plan my escape, to go somewhere else, another city, another life to learn about the Lord, the God who had warned Omer to flee for his life. Or I could go home with Ash and keep our family together.

Fewer than a dozen heartbeats passed before I said, "I'll come."

* * *

Entering the palace, I felt as if I'd been gone a year, not a few months. I sensed my father's absence immediately. Hand in hand, Ash and I went to the throne room, where his body had been laid upon a bier. A shroud covered him completely from head to toe to conceal his severed head. I hesitated, my stomach twisting as I thought about the brutal way he'd died. After a moment, Ash tugged at my hand. We had to pay our respects. It was time.

A few court people filtered in and out of the room, speaking in hushed tones. But they moved to the side as Ash and I walked slowly forward and stood before our father's shrouded body. His physical body might repose before us, but my father was no longer there. The absence of his soul was plain among the forlorn walls. I avoided looking at where his body met his neck; I didn't want to dwell on his fatal injuries.

I reached out, toward the outline of his arm and hand. I could see the rings on his fingers pushing against the shroud. My hand hovered above his hand, and then I rested my palm against his fingers. I flinched at the touch—through the shroud I felt the cold, claylike skin. But this was my good-bye, and I rested my hand on his for as long as I could.

I left the room and made my way to my chamber. Everything was as I'd left it. Exhaustion consumed me, and I climbed onto my bed and slept until late afternoon. Waking, I felt hungry, but I also wanted to see for myself if Lib still worked at the palace.

Sara greeted me as I entered the cooking room. "Welcome back, Naiva. We are sorry about the king."

"Thank you," I said. "Where is Lib?" The other servants looked up at me, their gazes nervous.

Sara pointed to the herb room, and I followed her direction. Stepping into the cool and fragrant interior, I noticed Lib in the corner, sitting on a stool. He looked up, his hands pausing in their work of crushing something in a bowl.

"You're still here," I said.

Lib set down the bowl, his eyes wary. "Are you back for good?"

"Yes." I looked down at my hands. "I wanted to apologize for getting you in trouble."

His expression relaxed. "We shouldn't be seen together."

"You're right," I said. "But please accept my apology. I never meant you harm."

He nodded. "I'm sorry about your father." He looked as if he wanted to say more, but instead he pursed his lips together and picked up the bowl.

I left the herb room and hurried along the corridor to my chamber. My heart sank when Akish came from the opposite direction. He stopped, and I stopped. I tried not to stare, but I wanted to see if I could detect deceit in his eyes.

"Ash told me you had returned," he said.

"Yes," I managed to say. His eyes were darker than I remembered, and as I stared into them, I thought of my father's still heart, his cold body. A chill spread through me; there was no life in Akish's gaze—only a deep well of betrayal. I took a shallow breath, dizzy with the desire to get away. I felt nothing but repulsion toward the man who had killed my father. I wanted to escape his gaze, to be in a place where he didn't share my space.

Thankfully, a servant came down the hallway, interrupting Akish's stare. I hurried past him without giving him a chance at further conversation.

Tonight my father would be eulogized, and that's all I wanted to think about.

CHAPTER 15

IT SEEMED THE ENTIRE CITY had come to mourn my father. His body
and head were covered in a sheath and set upon a platform in the front
courtyard of the palace. Torches burned in abundance, brightening the
darkness that had crept in with the night.

The head priest of the Sun Temple chanted, surrounded by the other
priests, men I'd come to recognize.

Ash and Akish stood on one side of the bier, my sister looking stoic
and forlorn at the same time. And I knew the people would love her more
for it. After a week of mourning, she would declare herself the new queen,
with Akish as king at her side.

A hand touched the small of my back. I knew who it was before I turned.
Levi's gaze remained focused straight ahead. He didn't move otherwise, yet
his hand remained, offering a measure of comfort, a showing of support,
and an acknowledgment of my loss.

I wondered if he knew I'd been in the temple. I wondered if he knew
why. If he believed in Omer's God, he'd surely disapprove of the rituals
that went on between priests and priestesses. I wanted to ask him what he
thought of it.

But I knew how dangerous it would be if I were to ask him. The
punishment for speaking to Lib would seem like child's play.

Levi's scent was strong, earthy, just as I remembered. I didn't need to
look at him to remember the color of his eyes, the set of his strong jaw,
or the disapproval in his expression. Had he believed Akish's story of my
father's death?

I turned toward Levi, and his hand dropped. His eyes met mine, and
for an instant, he looked like his brother, the darkness turning his eyes
black. A chill ran through me. *They are nothing alike*, I told myself.

Levi leaned down and whispered, "I need to speak with you."

I nodded, not knowing what to say, not knowing what I could say when the chanting filled every corner of the courtyard and we stood surrounded by people. We had no privacy here, and it was too easy for someone to see me with Levi.

"I'll find you," Levi whispered then straightened, reestablishing the space between us. A coolness settled around me as he moved away and blended into the crowd of mourners. The high priest had finished and was now sprinkling oil on my father's corpse.

Ash turned toward Akish, wrapping her arms around his waist, leaning her head on his shoulder. One arm encircled her, but Akish's gaze didn't change. It was a demonstration for the public so they would know the royal family was united. Another reason I'd been brought home. But Ash and I knew we had an enemy among us.

* * *

The next morning, Levi found me in the herbs cellar. I was going through the hanging herbs to replenish my dye collection when he entered. He stooped to get through the entrance of the small drying room. Thankfully his green eyes held nothing of the blackness of the night before.

"Is it true?" he demanded.

"What?" *Here it is*, I thought. He'd demand answers about my father's death, and I wouldn't be able to give them to him. I had promised—upon my life—not to reveal anything my sister had told me.

In two strides, Levi crossed to me, standing close enough that I felt the heat radiating off his skin. His torso was bare, his face and chest glistening with light perspiration, as if he'd been working in a field or other such labor. Perhaps he'd agreed to train the soldiers after all.

He grasped my arms and turned one then the other over, examining them, running his fingers from my wrist to my elbows. Then I understood. He knew I'd been to the temple.

"They didn't mark you?" His voice was quieter, calmer.

"No. They don't do the formal initiation until eighteen." My heart pounded at his nearness.

"My brother will hear about this." He released my arms as if he'd been burned. "Was it your father who sent you or your sister?"

I lifted my chin to meet his gaze. "Your brother convinced my father that I was a traitor and that I should be sent to the temple."

Levi's brows arched above those captivating eyes—eyes that I decided not to get caught up in. *This man is the brother of a murderer. Who knows what* he *is capable of?*

"Why would Akish send you to the temple?" But it wasn't a question to me. Levi turned away, his hand rubbing his neck.

I wanted to know what Levi thought of his brother, if he suspected foul play, but I hesitated. A servant could walk in at any moment, and what was to prevent someone from overhearing our conversation here?

Besides, I was afraid Levi might be involved in my father's death somehow, despite his earlier claims to not support his brother's beliefs.

He turned to face me again, his expression unreadable, his brilliant eyes now muddy. "I'm sorry about your father."

Before I could respond, he left the room without so much as a good-bye, leaving his earthy scent in his wake.

I gathered up the roots and herbs, careful to take only what I needed. Then I left the room, thankful to get out of its stuffiness. I passed through the cooking room, and Sara lowered her eyes. Other servants avoided my gaze as I passed through the corridors. Since my return from the temple, everyone seemed to avoid me, or maybe they were avoiding everyone in the royal family.

One king had fled. Another king was dead. I had come out of punishment. Things were uncertain. The fear was tangible.

I passed Lib in the hallway. He hardly gave me a glance; his face was pale as if he were afraid to even be near me. I wanted to stop him, to apologize again, to ask how he was doing, but it seemed the very walls breathed—seeing and hearing everything.

When I reached my chamber, I locked the door, wishing I could lock more than just that. I spent the next hour mixing dyes then the rest of the morning painting my sister sitting on a throne and wearing the headdress of a queen. It would be a gift that would bring a smile to her face.

I sat back, surveying the painting. Ash's eyes were wide and dark, beautiful, and her skin luminous with the use of safflower seed to make the copper-colored dye. Her hair fell like a rushing waterfall over her shoulders, adding to her mystical beauty. Her lips were set firm but full, and as only an artist could do, I had rounded her belly so that no one but the most discerning would notice that she was with child.

The afternoon light streamed across the painting, warming the colors and, in turn, warming my heart. My sister would be queen. After all that had happened, she would finally take her place among the great rulers and command men and armies.

The thought had just begun to fill me with satisfaction when a high-pitched scream rent the air.

CHAPTER 16

I RAN DOWN THE HALLWAY toward my sister's chamber, not caring that my hands were stained with dye, my appearance in disarray. I knew my sister's cry anywhere, and no one could comfort her like me—no matter what had happened.

The door stood open a sliver, and I first noticed the back of a man standing near the bed. If Akish was hurting her, he'd have to contend with the both of us.

The scream came again, sending a jolt through my heart.

I burst into the room, and the man turned. It was the shaman. It took a moment to understand that it wasn't Akish and I wouldn't be throwing myself at him like a crazed beast. My eyes went to the bed and my sister on it. Her bedding was soaked in blood.

She stared at the ceiling, her hair wet and tangled. Had she been stabbed? Was she Akish's second victim?

"Ash," I cried out, stumbling to her bedside. Her wild gaze found mine, and her trembling hands reached for me.

"The baby," she gasped. "I've lost my baby."

Understanding seared through me, and I took her in my arms.

"The baby was my hope," she cried. "My salvation. He's left. He says I've betrayed him."

It took me a moment to comprehend she was now talking about Akish. "These things can't be helped," I said. "Many women lose babies."

She shuddered in my arms. "He says I must have been unfaithful for such a curse to come upon me," Ash said.

I shuddered too but for an entirely different reason. We should be cursed for plotting to overthrow our grandfather. Or cursed because we were letting Akish go unpunished. Not cursed by Ix Chel, the fertility goddess. My sister knew no man but her husband.

"Akish is just upset," I said. "You're young and healthy; there will be many children."

She sagged against me. After a moment, I asked the shaman to call for Sara to help with the cleanup. Sara was one of the servants I trusted to keep things private.

Ash said nothing as we made her comfortable and changed all of her bedding. When Sara left, I helped my sister to a set of cushions by the window. I kept hold of her hand as I sat with her.

"I miss Father," she whispered.

I nodded, my heart clenching with new pain. I missed our father as well but not in the way she did. I missed him because a child wasn't supposed to lose both of her parents so soon.

"What if Akish doesn't come back?" Her voice was riddled with a fresh wave of pain.

"He wouldn't miss the coronation," I said.

Her face brightened for an instant. "I guess not. A king doesn't miss his own crowning."

I nodded. "He's just as devastated as you about the child. He'll return as soon as he realizes you need him." I didn't know why I was defending him, but it brought comfort to my sister. I just hoped what I said would come to pass.

"What will you wear for the coronation?" I said, hoping to distract her and thinking of my painting.

Ash waved a hand, and I looked in the corner of the room. A dozen bolts of cloth were piled haphazardly. I released her hand and rose. I examined the various selections of cloth, relishing the smoothness of the material in my fingers. It was a luxury we hadn't enjoyed for a long time. A shiver traveled the length of my arms as I thought of my sister being crowned as queen.

I turned to her. Her face was flushed, as if she were thinking the same thing, despite her sorrow over her child.

Then I realized someone stood in the doorway. Akish strode into the room without a glance at me and knelt in front of Ash. He took her hands and kissed them. She threw herself into his arms, sobbing.

I left the room without a sound, tears in my own eyes. I was torn between hating my brother-in-law and knowing my sister needed him.

* * *

The throne room glowed brightly, lit with a thousand oil lamps. Akish and my sister were radiant as they stood together before the room packed with people. Ash's gold tunic shone lustrously, and her robe emanated a deep indigo. The combination flattered her skin color.

I had not seen Levi since the day he found me in the herb room, but he now stood across the room, surrounded by the men of the court— all the important and influential men. As brother to the new king, Levi was certainly someone to contend with now. People would press him for favors, hoping to gain audience with the king. I wondered if Levi had questioned his brother about sending me to the temple and, if so, what he'd discovered. And whether the discovery pleased or upset him.

His face bore little emotion, and I couldn't tell whether he was satisfied with the turn of events. Was he a man who sought power like his brother? An envious man? A man who would stop at nothing to get what he wanted? He didn't seem to be, but I'd learned in a short time that there were few to be trusted, and perhaps no one.

The court quieted as the head priest of the Sun Temple began to recite the long history of kings, beginning with Jared and his brother and those who had originally settled this land. I stood at attention as the list of names was recited, the room growing very warm, while the people remained ever so quiet. It seemed I had heard this speech all too recently, at my own father's coronation. The head priest had become a regular fixture at our palace. Perhaps he'd have his own chamber established here soon.

I watched my sister and studied the pallor of her skin. She glowed in her finery, her hair carefully arranged beneath her massive headdress. Her lips were painted bright scarlet, making up for the unusual paleness of her face and darkness beneath her eyes. No one but those closest to her knew about the lost child. I marveled at her stamina and strength to stand for so long, and I thought she must be using every bit of control to keep up her pretense of good health.

The head priest at last finished his recitation, and my sister was crowned queen and her husband crowned king.

The music began right away, and the court burst into lively conversation, laughter, dancing, and feasting. The sorrows of the past week were forgotten. Nothing could touch the young, beautiful royal couple. Their future was dazzling to comprehend and their prospects vast. I could see it in the eyes of the court as Akish and my sister accepted congratulations and honors one by one from the people.

I milled about, speaking to a few women here and there. For the most part, the conversations were of the food, what my sister wore, what Akish wore. No one mentioned my father or the mystery surrounding his death. No one wanted to think of past sorrows; they wanted to begin anew by ushering in a new era.

My sister called for me above the din of the crowd, her jeweled hand extended toward me, and I went to her. I stood beside her and her husband and became surrounded by the well-wishes. Gifts of shell necklaces and jeweled bracelets were pressed into my hands. Kisses bestowed on my cheeks. Blessings of prosperity and health conferred upon my head. I was given as much credence as the new king and queen, and I spent the rest of the evening with them, my mind caught up in the extravagant attentions but my heart grieving.

CHAPTER 17

6 Months Later

ASH SPOILED ME THE DAY I turned eighteen. For six months we'd lived an enchanted existence. Akish made his adoration for his queen no secret. He sent her flowers and gifts each day, which she received with relish.

He was nothing but courteous toward me. Although he was still too affectionate for my taste, I had grown used to his casual touch and kisses on the cheek and decided it was who he was and would always be. With the death of my father, Tirzah the storyteller hadn't been invited back to court. Perhaps Tirzah was too much of a reminder of Akish's guilt.

Yet, despite the attention he lavished on Ash, there were plenty of times he was away during the night. I never questioned Ash on what he was doing; I decided she'd tell me if she needed to.

Ash knocked on my door before the morning meal was served. "We have it all set up in the garden. A full meal, musicians, and a merchant here to show us his exotic goods from the hills of Shim."

I practically leapt out of bed and dressed, with Ash laughing at my eagerness. She forced me to sit while she combed my hair. A rare interchange, for it was I who usually took care of her. She spoke to me in her melodic voice. "Akish has invited one hundred guests tonight to honor your birth date."

I gasped. "Where will they all sit?"

Her face flushed with pleasure. "We'll set up a feast in the outer courtyard and light torches so we may eat beneath the light of the moon."

The image that came to my mind was beautiful and incredible. I grinned, imagining myself the center of attention for one evening.

"Come on," Ash said, putting the comb down. "They're waiting for us."

The rest of the day was a whirlwind. Apparently, the one hundred guests weren't to wait until the sun set to arrive. Every hour more people came, bringing gifts for me and the king and queen. I had nowhere to put them all.

Akish had had a roof of palm fronds made and erected in the garden, providing shade for me to greet and thank the guests one by one. With each approaching guest, I wondered if the next would be Levi. I had only caught glimpses of him over the past months, but mostly he stayed away from the palace. Ash told me he was training soldiers near the border of the city. Each time I saw him, he looked tanner and stronger, his eyes an even deeper green. But there had been no conversation shared between us.

As the sun turned orange and sank against the horizon, Ash escorted me to her chambers. She shut the door, a secretive smile on her face. "Wait until you see your final gift."

"You've done too much already," I protested but couldn't contain my excitement.

Ash held up a deep indigo-colored tunic with silver embroidery at the bodice and hem.

"It's beautiful," I said.

Then she lifted up a scarf of a lighter blue but with similar embroidery. "You'll be the envy of every woman and have the attention of every man."

I touched the soft cloth and shook my head. "I could never outshine the queen."

My sister laughed, her voice tinkling a melody. "Tonight you shall." She held up her final gift, a miniature statue of the goddess Asherah, made of pure gold. The tiny goddess hung from a heavy chain.

I took the necklace and turned it over. My eyes pricked with tears because of the beauty of the gift and because of the commitment I had made to worship this silent goddess of my sister's. My fortune only seemed to increase with time, so perhaps I had made the right choice after all.

"Thank you. This is beautiful. Fit for a queen," I said. Here was payment and confirmation enough that I'd made the right choice to return to the palace. We embraced, and I was careful of her protruding stomach, for she was with child again.

I dressed, luxuriating in the fine clothing. Ash called Sara in to oil my body and perfume and comb my hair until it hung in glossy waves down my back. When she was nearly finished, Sara said, "Perhaps tonight you'll find a husband."

I flushed, having wondered about that very thing. Strangely, Ash didn't comment. I wondered if she and Akish had discussed my marriage prospects. After all, I was the sister to the royal couple and would certainly be matched with an aristocrat.

"That will be all, Sara," Ash said, rather sharply.

Sara didn't seem to mind but simply replaced the comb, bowed, and left the room.

By the time Ash and I reached the courtyard, the entire place had been transformed. Dozens of torches were staked along the walls and next to the tables piled with food. The merry glow of the flames contrasted nicely with the falling darkness. Everyone greeted me by name. Everyone complimented me on my appearance and my fine necklace. A few men proposed; their wives swatted their arms. Envious eyes followed me throughout the evening, and I realized my sister had been right. Today, I outshone even the queen.

The great feast began. Akish stood, a wine goblet in hand, calling everyone to attention. "Tonight we celebrate the birth of my dear sister-in-law. To Naiva!"

The crowd tapped their goblets and called out well-wishes. I smiled my best smile and raised my own goblet. It was then I saw Levi toward the back of the courtyard, separated from the main crowd. He had no platter or goblet in hand but simply watched, his gaze steady. My face heated again, and I looked quickly away. It was mere seconds though before my eyes were drawn back in his direction. But he had disappeared.

My heart pounded at the thought of him watching me unaware all evening. Why had he not joined his brother at the front? Or at least used good manners and greeted me?

I set my goblet down, and Sara immediately refilled it. She leaned down and patted my shoulder. "Birth date greetings," she said.

"Thank you."

Yet instead of moving away to fill another's goblet, her touch on my shoulder tightened. She leaned closer and whispered, "It's not right. What they are doing . . . keeping you for themselves."

"What?" I turned to look at her, but she let go of my shoulder and moved on. I watched her for a moment as she filled goblets one after another. But she didn't look in my direction again. I took a long swallow, letting the wine wash its sweetness over me. The lights, the music, the feast, the guests— that is what I would focus on tonight. Not some servant's rambling words.

I danced and danced—it seemed with every man who was present. Trading one set of arms for another set, I wondered if Sara's words when she was combing my hair would bear any weight. I hadn't discussed who I'd marry with my sister since my father had become king. I didn't know why I was holding back. Perhaps because all we did was talk about her—until today. Today was my day. Tonight was my night. Perhaps she'd indulge me. After all, I was eighteen now.

It was early in the morning when I finally fell into bed, but I couldn't sleep. My mind kept replaying the events of the day, from the beautiful garden meal to the feast in the courtyard. I was too tired to paint but not ready to sleep, so I put on my robe and walked out into the gardens just as the black sky softened to purple.

I watched the sunrise, felt the promising warmth of a new day, a new year, upon my face. The goddess necklace hung against my skin, reminding me that perhaps I was watched over. Perhaps I was fortunate.

Yawning, I headed back inside. It was still early for the servants to be up and around, so I was surprised when I heard voices coming from the cooking room. I slowed as I approached and was even more surprised to hear Akish's voice.

I stopped, waiting out of sight, not wanting to pass by the doorway and be noticed.

"She has made her choice," Akish said.

"You haven't given her a choice," another man said.

My heart thumped. *Levi.* What were the brothers speaking about?

"A threat is not an honest decision," Levi continued.

"You're welcome to ask *her,*" Akish said, his tone triumphant.

"I plan to do that."

Before I realized the conversation was over and before I could exit the corridor, Akish and Levi came out of the cooking room.

Levi looked surprised to see me, but Akish simply smiled. He crossed to me and planted a lingering kiss on my cheek. "My dear sister, you're up early on the day after your celebration."

My cheeks flushed, and I couldn't form a reply. Akish didn't seem to notice. He cast a glance back at Levi then strode down the hallway, leaving the two of us alone.

Levi studied me, and I tried to look anywhere but at him, feeling chagrined that I'd been caught listening. Levi remained still, and I finally looked up at him. His eyes were on my necklace. He closed the distance between us and lifted the miniature statue from its place. Confusion crossed his features as he stared at it. Then he let go, his fingers brushing my neck. My heart started again.

"Is this your choice?" he asked.

I lowered my eyes, unable to look at him. How could I explain? How could he understand the love I had for my sister and how much she needed me? With women it was different from men. "My sister needs me."

"So this is your sacrifice?"

I looked at him in time to see his eyes turn dark. "My family is not a sacrifice."

He continued to stare at me. "Lib told me of your discussions and why you were sent to the temple."

Anger swept through me. How dare Lib discuss me with this man, and how dare Levi force it from him.

His voice softened, and his eyes returned to green. "Do you still want to know more about the Lord?"

I took a step back, feeling as if I'd been punched in the stomach. Levi was too late. And I was too afraid. I'd rather put up with Akish and my temperamental sister than be returned to the temple. I knew they had every power to do it.

"You're a grown woman, Naiva," Levi said. "You can decide for yourself."

"Of course I can decide," I said, resentment snaking into my tone. "I have two choices. I can choose to worship their gods and goddesses and live with my family. Or I can reject them and be forced to live in the temple, where I would serve the sun god the rest of my days."

"There's a third choice." Levi moved closer, erasing the distance I'd put between us.

I blinked back tears. "I'd have no home."

"You can stay with me." His voice was quiet, his eyes determined.

I blanched. Was he serious? "Live with the soldiers? As what? A servant? Or a harlot?"

"Don't insult me. Or yourself," Levi said with a shake of his head. His hand closed around my arm. "As my wife."

Our gazes locked, and when his fingers, rough and calloused, touched my jawline then slid behind my head, I realized he was serious. I closed my eyes, inhaling his earthy scent, anticipating what this closeness might bring—wondering what my first kiss would be like. My stomach quivered with nerves, but I tilted my head up, waiting.

Levi unclasped my necklace and slid it off.

I opened my eyes and stared at the gold figurine he held in front of me. The warmth that had just encompassed me fled, leaving me cold all over.

"No wife of mine will worship false idols."

I opened my mouth, stunned. Here was another man telling me which god to worship. Ordering me into *his* beliefs. I snatched the necklace away. How dare he take my sister's gift.

His eyes flashed, and a myriad of questions flitted across his face.

I stepped back, away from his towering body and bronzed skin. I raised my shaking hands to my neck and reclasped the necklace.

His face hardened, but I didn't care. Let him find some serving girl to command.

I turned away, fighting tears but resolving to walk slowly. I didn't want him to know how much he'd affected me. He could go back to his company of soldiers.

Levi stopped me, grasping my hand, his skin rough to the touch. I refused to turn, but he leaned down and spoke in my ear. "Naiva, someday you'll put God first in your life. And when you do, I don't know if I'll still be waiting."

I tugged away from him. "Then don't bother waiting." I hurried down the corridor now, hoping I hadn't just made the greatest mistake of my life.

CHAPTER 18

I DIDN'T KNOW IF I loved Levi. I didn't know if he loved me. Marriage between a man and woman wasn't necessarily based on love. *That* I knew well.

My sister and Akish were fighting again. Only one day after my birthday and I had turned down a marriage proposal then landed myself in the middle of Akish and Ash.

I was to blame, certainly, but could I truly be blamed? "Was I right to turn him down?" I asked Ash, hours after Levi had left the palace, angry and probably never to return again. I'd told her about his proposal but not about his demands that I give up worshipping my family's idols.

"He'd take you from the palace and from me, Naiva." Her face was pale, likely from celebrating most of the night. "You don't want to be a soldier's wife." She waved her hand about her luxurious chamber. "You'd have to give up all this."

She rose from the cushions by the window, her movements fluid and graceful. She crossed to me, where I had been pacing and ranting. Her slim hands took mine and held on firmly. "I couldn't bear it. Who would I have if you left?"

Akish, I wanted to say but didn't. Looking into her luminous eyes, I knew I wanted to be that person for her. I ignored the tugging in my heart, the way my pulse had hammered when Levi had stood so close to me. His words were empty to me now. I wasn't going to live in a hut in a dirt field and be told which god to worship.

I was going to live in a palace with my family . . . and be told which god to worship.

Ash's grip tightened as the color drained from her face. "Oh no!" she cried before she fainted.

I screamed for help, but it seemed like hours before anyone came.

When Sara rushed into the room, we carried Ash to the bed. But by the time we had laid her on the bed, a dark red stain had spread below her waist. My sister had lost another child.

* * *

I lit an oil lamp then knelt before Ix Chel, the fertility goddess, my cheeks wet with tears. "Please," I whispered. "Please heal my sister quickly and give her the son she desires. An heir will secure the throne and keep our royal lineage strong."

The goddess regarded me, her gaze bland, her exaggerated body unmoving. I touched the miniature replica of the goddess of heaven hanging about my neck, hoping for some sense of peace, some answer. Hoping that with the combined forces of the two goddesses something might happen.

I placed my forehead to the ground, my tears dripping onto the prayer rug. I repeated the words over and over. "My sister is queen. Blessing her is blessing the land. Grant our family your benevolence."

Ix Chel remained in her gold-crafted encasing without a word.

Much later, I rose from the rug, feeling stiff and achy. My days had been spent tending to my sister's grief and her husband's hostility. His sporadic absences during the night had now turned into disappearing during the daylight as well, sometimes not coming home until the next day.

Although my sister hadn't complained to me directly, I felt that my worst suspicions were confirmed. At least he was smart enough to not bring the harlots into the palace, but my sister and I knew he found comfort in other women's arms.

The rumors didn't necessarily reach us first, but they always reached us eventually. Akish was known as a patron at many of the taverns in the city, going from place to place, as if seeking for something he'd never find at home. Filled with drinking, games, gossip, and women who dressed in next to nothing, the taverns slowly separated husband from wife, night by night, minute by minute.

Another child lost. A marriage crumbling. But still, they formed a united, if false, front at all celebrations and festivals. Ash immersed herself in throwing the most lavish events, and Akish became obsessed with fortifying our city and building the strongest army in the land, leaving me to comfort my sister in his absence.

I would have done anything to ease her pain, to bring the sun back into her life and heal her family.

I turned from Ix Chel, dejection settling into the core of my soul. Her cold, gold face gave me no comfort, no promise.

As I made my way back to my room along the dark corridor, I thought of Lib's faceless God—a God with no idols, a God who had warned a king of danger. Would this God have warned Ash of Akish if we had worshipped him?

I shook my head, trying to rid myself of the traitorous thoughts, but they returned again and again. When I reached my room, I discovered Ash sitting on my bed. I braced myself for another night of listening to her complaints about her husband. If she was in my chamber, then obviously Akish wasn't home.

But there were no tears in her eyes. In fact, she smiled as I entered. "Did you make a late-night trip to the cooking room?"

"No, I was in the prayer room."

Her face fell for a moment then brightened. "Did Ix Chel tell you about my new plan?"

I looked at her, puzzled. None of the goddesses had ever spoken to me like my sister claimed they spoke to her.

"Of course not," Ash said with a giggle. "You're not queen."

I sat next to her on the bed, unease creeping through me as I wondered why my sister was here so late at night in such a pleasant mood.

She clapped her hands together. "I've come to tell you why Akish and I haven't chosen a husband for you."

My stomach knotted in anticipation. Would they send me to the temple after all?

"I was so stubborn when Akish first suggested it, but it turns out that he is right, which has only been confirmed by my losing two babies." She smiled, but it was eerie, not comforting. "It appears that it's Ix Chel's wish as well."

"*What* is Ix Chel's wish?"

Ash exhaled and took my hands in hers. "I need an heir to the throne. If I don't have a son, someone in Akish's family will take over if anything happens to him. If I die without producing an heir, our family will lose all its power."

"You aren't going to die, Ash," I said. "You're young and will have plenty of children."

Her strained smile was back. "I plan to have more children, and I pray constantly that I will have many sons. But the sooner the throne is secured, the stronger our power and claim to the throne will be."

I knew all this. But Ash hadn't even been married for a year. Why was she so impatient? Besides the fact that it was her born nature.

Ash leaned forward and said, "The heir must come through *you* if I fail."

Was this about Levi and the proposal I turned down? Mixed thoughts tumbled through my mind. Even with my sister's blessing, was I willing to marry a man who wanted to control me?

"I don't know if I want to marry him."

Ash barked out a laugh. "I wouldn't allow you to *marry* him. You'd be his handmaiden, and the children produced would be legally mine."

I stared at her, confused, and then slowly the horror of what she was saying sifted into my mind. "Are you talking about *Akish*?"

"Of course." Her brows quirked; then she let out a full laugh. "The heir to the throne needs to be as pure as possible. Having a child through you and Akish is the next closest thing to an untainted line of authority."

Nausea tore through my stomach, and I pulled my hands from hers. I covered my mouth, inhaling, trying to block out what she was suggesting. It couldn't be true. I looked back at her, hoping this was a dream and she'd evaporate like a column of smoke. But she returned my gaze calmly, expectation in her eyes.

There was a time when I would have embraced being the wife of Akish, but that was before my sister had married him. Before my father had been murdered by him. He was not a man I'd ever consider marrying, let alone producing children with, no matter the reason.

"He cares a great deal for you, Naiva," Ash continued. "I know that at one time I was jealous of the affection he showed you, but now I realize it makes this all that much more natural and easy for both of you." She ran her hand along my arm, trying to draw me back to her. "It will be duty, yes, and a sacrifice, but it won't be as terrifying as you think. Akish is truly a sweet man, and he'll be gentle with you."

Sweet. Gentle. Not words I'd use to describe my brother-in-law. Bile burned hot in my throat, and I leapt from the bed. I stumbled to the wash basin and vomited.

"Don't make a bid for my sympathies, Naiva," Ash said, her tone exasperated.

As I rinsed out my mouth, Ash crossed the room and put her hand on my shoulder. "You'll get used to the idea soon enough." Her voice held no trace of sympathy. "Understand that you're the hope of our kingdom, of our *family*, and this is an incredible honor."

"I can't," I gasped. The bile was back, and I hunched over the basin until my stomach muscles relaxed. I turned to her, my head throbbing, but I wanted to make myself clear. "I love you, Ash. And I'll do anything to ensure that your children gain the throne. But I'll not have a child with your husband."

Her eyes didn't even register surprise, just a tinge of sorrow. "I knew there would be some resistance. I wouldn't expect anything less. In fact, if you'd been excited at the prospect, I probably *would* send you back to the temple." She laughed at herself, the sound high-pitched and unnatural.

I turned away, unable to look at her glowing eyes. "I can't, Ash. He's my brother-in-law."

Ash's voice became hard. "It's for our future. Do you want to hand over the kingdom to a *stranger?*"

"Of course not," I whispered. "But you and Akish have many child-bearing years ahead. Any child I might have would be no one compared to your children."

"We can only hope for that," Ash said. "But I can't risk it right now. Ix Chel has spoken, and we must obey her, or I'll continue to be put through the torture of losing my babies."

You mean Akish *has spoken,* I wanted to say but didn't.

"Akish will be here tomorrow night," Ash said in a firm voice. "He has concerns as well, but he's willing to make this sacrifice, he says, for the good of the kingdom."

I wrapped my arms around my torso as my sister left the room, shutting the door silently behind her. I stared at the door for several minutes until my eyes started to water. I had to find a way out, but helplessness consumed me. I climbed into the bed and pulled the coverlet over my head, blocking out the world in which I lived.

CHAPTER 19

I WOKE WITH A SILENT scream on my lips. My sister's words from the night before came flooding back all at once, bringing a new wave of revulsion. Had it been a dream? A terrible dream that had encompassed my worst nightmare?

I sat up, keeping the covers pulled to my chin as I looked around my room. Everything appeared the same, unlike the tempest I had expected. When my world caved in, shouldn't the physical things around me be destroyed as well?

Perhaps it was all a misunderstanding. Perhaps Ash would visit me today and tell me it had all been a cruel trick. She had been testing me. She had wanted to see my reaction in order to put to rest her envy about her husband's interest in her sister once and for all.

I scrambled out of bed, my head throbbing with all the crying I'd done the night before. I had miraculously fallen asleep, even if it had only been for a couple hours.

I washed and changed then brushed my hair furiously and smoothed it into a tight knot at the base of my head. Then with trembling fingers, I fastened the goddess necklace about my neck, a symbol of my loyalty and sacrifice for my family. I hoped it would be enough. But I wasn't above groveling.

Ash was in the throne room with Akish. I almost turned and ran, but I had resolved to face this directly. I took a deep breath and entered. Several other court members were there. They greeted me, but their words died on their lips as I ignored them and headed straight for the king and queen.

As customary, I dropped into a low curtsy when they both noticed me.

"Naiva, it's so good to see you this morning," Ash said, her voice elevated.

I lifted my head, the painful throbbing back. Akish's eyes were on me, dark and contemplative. Ash held her hands out to me, but I refused to move.

"I have made many sacrifices for our family, Ash," I began in a raspy voice. The crying hadn't done much good for my throat.

Ash's eyes narrowed; then she turned to the court members. "Please leave. This is a private matter."

Footsteps scurried around me, and seconds later, the throne room was absolutely quiet.

I didn't wait for permission to speak. I had to spill it all out while the courage burned hot inside. I didn't care what they did to me, what my punishment was, but I would *not* become a handmaiden to Akish.

"I've spent my life in your shadow in order to help you achieve your destiny as queen," I said.

"It is your destiny as the second daughter to serve me," Ash spat out.

"I know," I said, keeping my tone calm. "And I have done it with pleasure and will continue to do so." I couldn't look at Akish with the next words I spoke. "Part of my loyalty to my sister, and my queen, is to not interfere in her marriage and to not—"

"This is not interference, Naiva," Ash cut in. "This is a command from your king and queen. It's an order but also a very high honor." Her voice softened by a margin. "I could choose any woman as a handmaiden. But I chose you. Just that fact alone proves my love and concern for you and for our family's pure bloodline."

My eyes welled with hot tears, no matter how much I didn't want to cry.

"Just think, dear sister, one of your sons might be on the throne. He might be in a position that you could never be in yourself, but *through you*, he'll rule the entire kingdom."

I knew what she was doing. Twisting. Tempting. But I had been born a second daughter, and I had never aspired to her desires, either for myself or for my future children. Yet how could I turn them down without incurring their wrath?

I sank to my knees, desperate, not caring if I looked like a childish fool in front of Akish. Perhaps it would dissuade Akish from coming to my chamber tonight. "Please," I begged, trying to keep my shaking voice steady, "let me serve you in the ways I've already served. Don't add this to my lot."

"Don't you think I'd seek another way if there was one?" Ash rose to her feet, her face a mass of anger.

Akish put a hand on her arm. "Let's give her some time," he said.

Time wouldn't change my mind, but a small well of relief opened in my chest. Perhaps time would change *their* minds.

My sister assented to her husband's suggestion with one condition. "She must be well guarded, then." Her eyes narrowed as my face flushed. I was too easy to read.

I left the throne room, my eyes red and blotchy, my face swollen, and my legs ready to collapse at any moment. Two guards followed and stationed themselves outside my chamber.

I spent the rest of the day on my bed, alternating between acute nausea and disbelief. I burned with anger and hatred. I had to find a way past the guards, I decided. The windows were too small to fit through, and the door was blocked, but I still plotted. As the afternoon shadows collected in my room, I packed a satchel of clothing. I included only the necessities, hoping that whoever had the compassion to take me in would allow me to work for my keep.

I finally fell asleep, exhausted, as the orange afternoon sky turned lavender. I was settled on my plan to escape in the middle of the night.

It was dark when I awakened. Confusion filled me, then my mind suddenly cleared as I recalled what was supposed to happen tonight. I scrambled off my bed and straightened the covers. I didn't know when the chance would arise, but I wanted to be prepared to flee at the most opportune moment. I didn't know exactly where to go, but I remembered Nelise telling me about her home in the Isla village. I hoped her parents might take me in for a short time.

I decided I might be able to sell my paintings, so I turned to add my set of dyes to the satchel. Then I froze.

"Hello," Akish said. He sat near the window, silhouetted by the moonlight.

Fear took possession of every part of my body. How long had he been there watching me sleep? Had he seen my loaded satchel by the wash basin? Had he wondered why I was straightening the covers when evening had descended?

He stood, and my heart nearly stopped. How could I get out of this? How could I explain? I had thought of a hundred different ways, but now that he stood in front of me, I couldn't think of one.

"Don't be afraid," he said in a soft voice.

I took a step back, my legs hitting my bed frame.

"Screaming won't help either. I've dismissed the guards." His lips moved into a smile. "They wouldn't dare interfere anyway." He took a few steps closer. "I know this is not what we hoped for from the beginning. Do you remember when I told you there was something powerful between us?"

I don't know if I nodded; I don't know if I even moved. I could only stare at him.

"There still is . . . something between us." He touched my cheek, running his smooth fingers down to my neck then resting them at my collarbone. "No matter what reason Ash gives—or the goddess, Ix Chel— we were meant to be together. And this is our opportunity."

His touch sickened me.

"I love you," he said, pulling me into his arms. I tensed, hating to feel his body against mine, hating that I might have once welcomed it. "You're the sister I saw first," he murmured. "And the sister I see now. I can give you everything you desire. My love has no limits."

He held me gently, but it was as if his arms were iron shackles. I knew I couldn't overpower him. I knew his wicked heart would have no problem snapping my neck or driving a dagger through my heart. I would be another accident at the palace that he'd get away with.

I pushed the rising nausea back down, wrapped my arms about his neck, and pulled him closer. "I'd like to wash and prepare myself for tonight," I whispered against his warm neck.

He chuckled and held me tighter. "You smell delicious."

"No," I breathed. "I want to be special for you."

"How long will it take?" he said, his fingers threading through my hair before releasing me.

I met his black eyes. "Not long."

"I'll be right outside the door, then." Akish touched my lips as he spoke, and I kissed his fingers. A small growl escaped, and he leaned in, but I put my hands on his chest and playfully pushed him away.

"Patience," I whispered. "Bring some wine while you're working on that patience."

He gave me an adoring look, one I'd seen him give my sister many times. When the door clicked shut behind him, I knew I had only a few moments before he would return, goblets in hand.

I dumped my collection of dyes into my satchel, took one final look about my room, and opened the door. The corridor was dark and silent. I heard nothing over my pounding heart. To the right was the cooking room where Akish had likely gone to fetch the wine. To the left was the king and queen's chamber, the throne room, the entrance to the palace.

My choices were limited. If I ran into Ash, I hoped to be faster than her. If I ran into Akish, heaven help me.

* * *

I approached the guards at the entrance of the palace. "Akish needs assistance," I said. "He says he needs help from every able guard."

The first guard looked at the second then nodded. They both abandoned their post and hurried into the palace. It would only take a few minutes before they discovered my lie.

I hurried across the courtyard. The moon had never seemed so bright and the sky so clear. Everywhere I looked was bathed in silvery light, limiting the shadows that might conceal me on my journey. Once outside the gate, I ran along the wall until I reached the line of trees that bordered the palace grounds. I didn't dare head straight into town.

Instead, I circled the palace until I reached the practice fields. I imagined torches being lit, shouting through the corridors, and men searching for me. The thought propelled me to move faster until I was sprinting across the expanse of field, lifting my tunic so my legs were free to run. I reached the thick set of trees that separated the first field from the second, and I stopped in the shelter of the deep shade to catch my breath.

Sure enough, various torches shone from the palace. Was Ash awake and caught up in the search? My breathing slowed, but my heart continued to hammer. One more field and then I'd be in the hills of Ephraim. On the other side of the hills was the city of Cerros. Then through the next valley, I'd arrive at the village of Isla—home to Nelise.

Then I froze. Men carrying torches had appeared at the back courtyard walls. I could almost see their faces from across the field, garish in the orange flames. I didn't wait to see if one might be Akish. It didn't matter.

I turned and ran through the trees, the underbrush clawing at my tunic and legs. Fear pulsed through me, making me run faster and faster despite my ragged breaths and aching muscles.

I sprinted across the second field, my satchel knocking against my hip, but I didn't slow until I reached the next group of trees. Everything was uphill from here, but I was determined to put plenty of distance between me and the palace.

I turned again, the curiosity too great to not know if I was being pursued.

The moonlight seemed to detail every bush and clump of grass in the field. The wind was gentle tonight, barely moving the leaves overhead and not strong enough to disturb the grass or wildflowers.

I'm free, I thought then quickly pushed it away. I wasn't free yet. For a moment, I wished I'd brought a waterskin. The path to a nearby river wasn't far away, but I didn't want to travel anywhere that Akish might think to look. I started up the hillside, heading east, away from the palace and away from the river.

Though exhausted, I decided to walk through the night and arrive at Nelise's village by morning. I reached the first ridge and turned to look over the escarpment. I hadn't traveled as far as I'd thought, and the palace still seemed relatively close. The torchlights were more spread out now, with a couple in the first field and several along the perimeter of the palace.

Please, I prayed to whichever god might be listening, *please send them in the wrong direction.*

I crested the ridge and started down the other side of the hill. At the base was a narrow river. When I reached it, I drank the water and felt a measure of energy restored. My head throbbed, and my breath was still far from normal, but with each step, hope grew stronger.

I stood and looked up at the next hill looming over me.

A rush of air touched my legs, and something heavy crashed into the back of my head. I was so stunned I barely put my hands out in time to brace myself from falling into the river. I landed hard on my knees, scraping them against the rocks, my hands flailing to find purchase.

Someone wrenched my arms behind me and lashed them together. I screamed. A cold hand clamped over my mouth, and I was dragged to my feet. I kicked at my assailant and tried to pull away. I slipped on the rocks.

The man jerked me painfully to my feet again, and I came face to face with the guard I'd lied to. His lips parted, and he sneered at me before calling out, "Got her!"

The footsteps that scuttled over the rocks made my heart sink. I might have had a chance against one man but not against several.

The guard forced me forward, and I nearly stumbled into Akish.

"Well, well," he said in a quiet voice, looking me up and down.

A shudder went through my body as I met his gaze. Hatred seemed to pour into me. I'd never seen or felt such fury. I broke the gaze, my fear turning into outright panic.

"I'll take her," Akish said. The guard handed me over, and Akish's strong fingers closed around my upper arm. He started forward, practically dragging me along. I willed myself to walk, though my hands and knees were scraped, my head throbbing, and my legs exhausted.

We retraced my steps almost exactly, making me wonder how free I had ever been. I hadn't even heard them, let alone seen them.

When we reached the first field, Akish told the guards, "Go ahead and prepare the prison. I'll bring her in the rest of the way."

The three guards hurried ahead, their mission almost complete. No one would be reprimanded tonight for doing a poor job—no one but me.

Akish pulled me firmly to his side. "A woman in love doesn't run to the hills."

My blood chilled as he slowed his step significantly. Would he ravish me right here in the fields beneath the open sky?

I wanted to bite my tongue but didn't. "A man in love with me wouldn't tie me up."

He exhaled with what sounded like a cross between a sigh and a snort. Then he came to a complete stop and put both hands on my shoulders.

"Naiva, I would never force you." His eyes burned into me. One smooth hand touched my cheek. "I would have you come to me willingly. What brute of a man do you think I am?"

My expression must have said it all, for his hands slid from my shoulders to my upper arms.

"I will not be accused of assaulting a defenseless woman, not even in your mind," Akish said. The anger was back. "You'll be punished for disobeying your king. And when you're ready to be loyal to your family again, I'll personally escort you from prison." His hand touched my chin. "One of these days, you'll tire of your shackles, and you will be mine. Completely."

Although his touch was fashioned as a caress, my fear only multiplied.

Help me, I pled silently, though I wanted to scream the words. There was no one to help me. Not even the gods and goddesses had been listening. I had been captured, hadn't I? And now I'd be imprisoned. The queen's own sister.

CHAPTER 20

FILTH SURROUNDED ME. DAMP AIR permeated my skin. I felt the dirt in my hair, in my clothes, and beneath my feet. I had no idea prisoners were kept in such poor living conditions. Not that I'd ever thought being kept prisoner in a hole beneath the earth was anything luxurious, but I thought at least the holes were cleaned out periodically.

Akish had lowered me into the cavern, sending an oil lamp with me. I supposed it was as an act of mercy on his part, since it was still dark outside and I wouldn't have been able to see my prison until the sun had risen. I set the lamp in the middle of the small cavern and looked around.

A wide-mouthed jar stood in one corner for a privy. It smelled as if it hadn't been cleaned out since the last prisoner, whoever that poor soul had been. A mat lay against one side of the cavern. I couldn't decide which looked dirtier, the ground or the mat. There was no rug for warmth or any food or water in sight.

I sat in the middle of the cavern, ignoring the mat, and hovered over the flame of the oil lamp. It gave off little warmth, but somehow staying near it brought me a sense that I wasn't the only living thing in this hole. I wanted to preserve the oil, but if I blew out the flame, I had no way to relight it. I doubted new oil would be among any standard prisoner supplies.

As I stared at the flickering orange, I imagined Akish returning to the palace and telling Ash that her sister was sitting like a filthy varmint at the bottom of a hole. I pulled my knees up to my chest and wrapped my arms around them. I imagined Ash's surprised reaction, her possible horror, then her demand that her sister be released. No member of the royal family should be treated this way.

I wondered if Akish would tell her that I would be released when I promised to become his handmaiden.

Ash would tell him he'd gone too far, that I should be locked in my room or sent to the temple again. What would people say about the queen's sister being imprisoned?

The hours passed, and no Ash. I curled up and lay on the floor, barely keeping my eyes open to watch the flame.

The darkness dissipated, replaced by a gray light. Morning had arrived. Still no Ash. I was forced to use the privy jar; then I scurried back to my place at the center of the cavern, next to the now-extinguished lamp. I lay back on the ground and watched the changing colors of the sky through the opening at the top of the hole. Gray. Blue. Violet. Indigo. Black.

Still no Ash.

She hadn't come for me.

* * *

On the second day, they fed me—two tortillas and a waterskin dropped down the hole. I forced myself to eat slowly after I practically inhaled the first tortilla. My stomach had alternated from starving to nausea to nothing.

Every minute of waiting was agonizing, and I could only hope that my being in prison was agonizing for my sister too. Why didn't she come? I also wondered why Akish didn't come, even if only to ask if I'd changed my mind. But death seemed a better alternative than becoming his handmaiden. Even if he were to give me the status of a second wife, I would refuse.

I had heard the stories of old and how the two wives of Lamech turned against him when they found out what he really was—someone who had entered into a secret combination. Someone who was a murderer. The two wives had rebelled and revealed his dark secrets to others. Lamech was despised and cast out.

But I knew marrying Akish would only drive my sister and me farther apart. And it would only plunge us into greater darkness.

The sun set on the second day.

The third day.

The fourth day.

I awoke with a start. I'd taken to sleeping in the moon-lit patch on the ground so I felt as if I were still a part of the living world. Someone had spoken; I was sure of it.

"Naiva," the whisper came again.

I sat up, my body weak and stiff. Peering at the incoming moonlight, I saw the silhouette of a head looking down on me.

"Lib?" My voice scratched since I hadn't spoken aloud in several days.

"Yes," he hissed back. "I brought you some things."

"All right," I said. "Throw them down." I stepped out of the direct line of the opening, and seconds later, a thick woven rug landed at my feet. I picked it up and held it against my chest. The nights grew cold down in the cavern.

Something else landed on the ground, and I picked up a small tied basket. Inside, I found a guava, an avocado, and a pouch filled with pistachios. "Thank you," I called up to Lib.

"I'll try to come every night," he said. "I've been praying for you. All of us from the cooking room have."

Unexpected tears came to my eyes, but I quickly brushed them aside. The gods had been silent to me. Apparently, they had more important people to help.

I touched the idol that hung about my neck, thinking of the desperate pleas I'd sent to her.

"Naiva." Lib's voice came again. "I know you may not believe this now, but the Lord is watching over you. He'll bless you if you but turn to Him, and only Him, in faith."

I sputtered out a laugh. I didn't want to hurt Lib's feelings. I was grateful for the kindness he'd showed me, but his words of faith rang hollow in my mind. "Why are you here?" I asked. "Aren't you afraid you'll get caught?"

"The risk is worth it."

"It's not worth it," I said. "You shouldn't be here. We've already been in trouble once for talking about your God. This time they might throw you in prison."

"They might," Lib said. "But the Lord will protect me wherever I am."

"Prison isn't a protection," I nearly shouted.

"It's protecting you from Akish." His response was quiet, just above a whisper.

"I know." It was true—for the moment I was safe from my brother-in-law. I exhaled, trying to take comfort in the bit of realization. I looked up again. "Does everyone at the palace talk about me? Does my sister worry about me?"

"Your sister is who she's always been," Lib said.

I didn't have to ask him to explain. I knew exactly what he meant. Ash wouldn't be coming for me. She'd stand by her husband's decision and allow me to be made an example to the people. I sank to the floor, pulling the rug about my shoulders.

"I don't know if I'll ever be released from this prison," I said. "I can't be a handmaiden to my sister's husband." My voice cracked, and I wished to be alone again, to grieve in private.

"We're praying for you," Lib said. "Have faith in the Lord. He has the power to deliver you."

I said nothing in reply, and after a few moments, he said, "I'll try to return tomorrow night."

"Thank you," I whispered, and then he was gone.

I lay on the ground, the rug pulled over me, and curled around the basket of food. I'd eat it in the morning. My stomach wasn't complaining too loudly now. I'd received the customary two tortillas just before sunset.

* * *

As the days and weeks passed, Lib came almost every night, bringing me food and other comforts. I engaged in the habit of asking him about those at the palace, without mentioning my sister's name. But he'd always give a report on her and her activities. Although I wanted to rant against the life of excess she was living, I listened patiently, grateful for any conversation with another soul.

I'd lie on my back in the moonlight, while overhead, Lib's voice calmed and comforted me as he told me tales of how the Lord had delivered prophets and entire groups of people. They all had the same thing in common: enduring through their trials and praying with faith.

"But they still had trials."

"Yes," Lib said. "That is part of our life's journey."

"If the Lord can deliver us, why do we have to go through the challenge in the first place?"

"To make us stronger," Lib said.

I thought about it for a moment, but it still didn't make sense. "I'd be a lot more grateful if I *weren't* in prison."

"When you get out of prison, you'll see the world with new eyes. Your gratitude will increase ten-fold."

I closed my eyes, imagining what it would be like to feel the breeze on my skin, smell the sweet scent of a flower, wade into a river of rushing water. "I'm ready to be delivered now."

Lib let out a soft chuckle. "In the Lord's time."

I propped myself up on my elbows. "Can I speed it up?"

Lib laughed again. "You can try. Prayer might help."

Prayer. I'd said the words of prayers many, many times. But I'd never felt the peace that I felt when talking to Lib about his God. Was it Lib or was it his God? Or was I just so desperate for another human to talk to that I created this emotion when Lib visited? "Does Sara know about your visits?" I asked.

"Yes," he said without hesitation.

"Is she praying for me?"

"Yes."

I sat up now. "Who else is praying for me?"

As he named every servant I knew at the palace and even some I didn't, tears stained my cheeks. When he finished, the silence stretched out between us.

"If all those people are praying for me," I began, "and if your God is real, wouldn't He have answered them by now?"

"The Lord's answers don't always come in the manner we expect," Lib said.

I pulled my knees up to my chest. "So that's what faith is?"

"Exactly."

After Lib left that night, I moved to my knees and lifted my head and hands toward heaven. "O Lord, I kneel before Thee with a humble heart and broken spirit. Please, Lord, deliver me from this prison. Please spare me from becoming a handmaiden. Please guide me, O Lord."

I lowered my hands and noticed I'd started to perspire. My heart thudded. My prayer sounded weak, and Lib probably would have laughed if he'd heard. But it was a start. Feeling strangely content, I lay back down and fell asleep.

CHAPTER 21

5 Weeks Later

"How long has she been down here?" The voice floated over me, just out of reach. Someone touched my forehead.

My eyes snapped open, and I found myself staring at a man I thought I'd never see again.

"Ah, you're awake," Levi said.

A dream. I was certain of it. With no desire to dream about Levi, or any other man, I turned over and closed my eyes.

"Naiva," his voice came again. He touched my shoulder briefly. Feeling the roughness of his hand reminded me of how opposite he was to his brother. Akish's hands were as smooth as a woman's.

I kept my eyes shut, willing my dream to fade. I'd been praying every morning and night for three weeks. In fact, I'd been praying every waking moment, petitioning Lib's God so many times that I was sure my prayers were simply being ignored. I had tried, and so far it had failed. But each time Lib's head appeared at the top of the cavern, I didn't have the heart to give up. So I continued in faith—at least as much as I could muster.

"She hasn't been eating much." Lib's voice. "She used to finish what I brought, but now she eats only half."

I opened my eyes. Lib was a part of my reality, not a part of my dreaming world.

His wide eyes stared down at me. My gaze moved from Lib to the other man who occupied my cavern.

What was Levi doing here? His large frame seemed to fill the space of the cavern. He didn't belong here—he was clean, well fed, and strong. I was filthy and weak. I scooted away and rose to a crouch. I didn't want him here. I didn't want anyone to touch me.

Lib must have seen my confusion. "He can help you, Naiva. You've been ill."

My eyes watered, but I refused to let the tears fall. I had so little left inside me to cry anyway. "Am I to be set free?" I croaked.

Levi's jaw tightened.

"Not yet," Lib said in a careful voice. "The guard allowed Levi down here to check on your condition . . . as a healer."

"He's no healer," I said. "He's a soldier under the rule of the king." I looked directly at Levi. "Tell me why you've really come." My stomach tightened at the thought of being forced into something. "Are you taking me to Akish?"

"No," Levi said. "I don't want you near my brother."

Relief filled me. "Has Akish changed his mind? Will he set me free?"

Pity darkened Levi's eyes. "He hasn't changed his mind. But he can't stop me from checking on your condition."

I folded my too-thin arms, wishing I were strong enough to stand. The compassion in his eyes only made me feel weaker. "My health is none of your concern."

"You haven't been eating," Lib said.

"I'm not hungry."

"You're starving yourself," Lib broke in, his voice trembling. "Please don't give up, Naiva."

I looked down at the ground, the floor of what had been my home for many days, perhaps several weeks now.

"You have to talk to her, Levi," Lib said. "Tell her to have faith."

"Faith?" I cried out, not caring if I sounded like a madwoman. "Your God has been nothing but silent. I have prayed to Him every hour. He's no better than the stone statues that litter the city." I'd discarded my goddess necklace in favor of praying to Lib's God. But nothing had come of it. I had received only Levi in my cavern to pity me.

"Naiva," Levi said.

I turned away from them. I didn't want to see their clean faces, their clean clothing. I didn't want to see the sympathy in their eyes as they took in my disgusting surroundings. "Leave."

Despite my request, Levi crossed toward me and set a waterskin next to me. "It has orange blossom inside. You should drink it all. I'll bring more in a couple days."

I picked up the waterskin and hurled it at him. It dropped with a thud at his feet, missing its mark. My arm strength was next to nothing now.

Without another word, Lib and Levi left the cavern, one of the guards above pulling them upward with a rope. I was furious that they dared tell me what I should and should not be eating or drinking. Why did everyone insist on commanding me at every turn? But what did it matter? Unless they could convince the king and queen to free me, I had no hope.

I pulled the rug around my shoulders, even though I wasn't cold. It had become the only comfort to me in the dark cavern.

I must have drifted off to sleep because I awoke in the dark with Lib calling my name.

I grunted in reply.

"He's only trying to help, Naiva," Lib's voice sailed down to me.

"Then tell him to free me."

"He doesn't have the power."

"Why does he pretend to be concerned about me, then?" I asked, allowing bitterness into my voice.

"He doesn't pretend," Lib said. "Levi was traveling from city to city, recruiting soldiers for the borders. He didn't return until yesterday, and when he heard of your imprisonment, he came immediately."

I let Lib's words settle into my soul but not my heart.

"I know he asked you to marry him."

I remained silent. If Lib knew about the proposal, he likely knew what my reply had been.

"I brought you something," Lib said in a soft voice.

A wrapped bundle fell from the top of the cavern and landed a couple paces from me. I had no interest or desire to open it.

"Please keep the faith," Lib said. "We're still praying for your deliverance."

I didn't have the strength to counter him.

* * *

The days and weeks passed in a blur, the darkness periodically filled with the light of an oil lamp, with someone forcing me to drink a bitter orange tea. Sometimes I opened my eyes to see Levi's worried face; other times I turned my head away and refused to respond.

I wasn't sure exactly how much time had passed since the first visit from Levi, but I did know the nights had grown much colder. The harvest season must be over and the monsoon well into its first month. I'd taken to sleeping against the wall, as far away from the rain-soaked center as possible. Lib had sent down another rug, which provided extra warmth, but I continued to lose weight.

I had no appetite and no desire to make the concessions needed to escape my prison. There had been no change in the king and queen's decision, and there had been no change in mine.

I slept most of the days and lay awake most of the nights, the changing light from the cavern opening my only indication of passing time. It was dark when a rope cascaded down the opening of the cavern now. I barely registered the movement and languidly watched the person who lowered himself down the hole.

This time his voice reached my ears but not my mind, so I wasn't sure what he was saying. He lifted me up, and I had no strength to resist. I stared at nothing as he carried me to the rope, tied it around my waist, and tied it again beneath my armpits. Someone slowly raised me out of the cavern into the yellow moonlight. Stars littered the night sky, so far away yet so close. Other men were there, yet I couldn't focus enough to recognize any of their faces or voices. Someone lowered me into a cart of sorts, and the jostling began. I wanted to ask where I was being taken, but my voice wouldn't obey.

I imagined being hauled to the center of the town to be executed. Or perhaps I'd be dumped someplace and buried. I was close enough to death; why wait any longer? A hand touched my cheek, a rough hand that I remembered. But I didn't turn my head, nor did I open my eyes.

I let out my breath, hoping it would be my last.

It wasn't, as I found out when I woke to a blinding light.

I covered my eyes with my hand.

"There, there," a woman's voice said. "Keep this cloth over your eyes for now." She pressed a coarse-woven cloth into my hands.

I placed it over my eyes and opened them. An incredible light filtered through the indigo fibers of the cloth. I felt strangely comfortable and relaxed. And clean. Perhaps I'd arrived in the afterlife.

"Are you the sun goddess?"

The female voice chuckled, and a hand gently grasped mine. "No, my dear. You are at my humble home in the village of Palo."

I'd heard of the village; it was north of Nelise's home, the original location I was trying to escape to. "How did I get here?"

"My grandson brought you in the middle of the night."

The vague memories of traveling the night before came back to me. I wasn't entirely sure who had brought me out of the prison. I lifted a corner of the cloth and squinted at the woman who sat next to me.

Deep wrinkles lined her face, but she had perhaps the kindest and warmest eyes I'd ever seen. They were the color of forest leaves.

"Levi," I said.

"Yes. My grandson." The woman cracked a smile. "He'll be returning later today to make sure I've taken good care of you."

"Why did he bring me here?"

The woman touched my arm. "You can discuss that with him. For now, you should try to eat a little then get plenty of rest." She held out a steaming bowl and spooned up a thin soup. My first instinct was to clamp my mouth shut, but the woman's eyes looked so kind that I swallowed the first spoonful.

Several bites later, I couldn't take in anymore.

I leaned back. "What's your name?"

Another smile. "Virai."

"Why are you helping me? What will happen when the king finds out?" *Your other grandson?*

Virai patted my arm. "Don't you worry about Akish. He won't find you here."

I doubted her words, for how could Akish not hear news about his own grandmother harboring his sister-in-law? It wouldn't take the neighbors long to learn of my existence, I was sure, and to learn the news that a prisoner had been smuggled out of the king's prison.

"Go to sleep now. You're safe here." Virai's voice was so confident, so reassuring, that I closed my eyes again, keeping the cloth over them to darken the bright sunlight in the room.

CHAPTER 22

ON THE FIFTH MORNING OF my stay at Virai's home, I finally felt strong enough to venture into the yard. Levi had visited that first day but had only stayed for a few moments before his grandmother had ushered him out. I had been too tired and annoyed with his persistent questions about my health to pay much attention to him.

But today as I exited the back door and stepped into the lush greenery of Virai's garden, I wished I hadn't been so hardhearted toward Levi. He'd taken a great risk and would face punishment for it when he was inevitably found out. His grandmother told me it was all done in great secrecy, and no one spoke about it openly, though a reward had been offered for any information about me. I wanted to ask Levi what was going to happen next. To me. To him.

"That's enough," I heard a voice command nearby. I froze, wondering if someone had spotted me.

I turned a slow circle, my heart hammering, but saw no one.

The voice came again. "I'll be fine, Grandmother."

Levi? I continued on the winding path and arrived at a small opening in the garden. Levi's back was positioned toward me, bare and exposed. Deep red welts crisscrossed his flesh.

I gasped, and both Levi and Virai turned.

"What happened?" I asked, ignoring the astonishment on Levi's face at seeing me.

He stood, keeping his back from my view. "Are you doing well?" He glanced at his grandmother. "You didn't tell me she was up and walking."

"She's up and walking," Virai said, a smile creasing her wrinkled face.

I kept my gaze on Levi. "Your back . . . Was it Akish?"

His mouth pulled into a line, and he slipped on the shirt that had been hanging from his waist.

"He whipped you for taking me out of prison, didn't he?" I whispered, horrified that Akish would beat his own brother.

"Akish doesn't know anything," Levi said. "He only suspects."

"What about the others? Lib? The guards?"

Levi hesitated, his face like stone.

Virai put an arm around me. "She's strong enough to hear the truth."

Still, Levi hesitated. His grandmother gave him a firm nod. Finally he said, "Lib is in prison now. The guards were executed."

The breath left me. Virai's arm tightened around my shoulders, and I leaned against her for support. I closed my eyes, thinking of the lives that had been lost in my behalf. Although I hadn't asked them to rescue me, I felt even worse knowing they'd willingly helped Lib and Levi.

"Who will take care of Lib?" I asked, opening my eyes again.

"Sara has fussed over him plenty," Levi said. "He's strong. He'll be all right."

"How long will he be in prison, or has he been forgotten like I was?"

"You were never forgotten." Levi's gaze was so intense I had to look away.

My eyes burned. "The price of my rescue has been too high." I didn't want to cry in front of either of them, but it was hard to hold back the emotion once it surfaced.

Virai squeezed my shoulder. "You had no say in their fates."

"That's right," I said. "I had no say. I didn't ask to be rescued either." I looked at Levi, knowing he could very well see my tears. "Why did you do it?"

He held my gaze. "I didn't have a choice."

I was about to ask what he meant when Virai said to Levi, "I need to fetch more poultices for your back."

She slipped away, leaving Levi and me alone in the garden. When I turned to look at him, he'd taken a step forward. "How can you even ask why?" he said in a low voice.

The tears bubbled up again. "Because two men have died, Lib is in prison, and you've been tortured by your own brother. I deserve to know why so much was risked for my rescue."

He moved closer until I could look nowhere else but into his eyes. "I told you how I feel about you."

"You asked me to marry you." I tried to keep my voice steady, despite his nearness and despite my erratic pulse. "Then you asked me to give up my gods." My voice dropped to a whisper. "You never told me how you *felt*."

Both his hands cradled my face.

He closed the distance before I could take a breath. His lips pressed against mine lightly, hesitantly. My hands went to his chest; warmth radiated from his skin through his shirt. My touch encouraged him, and his kiss became more possessive as he pulled me into his arms, wrapping me in his security. For a moment, I believed that nothing could touch us, nothing could harm either of us. He slowly kissed my cheek, my eyelids, my neck. A torture of a new kind.

Then he pulled away, his hands resting on my shoulders. He stared at me with an intensity I'd not seen before. "I love you, Naiva. You must know you're in my every thought, my every breath."

It took everything I had to not fall into his arms and be swept away into our own world. I tentatively ran my hands along his chest, down his arms, absorbing his words.

I wanted to tell him the same thing—to confess my heart—but I was afraid I wasn't who he thought I was. Nor could I ever be.

"If your brother finds out, he'll kill both of us."

"My brother is destined for hell," Levi said in a harsh voice. His fingers traced my cheek. "I'd kill him before he has a chance to touch you again."

His words were bold. And untrue.

"The king has armies," I said.

"And I have the truth."

My gaze faltered. Levi's truth was different from mine. I didn't know what the truth was; I hadn't found it yet. I wondered if I ever would.

"The Lord will bless us," he said. "You must have faith in that. It doesn't matter how long we live on this earth. We'll have an eternity together."

My throat tightened. Levi spoke as if he'd willingly go to the palace, confess all, then present his head for execution. "I won't be responsible for any more deaths," I said, my voice shaking. "And I can no longer stay here. I'll be found out eventually, and you and your grandmother will be punished." My breath caught as I thought of dear Virai.

His hands slid to my shoulders. I wanted to be in his arms again, to forget everything—forget that a king and queen were looking for me.

"You'll do nothing so foolish," he said, his breath warming my face.

I lifted my chin. "I'm not worth it, Levi."

His eyes narrowed, and I knew he was about to argue, but I plunged ahead. "I prayed to your God while in prison. There was no answer—" I held up my hand "—and don't say that being rescued by you was an answer.

We're even worse off. It's not just me who's involved now. It's many more people."

"My grandmother makes up her own mind." His hand touched my cheek then slid behind my head, making it hard to concentrate. "If she was worried or afraid, she wouldn't have taken you in." His eyes searched mine. "The Lord doesn't take away all of our trials. We still have to endure."

"Then what's the point of worshipping a God who won't do anything for us?" I asked.

Levi's eyes widened. "With faith in the Lord, our trials become bearable."

I blew out a breath. "All this worshipping, all this praying, and nothing changes." I pulled away from him and shook my head. "You and your grandmother have both been very noble, and I could never repay you for your kindness. But staying here is too dangerous for all of us."

He reached for me again, amused. "So you would live in the jungle?"

"No, I'll find a place to live and work where I'm not putting anyone in danger."

Levi's hands slid to my waist, pulling me close. "I won't allow it."

"You have no say," I said, but I was losing ground in his gaze.

"Marry me, and we'll live wherever you want." His lips pressed against my hair as he pulled me tightly against him.

I wanted to melt in his arms and block out every concern, every danger. But fear took over. I stepped back, out of his embrace, though he kept hold of my hands. "You need a wife you can live with in public, not have to go into hiding with," I said. "You need a wife who believes in the Lord as you do. How would we raise our children?"

"Some people's faith is slower to grow than others."

"What if mine *never* grows, Levi?" I asked. "What if you become an old man and regret choosing me?"

"Your faith will come; I know it," he insisted, tugging me toward him. But I resisted.

"I don't want you to marry me and always hope for something else, for someone I may never be," I said.

"I'm willing to wait." Levi tugged me forward again.

It would have been so easy to believe him, but I was no longer the girl I used to be—the one who had first been thrown in prison. I had to be true to myself, and I would not allow another to force his beliefs on me. "How long would you wait?" I raised my face to gaze at him. "And how will you feel when you give up your position as captain of the king's army?"

He leaned down and whispered, "That's nothing to me."

I closed my eyes as his breath touched my lips, but my heart hammered with fear for Levi. "Akish will hunt you down."

"We'll join another tribe in another land."

I opened my eyes and saw the determination in his eyes. "You would give up all of this for me?" I asked.

"Yes." No hesitation. No wavering.

I kissed him then. Kissed him because I knew it would be the last time. He was not thinking clearly. Months spent in a dark hole had taught me to think deeply, from all angles, to see life beyond the moment. He would regret marrying me. He'd forever be trying to change me. Everything would be lost to him, and the bitterness would slowly destroy us.

When I pulled away, we were both breathless. "Go," I said, my voice breaking. "I cannot marry you. I cannot destroy your life."

I turned to leave, but he grabbed my arm. "Someday, Naiva, someday you'll put the Lord first in your life, and when you do, you'll marry me."

* * *

Levi stayed away for three weeks. The only thing that was worse than three weeks of not seeing him was the time spent in prison. I'd made progress with my plans to survive on my own. Virai had discreetly procured vellum and dyes for me to create images. I had a collection of more than a dozen paintings ready to sell at the market. The market must be far enough away from the palace that my paintings would never make it into my sister's hands. She'd know immediately who the artist was.

The morning was still young when I heard Levi's voice. I dropped my brush on the floor. I hastened to pick it up again then surveyed my image in the reflective metal that hung from the wall. *Why am I so worried about what I look like?* I had turned down his proposal twice. Yet I was acting like a silly fool. In love.

I entered the cooking room, where Virai stood with Levi and was asking him questions. I couldn't take my eyes off him. It was like I had been living upon the desert sands and had just been given my first drink.

His gaze locked on me. "You look well."

I had gained some weight, and color was back in my cheeks. His eyes confirmed that and much more.

For a mad moment, I wanted to fall at his feet and declare that I had found the truth and would be his wife. We could live together in our own existence, far away from the rule of any king or queen. But I said none of this.

"We've found a place for her to live in another village," Virai told him.

"It will be best for everyone," I added, my voice almost a whisper.

Levi's eyes narrowed for an instant. "Where?"

"The Mesón Village," Virai said, thankfully answering for me. It seemed my voice wouldn't cooperate.

Levi's expression remained wary. "I have news from the palace."

"Do they know where I am?"

"Not exactly," he said. "Your sister came to visit me in the fields. She said she wanted me to deliver a message to you." His mouth pulled into a grimace. "She said *in case* I should happen to see you anywhere, I should tell you that she is with child."

I brought my hands to my chest. After all I had gone through because of her and her husband, she was with child again. Just as I'd told her she would be.

Levi shifted his stance. "She also wanted me to tell you that all is forgiven. That she wants you to return home. She no longer expects you to be a hand-maiden."

My heart leapt then froze. It was the same game she'd played before. She'd told me once she'd forgiven me, had lured me back home at my father's death. But once in her lair, she'd found a way to control me again.

"No," I whispered. Virai moved to my side, compassion in her eyes, as I said, "I can't face him again."

Relief swept over Levi's face. "Shall I pass on the message?"

My shock over, my senses back, I said, "Tell her you couldn't find me. If you pass any message, she'll have control over you." I searched Levi's gaze. "Do you think she was telling the truth? Or was she testing you to see if you knew how to contact me? Is she really with child?"

"She's with child," Levi said, his expression perfectly sober.

I exhaled. "Next time you see her, tell her I haven't been located." I was afraid to look into Levi's eyes again. Afraid of the raw feelings I saw there. "And my brothers? How do they fare?" What I really wanted to ask was if they were living at the palace now, so Levi's next words were very welcome.

"From all accounts, they are well. Shule and Ethem still study with Hearthom in their apprenticeship," he said, and I thought I heard a bit of relief in his voice.

"Thank you for telling me," I said with a quick glance at him, though avoiding his eyes. His nod acknowledged my thanks, and I took that as a good time to leave the room.

CHAPTER 23

As a young girl following my beautiful sister and mother around the palace, I never thought I'd live as a commoner. I never thought I'd relish living in a hut by myself at the edge of the jungle, with no one to keep me company but a pet goat.

The cold months had passed, and the planting season was in full force. I'd put aside my paintings, which only earned a meager income as it was, and hired myself out as a laborer. With every turn of soil and every seed planted, I felt as if I had lived one more second of freedom. I was surrounded by poverty and suffering, but I was also surrounded by the greatest happiness I'd experienced. The only thing that could have made this existence more complete was Levi.

I missed him with every corner of my soul. In the morning, I thought of his strength as I struggled to carry water jugs from the well. In the afternoon, I thought of his courage as I endured yet another endless day in the fields. At night, I thought of his touch, his kisses, his forest-colored eyes.

The months passed, softening the memories of my former life. My little hut became my entire existence, my neighbors the only people I ever talked to; the only news that filtered down from the center of the kingdom was a regular reporting of executions. Criminals seemed abundant in the land of Heth.

I had foregone all religious worship. When my neighbors gathered for ritual feasts, I joined them but never went home and added my prayers to theirs. Ix Chel had seemed to bless my sister, but the goddess had been just as cruel as she had been kind.

It was of my own determination, and no benevolence from the Lord, as Levi might have claimed, that I stayed clear of further punishment. If I had conceded to Levi's plan, we'd likely both be dead.

The sixth day of each week was market day. For a village as small as ours, there was not enough trade for a daily market. I always set up my paintings in the same corner of the square so I could paint the villagers as they sat for me. It had been disconcerting at first, but I had grown accustomed to having others watch me at my craft.

A young girl sat in front of me today. Her father had proudly escorted her to my corner and had handed me a silver onti. It was her eighth birth date, and for her gift, she'd asked for a drawing of herself.

I situated her on a rug, where the rising sun captured one half of her face, leaving the other half in shadow. She lowered her eyes, and her dark lashes fluttered against her cheeks. I swept her hair over one shoulder. She was an image of innocence and beauty.

As I began the first strokes, a messenger arrived in the village square. He asked to see our village chief, who hurried to meet him. Any news from surrounding cities was always an event. I put down my brush and crossed the square so I'd be able to hear the news as well.

The messenger wore the indigo cape of a royal messenger. My heart beat faster as I realized he was too well dressed; he could only be from the palace.

"I have an announcement for every person," the young man said. He stood with his head erect, his gaze encompassing the entire crowd that had now gathered. "The queen has given birth to a male child."

My heart leapt, and I couldn't help but smile. My sister had a child. At last.

A murmur of approval went through the crowd, and several people clapped.

"The royal guards will be coming in a few days to collect gifts for the new prince." The messenger straightened his cape. "We must praise the goddess Ix Chel for blessing Queen Asherah."

The crowd replied as one. "Praise our beloved Ix Chel!"

I was about to repeat the chant with the crowd when I realized the messenger was staring at me. I looked away quickly, trying to recall if I recognized him. I moved slightly to the left, behind another person, so I wasn't in the messenger's direct line of vision.

When the crowd finished their chanting, I pushed through the gathering, farther away from the young man. I didn't dare look at him but hoped his attention had been diverted elsewhere. I escaped between two huts and made my way down a side path to my own place. The young girl and her drawing would have to wait until I was sure the messenger was long gone.

I entered my hut, grateful to be in the cool, dark interior. I blew out a deep breath as I thought about how much the piercing gaze of the young man had unsettled me. I dipped a cloth in a jug of drinking water and smoothed it over my face and neck.

I put the messenger's questioning gaze out of my mind and thought about my sister holding a healthy infant in her arms at last. Happiness surged through me. She had done it, just as I had told her she would. Her happiness would be complete. The sacrifices and sorrows that had led up to this event were now things of the past. Hope was once again a part of her life.

I paced my hut, thinking of where I was now and where I had been. I was free from prison, and my sister had a new baby. Two blessings that could only come from a god. The question was still, which god?

I knelt in the middle of the floor, something I hadn't done since being in prison, and clasped my hands together. I closed my eyes and thought of the good fortune that presently surrounded me. If it was due to Levi's God, I should thank Him first. "O Lord, I kneel before thee to praise Thy work. My family has been richly blessed. Please provide for my sister and her new son. Watch over them. Give them health. Have mercy upon them." My eyes burned with tears as I thought about how much I missed my sister. How much I still loved her. And how I ached to see my nephew—my own family. "O Lord, have mercy upon my soul. I have been ungrateful. Please hear my supplication. My life is in Thy hands."

I kept my eyes closed for a long time, waiting, listening, feeling. It was slow to come, but when it did, I couldn't deny the warmth and peace that spread through every limb, from the top of my head to my feet. I sank to a sitting position and drew my knees to my chest. Pulling them in tightly, I let the tears fall. I was alone. I had been alone for many months. But I felt the presence of comfort. The same feeling I'd had when Lib first started teaching me about his God. It was back. Stronger and surer than ever.

All the times I had pushed away the teachings of the Lord, the ones Lib had so painstakingly risked telling me, flooded through my mind. Guilt settled over me, but even as I wallowed in the distress, Lib's words came back to me that the Lord was a merciful Lord. He was all knowing. He knew of my trial of faith. He also knew I would one day soften my heart enough to truly ask.

"Thank you, O Lord," I whispered then repeated it louder. Warmth enveloped me as no rug ever could, completely saturating me from the inside out with a sweetness I could find no words to describe. Strangely, even though I feared being discovered by the king and queen and being punished, I saw things differently now. It was as if I were stronger, more sure of myself, more courageous to move forward in what was requested of me.

I also had the insatiable desire to share my faith with my friends in the village. I suddenly knew their days of worshipping stone statues had been wasted. There was so much more to look for now. I thought of them with expanded love. I thought of my sister and even Akish and saw them as the Lord saw them. People with their own insecurities and challenges, people who wanted to be accepted and loved equally. I was no different.

I began to pray again, this time with fervency, thanking the Lord and asking for forgiveness of my stubbornness.

"Hello!"

I lifted my head, feeling as if I were just waking up. Someone rapped on the reed door, and my heart nearly stopped. My voice was too shaky to call out. I rose to my feet and hurried to the door. When I opened it, I clamped my mouth shut. The girl and her father stood there. Right behind them was the royal messenger.

CHAPTER 24

Don't leave me, I WANTED to plead to the father and daughter. They had led the messenger directly to my hut. How could I blame them or expect them to disobey orders from the king's servant?

I thought of my prayers and the warm assurance that still clung to my soul. I drew courage from somewhere deep inside, knowing it was from the Lord Himself, and I stepped outside my hut. I pulled the door firmly shut behind me, ready to face what I must. The father and daughter quickly left, having done their duty.

The king's messenger studied me. "Naiva?"

My heart sank. It was too late. I had nowhere to turn now. This young man was about my age, tall and strong, and could catch me before I got to the jungle.

"Yes," I whispered.

"The queen has a message for you."

I let out a sigh, wondering if he'd tie me up like a prisoner now or later. I said nothing but stared at the ground, too afraid to glimpse my fate in his eyes.

"You are Naiva," he said, "sister to Queen Asherah, correct?"

I nodded.

He cleared his throat. "She requests that you return home to the palace. She invites you to help her care for her son. You'll have your own living quarters and may come and go as you please." He lowered his voice. "She says that families must stay together."

He waited, as if he expected a response.

"Are you to take me there?" I asked.

His brows drew together. "She never gave me a command to bring you. She only wanted to send you the message."

I took a step back and leaned against the front door. The messenger made no move to detain or capture me. "Is that all?"

He gave a short nod. "Yes."

"Tell me of the news of the palace. Tell me of the king and queen. And of my brothers? How do they fare?"

"Very well," he said with a slight frown, as if he were annoyed I'd inquired. "The entire kingdom is celebrating the birth of the prince. Feasts every night. Your brothers have attended a few, but they continue in their apprenticeship most days."

"And the servants. How are they? What about Lib and Sara?"

"They are still employed at the palace. Lib is now an apprentice to the head cook. The king says he creates the best mixture of spices for the meats."

I hid a smile. In truth, my heart soared. Lib was out of prison, and he had been promoted. I took a deep breath. "What about the captain of the militia?"

"Levi? Brother to the king?" he asked. "Very well. He is set to marry next month."

I was grateful to be leaning against the door already, or I might have made a fool of myself and collapsed. The breath left me, and it seemed to take several moments before I could form a reply. "Thank you," I choked out. "The queen has made a kind offer."

We stood there a moment longer in awkward silence. Finally, the messenger turned and left. I stumbled into my hut. Tears followed as I berated myself. A man like Levi had every right to marry. He probably found a woman who had been faithful to the Lord all her life. She was certainly beautiful and loving in every way.

He said he'd wait for me.

Had I truly believed it? Had I really expected him to wait?

And now that I'd had my assurance that the Lord was real, it was too late.

* * *

Three days later, the king's royal guard came through our village, guiding chariots filled with gifts from neighboring towns. Our people added their gifts to a growing stack. I placed my offering in the mix. A painting of a mother and child. Ash would know immediately who it was from.

I spent the next few weeks praying and pondering about the next steps I should take in my life. What did the Lord want me to do? That was my primary question. My life's plan had deviated from what I thought I should be doing or the way I thought I should be living, but I wanted to be where I could best serve Him.

I could spend the remainder of my days living in this tiny village, sharing my faith, and hoping to convert a few brave souls. In the outlying villages, people were able to practice varying religious beliefs without too much scrutiny. It was those who lived within the kingdom who had to demonstrate their loyalty more openly.

Or I could return home, convert a monarchy, and watch as the entire kingdom was affected and able to return to worshipping the true God as they had under the rule of Omer.

I tried to imagine Akish and my sister humbling themselves before the Lord, asking Him for guidance. It was nearly impossible to imagine, but Lib had taught me the Lord could do the impossible.

Each night I was haunted by the responsibility of knowledge—was I to be an instrument in the Lord's hands for my family? The thought sent absolute fear through me. I loved them deeply, but I also feared that returning with this agenda would land me back in prison or something worse.

My sister was willing to welcome me back home but under what conditions? I wouldn't know until I got there.

I also feared seeing Levi. He'd soon be settled into married life. There was no place for me. But I owed one thing to him—I needed to tell him of my faith. In that, he could rejoice and perhaps feel justified for risking so much to rescue me.

The excuses for why I should not return home did not hold up to the Lord's prompting.

I had to act.

Putting aside my reservations and fears, I packed what I could carry into a satchel and left the rest for neighbors to divide among themselves. Then I began the several-day trek back to the center of the land. Back to a place I'd sworn to never travel again. But this time, I had a new companion—the Lord.

CHAPTER 25

I HESITATED AT THE OUTER gate of the palace. The guards' eyes widened when they recognized me. I suppose I hadn't changed so much. "I'm here to see my sister, Queen Asherah," I said in the most authoritative voice I could muster.

I didn't know if the protocol had changed, but visitors were usually kept outside the main gates until they were cleared by someone within the palace. So I was surprised when the guards stepped aside and waved me through. I felt the imprint of their gazes on my back as I crossed the courtyard to the steps that led to the front entrance.

Two more guards stepped up to assess me. I repeated my request, and only then was I stopped. One of the guards disappeared inside the palace. I waited beneath the hot afternoon sun at the top of the steps, sure I looked quite traveled in my appearance.

The passing minutes seemed like hours, and I imagined my sister receiving the news and what her various reactions might be. The doors burst open, and a woman came flying through in a flurry of robes and jewels. Before I could steel myself, Ash had wrapped me in a fierce embrace.

"You've come! Praise the goddess of heaven!" she cried out.

I pulled back, laughing despite myself. She was exquisite, maybe even more so now that she'd gained some weight with the baby. Her girlish thinness had been replaced by womanly voluptuousness. She was swathed from head to toe in luxury. "Is it really you?" Ash said.

"Yes, it's really me."

I was smothered again, enveloped in her scent of plumeria and spices. We giggled together like when we were young girls. I had so many questions, so many fears, but for the moment, I allowed myself to breathe her in.

"The baby, how is he?"

She pulled back, her eyes glowing. "Shez is perfect in every way. The most beautiful child to ever be born."

I could very well imagine that he was.

"He has my eyes," Ash said. "You must come see him right away."

She pulled me inside, our hands clasped together. She breezed through the palace, and I hardly had a chance to soak in my surroundings. The halls, the rooms, all were familiar, but I had forgotten so much—the memories rushed back. I braced myself for an encounter with Akish, but he was nowhere to be seen, and I didn't ask Ash where he might be.

We entered Ash's chamber. In the corner of the room, a large gold square of cloth hung from the ceiling. Ash drew aside the drapery, and there, inside a bassinet, was a sleeping child. I stared at him, tender emotions flooding my heart.

Ash lifted the babe, and his eyes fluttered open then shut again. "You can hold him."

I took him in my arms and instantly fell in love. I couldn't believe I was holding my nephew. I couldn't believe how small he was. He was a bundle of warmth and softness. I pressed my lips against his full cheek and inhaled his sweet scent. He smelled like his mother. "Only the Lord could provide such a miracle."

Ash drew her brows together. Her smile became forced. "The Lord? Do you mean Grandfather's God?"

I met her gaze. She may throw me out again, but she needed to understand I wasn't going to worship her idols. At least I had the chance to meet my nephew. My heart pounded, but I knew it was the right thing to share my beliefs. "The Lord is all powerful."

Her mouth pursed into a firm line.

"You can deny it. I used to deny it. But I have found the truth, Ash," I said. "As surely as I hold this beautiful boy in my arms, I know the Lord sees all. He is no stone statue, no creation of man, no God giving false promises."

"Naiva," Ash whispered. "Be careful what you say."

"I'm not afraid of you," I said, meeting her gaze. Her eyes flickered away. "I want to be a part of your life, of Shez's life, of all of your children's lives. I will be the most devoted aunt. But I'll not let you tell me who to worship."

Ash turned away, her arms folded. When she looked at me again, tears were in her eyes. "What has this Lord done for you?"

"He delivered me from prison. He gave me peace. He softened my heart and brought me back to you."

She fell quiet for a moment. "You must thank Him for me, then."

I shook my head. "You can thank Him yourself. I can teach you about His mercy and love."

Ash wiped the tears on her cheeks then gripped my arm. "Worship whomever you like. But I will not change my loyalty. Ix Chel and the goddess of heaven have brought me my son. I will not turn against the goddesses now."

I started to protest, but she cut back in. "You must hide your faith. Akish cannot know I've allowed this. If he does . . ." She turned away again, and I saw that her hands trembled.

So she still feared her husband. I took a deep breath, my pulse racing, but I had to ask. "Have you and Akish truly changed your minds about a handmaiden?"

"Yes," she whispered. Her eyes turned to me, her gaze desperate. "He has concubines all over the city. I do not interfere in whom he chooses. But with you, he's promised to let you live unencumbered at the palace. We'll be sisters like we were before."

"And if I choose to marry?" I didn't want to say it, and I didn't want to consider marrying anyone besides Levi—it was too late for us—but I wanted my sister to know that I might leave again.

Her eyes teared up. "Do not ask me that now. Just stay with me. Do not speak of leaving me so soon after you've just arrived."

My heart tugged against my chest. My sister was lonely, neglected, and afraid of her husband. A woman in her position had no one to trust.

"All right," I said. "We'll not talk of marriage yet." She surely knew about Levi's betrothal, but my heart was too fragile with emotions to hear her speak of him today.

I turned my attention back to the sleeping Shez. His pink lips pursed together, and a small sound came from him. His precious face filled my heart with warmth.

Ash grinned as I rocked and cooed.

"Does he keep you awake at night?" I asked. I was surprised he didn't have his own room with a nurse.

"He never bothers me. I can't seem to leave him alone for more than a few moments. We've spent many hours in the middle of the night rocking." She let out a contented sigh. "Akish sleeps in another room now . . . when he is home. He doesn't have the patience I do." Her fingers stroked her son's cheeks. "Shez is absolutely perfect. Even his crying is adorable."

I marveled that such a small being could be so endearing. It was as if he were a harbinger of love.

"Come, I've reserved your old room for you," Ash said. "You may wash up and change your clothing."

"You don't care for my rags?"

Ash smiled. "You're the sister of the queen. You must outshine every woman at court."

"Except for you."

Her smile broadened. "Except for me."

CHAPTER 26

I WASN'T PREPARED TO SEE Levi when I came face to face with him at the marketplace. I should have known, with all the soldiers milling about. Apparently, they had been given leave for a couple days before setting out on another expedition to the border. Skirmishes between the people of the land of Moron and our people had escalated over the past few days.

It had been a week since my return, and the only information I had been able to glean from Ash was that Levi was betrothed to a local woman. Ash claimed to not even know her name. I didn't dare ask the king anything about his brother.

The time must have been nearing for Levi's marriage ceremony.

Now, in the marketplace, I was examining a basket filled with shells, with thoughts of stringing them together to hang over Shez's bassinet, when I turned and nearly bumped into Levi.

"Naiva," he said.

I couldn't speak. I just stared at him then, feeling my face warm, looked away. I clutched my robe closer and wished I had worn my veil. The merchants certainly assumed I was a wealthy woman of the court by my dress, but not many of them would know I was the queen's sister. If they had realized I was part of the royal family, I would have been pressed to make larger purchases.

I didn't know which way to turn. I wanted to throw myself at him and ask him why he hadn't waited for me. These thoughts embarrassed me even more, and I was sure I was blushing a deep scarlet.

His hand grasped mine. The shock of his touch nearly caused me to gasp. But I kept myself as quiet as a statue.

"I need to speak with you," he whispered.

It was a miracle I heard him at all above the din of the shouting vendors, bleating animals, and running children.

"No." I turned away from him, moving through the crowd. Tears threatened. Surely he had lied to me from the beginning. I thought he'd meant it when he said he'd wait for me forever. It hadn't even been close to forever.

He caught up with me and grabbed my hand again. I halted, and he leaned down close to my ear. "In the grove by the Sun Temple."

I opened my mouth to tell him absolutely not, but he was gone, deftly slipping through the crowd. After a moment, I no longer saw his head above the others.

Don't go, I told myself. *He doesn't deserve to explain to me. He deceived me.*

I argued with myself until my mind spun in circles, mirroring the crowd as it moved about me, everyone with an important place to go.

I followed him.

Even without seeing him, I knew he was not too far ahead, going in the direction of the temple. I walked slowly, allowing myself to change my mind, to come up with newer arguments, but they were all the same. One part of me crying, *Stay away. Hurt him as he hurt me.* The other part wanting to hear the explanation from his own lips.

Curiosity won out, driving me toward the temple. The steps were crowded with people going up and down the stairs, presenting their weekly offerings to the priests. Although I hoped to catch of glimpse of Nelise or Raynelle, I knew I wouldn't. Priestesses were only visible to the public at festivals.

I veered off from the main road and crossed to the line of trees. The clearing Levi referred to was well known to the community. In the middle of the clearing was a statue of the sun god. Farmers often brought offerings of food and drink to place at its feet in order to ensure a healthy harvest.

Levi was the only one in the clearing. He turned upon my approach, and I tried not to focus too much on the haunted look in his eyes.

I stopped several paces from him, deciding that a good amount of distance would be in my best interest. But he had other ideas. He closed the space left between us. "I assume you've heard the rumor of my marriage."

"Congratulations," I said, hoping my voice sounded natural.

"There's no truth to it," he said.

I stared at him then looked down at my twisting hands. Relief and shock clashed inside me. "How, why . . . ?"

"I hoped *not* to see you in the city, Naiva," Levi said. "But apparently they knew just what to say to bring you back to the palace."

"It wasn't—" *It was.* I'd been too inquisitive. I'd ignored the possibility that my sister was manipulating me once again. Tears stung my eyes as I realized that perhaps Levi had truly loved me, and perhaps he still did.

His hands rested on my shoulders. "I'm sorry to have to break the news to you."

"That you aren't betrothed to another woman or that I'm a fool?"

"You were lured here." His eyes held a wealth of sympathy.

Confusion consumed me. My sister had seemed so sincere; she had said she'd allow me to worship the Lord in private, but she'd also been adamant we not discuss the possibility of me getting married. Did she think I'd never find out the truth? Or did she not believe any of her plans could be thwarted? Now I realized she'd fooled me—again. She'd brought me here to be as I used to be—at her mercy and under her command.

"And I'm sorry that you thought . . ." he continued, "even for a moment, that I had broken my promise to you."

I couldn't look at him then. I turned away, self-conscious of the tears that threatened to fall. "It was difficult . . . to understand."

Levi turned me toward him and wrapped his arms around me. I easily fell into his embrace. I closed my eyes, wanting to soak in this moment—to remember every second of it when I was back in my chamber. He wasn't betrothed to someone else. He was still mine, and he was holding me in his arms.

"I'm still waiting," he murmured into my hair.

My heart leapt. "You don't have to wait any longer."

He pulled away abruptly, and his hands cradled my face. "What do you mean?"

My voice trembled when I spoke. "I started praying again and pondering on many things after I heard my sister had delivered a healthy child. I realized the Lord did have His hands in the blessings surrounding my life." My tears were now of elation. "An incredible feeling of warmth and knowledge swept through me. And I *knew*." I offered a small smile. "I know He's there for me, for everyone, if we but seek Him."

Levi wiped the tears from my face with his thumb then slowly kissed each cheek. "I'll ask Akish for permission tonight. There's a feast that the upper echelon of the military has been invited to on our reprieve."

"Tonight? You would face your brother for me?"

"It's the only way. I don't want us to have to hide from him anymore. We should be able to live our lives in open happiness."

I was breathless, ecstatic. I threw my arms around his neck. He laughed and pulled me close. Our lips met, and at last my dreams became reality.

* * *

I glided, instead of walked, back to the palace. I'd spent more than an hour, a wonderful, delicious hour, with Levi in the grove, talking, laughing, and being near him. After so much heartache, doubt, and fear, my life had become filled with love and hope. First my faith in the Lord, second the miraculous arrival of my dearest nephew, and now I was nearly betrothed to a man I loved.

I felt nervous about telling Ash, but I'd find the right moment. It just had to be before Levi asked for the king's official permission at the feast tonight. I hoped to find her in a good mood, something there'd been plenty of lately. Shez had really brought a new light to all our lives.

I would promise to visit her every day. We'd raise our children together as the best of friends. Our sons would hunt together; our daughters would learn to embroider together.

Inside the palace, the halls were strangely quiet, especially if there was to be a feast tonight. I passed the banquet hall and saw that the tables had been laid, but there was no one in sight.

I made a detour past my sister's chambers to my room, and as I passed her door, I heard someone crying. At first I thought it was Shez and hurried to the closed door. Then I realized it must be Ash. I hesitated, listening for any other voices, of servants or Akish. What could be wrong? Was it the baby? I knocked, hoping I wasn't interrupting anything too personal.

The crying stopped. I called through the door. "Ash, are you all right?"

No response.

"Is it Shez? Is something wrong?"

"No," came the muffled reply.

Still, the anxiety wouldn't leave. "Do you need anything?" When she didn't answer, I tried the door. It was unlocked, so I pushed it slowly open. Ash was curled on her bed, facing me.

"Are you ill?" I asked. She didn't move or reply. Her eyes were open, staring ahead. I shut the door and crossed to her. Then I gasped. Her right cheek had a large bruise on it, and there was a cut near her eye.

"Did you fall? Let me get something for the pain. Has Sara seen—"

Ash grabbed my arm, stopping my speech. "I didn't fall." She closed her eyes and exhaled then winced in obvious pain.

I sat next to her, dread pushing its way into my heart. Maybe she'd run into a branch while on a walk in the garden. Maybe . . . I stared at her bruised face, an answer forming in my mind that I wanted to push away immediately.

"I don't want anyone to see me," Ash said. "No one can know the king beats his own wife."

I felt sick. To have it stated so bluntly only seemed to make it worse. There was no denying it; Ash had given no excuses. I thought my heart would break for my sister. The indignity of it shot anger through me, and desperate thoughts of revenge circulated.

"What can I do?" I whispered. It pained me to look at her. Pity and rage blended in my mind. Violence in households was not uncommon among our people, but my sister was a queen. She was also my sister. How dare Akish touch her in this way? "I'll poison him." The words were rash but strangely comforting as I said them.

Ash's laugh was bitter. "Don't think I haven't thought of the same thing." She sat up, sniffling. I wanted so badly to take away the pain in her voice.

"It's not the first time, as you can probably gather," she said in a subdued voice.

This was not the sister I knew. My sister was made of drive and passion; she was not a shrunken, defeated woman.

"He comes home full of wine, angry at something. He takes it out on me." Her words were so matter-of-fact, as if she were placing a grain order with a merchant.

I looked down at her fingers that picked at a loose thread on her tunic. "What about Shez?" I asked.

"Akish wouldn't hurt him," she said in a dull voice. "He'll return in a few hours, full of apologies. He'll be in his best form at the feast tonight and will act as if nothing happened."

I grabbed her hands. "We could go away. The three of us. We'll live in another town. Akish would never find us."

Ash's hands were cold and lifeless in mine. "My son will be king someday," she said in a voice devoid of emotion. "I'll endure whatever I need to in order to ensure that my son takes his rightful place on the throne."

I exhaled. "You can't let your husband do this to you."

"If I stand up to him or become angry, it only makes it worse." She pulled her hands away and looked past me. "I just need to learn to stay out of his way. Every time, I hope it will be the last time."

"Does his brother know?"

Her brows drew together. "No one can tell the king what to do."

I knew Levi would be livid if he knew about his brother's latest habit. "Levi needs to know. He can help us."

"No one can know. I've kept it secret this long—" Tears glistened in her eyes. "Levi can't make a difference; no one can." She leaned forward, and I embraced her. "Having you here in the palace brings me protection. If you had been home, he wouldn't have done this."

"I only went to the market for a few hours," I said, feeling guilty about the extra time spent in the grove with Levi. If I'd come straight home, perhaps . . . no, it wasn't my fault Akish was the most vile of men.

"We must always stay together," Ash said. "When you need to go somewhere, Shez and I will come with you too."

"It's not like it was before you were queen," I said. "The people will throng you. We'll have to bring guards to protect you."

Her shoulders trembled as she held me closer. "Then we'll send servants to fetch whatever you need."

"I can't be with you day and night."

"Of course not," she whispered. "But knowing you're just down the hallway at night brings me more comfort than you can imagine."

I buried my face in her hair, holding back my own tears. Tears of shame, of anger, of fear. How could I tell her about Levi now? How could I leave my sister at the mercy of her husband?

The bruising on her face had rocked me to the core. Our parents were gone. Akish could have his way against a defenseless woman and infant. Someone had to stand between them.

CHAPTER 27

THE FEAST WAS EVERYTHING ASH had predicted. Akish was in a glorious mood. I'd seen him crossing the courtyard that afternoon while I sat in the garden with Shez. Akish's arms were laden with gifts for his wife—gifts of apology, gifts that meant nothing and held no guarantee. I could only imagine their reunion—his apologies and my sister's stoic forgiveness.

Ash wasn't at the feast, and the king excused her in front of everyone for feeling tired from being a new mother. Sara brought out Shez and paraded him around for a few moments, and then even they disappeared. I sat at the head table, as was my place to do so, but I maintained no eye contact with Akish. His voice boomed above everyone else's, so it was impossible to miss his conversation.

At one point, I glanced at his ringed fingers. There seemed to be no redness, no bruising. Hitting his wife had brought him no injury.

Levi came late, nearly halfway into the feast. Akish immediately stood at the sight of his brother entering the room. The two men embraced, and when Levi pulled back, I cringed to see the excitement in his eyes.

It should have brought excitement to me too, but now it brought only despair. I'd have to tell him before he had a chance to speak with his brother privately. But how could I tell the man I loved that I couldn't marry him after all? That I was choosing my sister over him?

Levi caught my eye. I tried to return his smile but was self-conscious with all the surrounding people, and if I smiled, I might burst into tears instead. I'd have to watch and wait then somehow give him the message.

The feast continued on and on with toasts made by nearly every soldier in attendance. Then the dancing started. The men hooted and hollered as the dancers began their sultry moves. It was time to speak to Levi.

I rose and crossed behind the table. The men, including Akish, were caught up in the women, so I didn't have to worry about anyone's curious stares. At the far end of the head table, Levi had squeezed between two other soldiers. He was leaning back, looking down at something he held in his hands. The other two soldiers leaned forward, clapping along to the rhythm of the music as they ogled the dancers.

I touched Levi's shoulder, and he looked up, surprise turning to joy. He slipped something into the satchel at his waist. I motioned with my head for him to follow me. I escaped out a side door into the dark hallway and waited there until he exited.

He immediately swept me up his arms and spun me around.

"Someone will come," I whispered.

"Then let them come," Levi whispered back. He kissed me hard, demandingly, as if he'd held back all of his passion during our other kisses.

I clung to him and matched his fervency. There was a time when I'd thought I was saying good-bye to Levi for good, but this time, I knew I was and that this was our last kiss, the last time I'd hold him in my arms.

"Let's plan the wedding for next week," Levi said, pulling away for an instant.

"Levi." I pushed against him. But he was kissing me again, and it was too easy to succumb.

Finally, I was able to pry away. "I have to talk to you."

He kissed my neck, my ear. "Talk."

"Not this way," I said, pushing again.

He let go, surprise on his face. "What's wrong?" He looked down the corridor. "No one is around."

"My sister needs me at the palace."

His eyes narrowed. "You want to wait a few months?" A slight smile touched his face. "It will be hard, but as long as we can start the countdown—"

"Ash needs me to protect her from Akish."

"What do you mean?" His voice was sharp.

"When he gets drunk, he takes out his anger on her."

Levi was quiet for a moment. He reached for me and took me in his arms. I could feel his heart thumping hard. "I wish I could say I was surprised," he said in a low voice. He ran a hand over my hair and tightened his grip. "Has he ever hurt you?"

"No." My voice faltered, thinking of my sister's bruised face. How many other times had she missed feasts because she was afraid of showing herself?

Levi's voice turned hard. "I'll take care of it. Don't worry. He won't hurt your sister again, and he won't stand in the way of this marriage."

Now I was afraid. "Don't do anything foolish, Levi. Your brother is the king."

"My brother is a charlatan and a murderer. But even worse, he hurts women. No man should get away with that." He pulled away and took my face firmly in his hands. "I want you out of this place as soon as possible. Your sister is welcome to come as well."

She won't, I wanted to say, but I think he knew it already. By leaving, she'd give complete power to Akish, and he might divorce her, choose another queen in her place. My sister could never live through a blow like that.

"How will I know my sister will truly be safe?" I asked.

Levi's gaze held a faraway look.

"Levi?"

He refocused on me. "You'll know. Leave it to me." He kissed me firmly on the lips then released me. He left before I could offer any more warnings or pleadings. My heart hammered with fear. What would Levi tell Akish to make him stop being so cruel? I'd heard their arguments before. I was too afraid to return to the feast in case the argument became public.

I hurried to my room and sank to my knees, pleading with the Lord to protect Levi, to protect me, and most of all to protect my sister.

* * *

Lib found me an hour later. I was still on my knees, my door left ajar. He tiptoed in, thinking I'd fallen asleep.

"Naiva," he whispered.

It was as if I were waking up. I turned and blinked back the blurriness in my eyes. I had hoped to see Levi. But it was Lib instead, standing there with an oil lamp in one hand.

"What is it?" I scrambled to my feet, not liking the pinched look of Lib's face nor his hand gripped into a fist at his side.

"Sit down," he said.

His words sent a chill through me. "Tell me now," I said.

Lib blew out a breath; then his words came in a rush. "There was an argument between Levi and the king. Levi punched Akish multiple times in the face. And the king . . ." Here, he paused. "The king banished Levi from all the land."

I inhaled, my thoughts spinning. "Banished? What do you mean? How?"

"The guards dragged him out of the palace, bound hand and foot," Lib said. "They carted him to the borders where he was marked and left as prey for the wild beasts."

"No." I swiped a hand over my face. "How could he do this to him?" I'd heard of men being marked before. It was usually a disfiguring scar on their face or someplace where it would always show. The more extreme punishments included losing a hand or foot. "How was he marked?"

"I don't know," Lib said. "I only heard the orders."

"I must find him," I cried out, desperation hot in my breast.

"A couple of servants have already secretly left to cut his bands and take him supplies."

I sat down on my bed, feeling as if I'd received a blow to the stomach. I had to go to him. He went to see Akish because of *me*. Because of what I'd told him. I had hoped he wouldn't be foolish in his actions, but warning Levi of that did little good. His brother had finally exercised complete power over him. The worst had happened.

As the initial shock faded, rage collected inside me. Akish had taken everything good in my life and had mocked it, hurt it, or thrown it away. How dare he banish his brother for calling upon his own morals?

"Naiva," Lib cut into my tumultuous thoughts, "Levi gave me a message before he was taken away."

I looked at him with a mixture of dread and expectancy.

"He said Akish doesn't know about the betrothal yet and for you to be careful around him, or he'll take his revenge out on you to hurt Levi more."

"So the argument was only about the queen?"

Lib nodded. "Everyone who was cleaning up the banquet hall overheard the things that were said. The king didn't like Levi telling him what he could and couldn't do to the queen."

My stomach twisted. I imagined Akish bursting into my sister's chamber and taking his remaining wrath out on her. "Where did Akish go?"

"He's still at the palace. The healer was called," Lib said. "The king will probably rest tomorrow. His face was a mess."

A glimmer of triumph shot through me, but it quickly faded. I shuddered. "He's a wicked man. For once, he got what he deserved." I rose and pulled on a thick robe.

"Don't go," Lib said. "Akish will find out and guess the relationship between you." His voice softened as he noted the pain on my face. "Levi told me to make sure you didn't follow. He'll be impossible to find, and the living conditions will be difficult in the wilderness."

I squared my shoulders. "I'm not afraid of a few snakes."

Lib's hand touched my arm. "I promised Levi I'd keep you safe. And I promised him I'd talk sense into you."

I almost smiled at that, despite the fact that my heart ached. "He thought I needed sense talked into me?"

"He knew it."

CHAPTER 28

I COULDN'T SLEEP. COULDN'T EAT. All I had to comfort me about Levi was that he was alive—at least, when the servants left him he was. Several weeks had passed since that horrible night that he was banished. Thirty-eight days to be exact.

I didn't want my sister to know the true reason for Levi's banishment. She, of course, knew there'd been an argument, but Akish and the servants kept the real reason from her. And I wasn't willing to be the messenger.

I found my sister watching me carefully from time to time. She still thought I believed Levi was betrothed to another woman. I would keep up the pretense for now, until I was able to discover a way to change my fate.

"You've been so glum," my sister said to me one evening. We sat together in the garden with Shez, who was bundled up against the night air. With each day, he became more adorable, and I thought I could never love another being as much as my nephew.

"Is it because of Levi's marriage?" she asked.

I covered the shock on my face, surprised she'd spoken it so directly. "Do you think his bride followed him into banishment?"

She narrowed her eyes. "I hadn't thought of that."

I didn't want to discuss it anymore. At times, I wanted to rage at her and tell her it was her fault Levi was gone. If she had chosen a better-mannered husband, none of this would've happened. I wanted to scream at her and tell her how much I'd given up for *her*. Other times, I wanted to confess everything, my love for Levi, my grief at his absence, and my desire to take comfort in her arms. But I wasn't sure if she'd offer comfort if she knew my secrets.

Shez gurgled as Ash handed him to me. I pulled the wriggling, warm body close to me, inhaling his sweet baby scent. If I could spend the rest of my life in the garden playing with my nephew and block the rest of the world out, I'd die a peaceful death. But he would grow up, and my sister still had a kingdom to run in the more and more frequent absences of Akish. And my heart couldn't let go of Levi.

When the air cooled, we reentered the palace. Akish was gone, leaving everything in quiet peace. When he was absent, everyone's heart was light, and everyone breathed easier. I escaped to my room and took out my latest painting. It was nearly finished. I had drawn Levi in the center of an expansive field. The sky above was dark and threatening rain, but all around Levi, I had drawn light, representing my prayers. I hoped my prayers would sustain and protect him.

I finished the outline of Levi, remembering his broad shoulders and the way I felt secure in his strong arms. My hand wavered as tears stung my eyes. I closed my eyes for a moment, regaining control of my emotions, then reopened them and completed the last strokes.

I stared at the painting as the night deepened into black, the only illumination in my room the three oil lamps I had lit. I reached out a hand and let my fingers hover over the figure of Levi, as if I could somehow connect with him, touch him, or speak to him.

"Where are you?" I whispered. "Are you safe?"

My questions soon turned into a prayer as I pled with the Lord to keep him safe and to bring us together once again. The marking he'd received would brand him in the eyes of every person he met. They would know he'd been banished by the king. Everyone would fear taking him in for worry of bringing a curse on their home.

My eyes flew open. I knew of one person who wasn't afraid. Virai.

Would Levi have gone to her home? It was near the borders of the land, so he would have had to sneak in. But it would be a safe refuge for him.

No, I decided. The king would hear of it. It might have been possible to hide a woman but not a man like Levi. Was he living in the wilds of the jungles?

I hid the painting beneath my bed. I couldn't risk anyone finding it. In the morning, I'd wash off the paint and start over. But tonight it would comfort me to have Levi near me in some form.

I was just drifting off to sleep when Ash burst into my room. Her eyes were wide, her hair fallen out of its usual careful style.

"He's on a rampage," she hissed. She shut the door, turned the locking latch, then climbed into bed with me. She huddled against me, and I wrapped my arms around her trembling body.

"Where's Shez?"

"Sara took him as soon as she heard Akish come through the courtyard."

I exhaled with relief, but every muscle went taut in my body at the thought of Akish bursting into my room to find his wife. I heard shouting from somewhere down the corridor. The voice was unmistakably Akish's. My sister sniffled and burrowed even closer.

"What's he angry about?" I whispered.

Akish's voice boomed louder, growing closer to my room. "Where's that harlot?"

I flinched. "What's he talking about?"

"When he's drunk, he mixes me up with the women at the tavern. He thinks he's seen me among them—"

"Asherah!" Akish shouted, sounding like he was right outside my door.

This time we both jumped. I was grateful I'd doused the oil lamps before going to sleep. I prayed Akish would think I was in my room alone.

The door rattled, and Akish cursed. Then his heavy footsteps moved on. Ash sobbed in my arms.

"Hush," I said. "You don't want him to hear us."

Then the footsteps were back, and Akish rattled the door again. Panic shot through me, and I clung to my sister.

"Naiva?" His voice came out soft and plaintive, unlike his belligerent yelling just moments before.

I didn't move, didn't speak.

"Naiva," his voice was louder now, pleading. "Let me in."

If I responded, would he go away? Or would he break down the door?

"I know you're angry with me," Akish said through the door. I stiffened. Why was he talking like this—besides the fact that he was drunk? My heart hammered, afraid of what he might say.

My sister lifted her head to listen better.

"I'm sorry. I didn't want to banish Levi, but he stood in my way. When he came to me that night so full of anger, I knew it was due to you. He thought he loved you, but he doesn't. No one truly loves you like I do."

I wanted to vomit. After all this time, after all that he'd put my sister through, he was still claiming affection for me.

Ash pulled away. I could practically feel the horror radiating from her. She climbed off the bed.

"No," I whispered. "He'll hurt you."

She crossed the room, her hands bunched into fists. Then she yanked the door open.

Akish stumbled into the room. In the dark, his form looked massive. He staggered against the easel I had left up. The wood frame crashed to the floor.

I leapt off the bed and moved toward my dressing table. I wrapped my fingers around a comb, wishing I had a better weapon to defend myself.

Akish righted himself and reached for Ash. He pulled her into his arms and said, "Naiva, at last."

My sister shoved him away, and he lost his balance and fell hard onto the floor.

He sat up, rubbing his head. "N-Naiva, I come in peace," he slurred.

"I'm not Naiva," my sister spat out. "I'm your wife!"

I couldn't decipher Akish's expression; it was too dark. "Where . . . is s-she?"

"Right here," I said. The comb still in my hand, I picked up my wash basin and dumped it over his head. He scrambled to his feet, sputtering, then slipped.

I grabbed my sister's hand, and we tore out of the room. I didn't know whether to laugh or cry. We hurried to her chambers, where we bolted the door again. We waited together, listening for any shouting or banging. An hour passed, then more. Ash whispered, "What did he mean? About Levi?"

I hesitated. "Levi asked me to marry him. That day you were beaten, I was gone for longer than I should have been because I met Levi."

"But he's married already."

"No," I said, unsure now who had been lying to me. Was it possible Akish had fooled my sister as well? "There was no truth to that rumor."

"But—"

"Levi came that night to officially ask for my hand from Akish. I intercepted Levi and told him I couldn't leave you alone in the palace."

Ash reached for my hand. I squeezed it. "I told him that Akish had been horrible to you."

"And Levi confronted him?" she asked.

"Yes."

"Oh." Her hand slipped away from mine, and I heard her sniffle.

"It's done now," I whispered.

"Did you want to marry Levi?"

My eyes burned with suppressed emotion. "Yes." My voice cracked. "With all my heart." I closed my eyes as renewed loss filled me.

She let out a breath. "You're too good to me."

I waited for an apology or maybe more recognition of what I'd given up. But perhaps this was as much as she could offer. Was it reasonable to expect my sister to know the grief I'd endured from loving and losing Levi? Had she had the same love for another? And then lost that love? Perhaps she had for our father.

She remained silent, and we lay together, each of us listening for any sound of a tempest. She reached for my hand again. Finally we fell asleep, our hands still clinging together across the wide expanse of the bed.

CHAPTER 29

I PRAYED NIGHT AND DAY for Levi. I prayed night and day for Ash and Shez. Every moment of my life was filled with anxiety, with prayer, with longing, with renewed commitment to endure whatever challenge the Lord placed before me.

More than I had ever known or felt, I knew the Lord was with me. I felt Him in the smallest of things and received hope each day that He watched over me. For that reason, I put my trust in Him. Unlike my experience of relying on other gods and goddesses, where they were quiet to my pleas, the Lord heard my prayers. It was as if He understood what I was going through, and in that, I felt a great measure of comfort.

On the night Akish yet again declared his misguided love for me, my sister and I awoke to a corridor filled with lavish gifts. Ash opened the door cautiously then stared at the offerings delivered by her husband.

I went to find Shez, leaving Ash to sort through the merchandise.

We said nothing more about that night. She'd forgive him. Again. At least this time the bruising was only on her heart.

I saw Akish in a different light now. Since the night of his drunken escapade in my room, I no longer looked at him as a powerful and handsome man. I felt sorry for him. Sorry that he continued to stumble through life, missing out on the pure joy that could be found if only he'd learn the truth. I saw him as the Lord saw him, as a struggling soul who'd become mired in the deepest of mud.

At least my sister was willing to listen to me, though her position in the kingdom and her fear of Akish held her back from opening her heart. And I grieved over that but also saw it for what it was. When Akish was gone, we'd all be set free, in more ways than one.

I didn't exactly admit to myself that I wished an early death on my brother-in-law but could certainly see the convenience in it. The kingdom had become more and more slovenly. A new captain of the military had been appointed—someone as reckless as the king. I feared the next military campaign and anticipated that more lives would be lost than necessary. At the various feasts, the military men seemed to delight in telling stories of horrific bloodshed.

Each day, I watched Shez grow and discover something new, and my heart cheered for his ascension to the throne. I was walking with Shez one day in the gardens when Ash found me there.

"I have news." A smiled played on her lips.

"Well?" I had little patience for news. My mind always leapt to the worst conclusions.

She patted her flat belly. "I'm with child."

"Oh." I embraced her. I was happy for her, pleased that her family was growing. Numbers meant strength. Yet in my joy for my sister, I also worried that Akish might beat her again and cause her to lose the child. Tumultuous thoughts had been circulating in my mind lately about how my sister might have lost her first two babies.

I pulled away to study her features. "How are you feeling?"

"Divinely nauseated."

I laughed then bounced Shez in my arms. "You'll soon have a brother to terrorize you," I told him. I stopped short, realizing what I'd said. In no way would Shez and any brother of his be like their father.

It was as if my sister knew Akish had crossed my mind. "Akish never bothers me when I'm with child."

I nodded and kept my focus on Shez, on his round eyes and dark brown tufts of hair that seemed to grow thicker by the day. I'd never asked my sister about her intimate life with her husband. There are some things a sister never shares, but now I wondered how she felt sharing a bed with a man who spent many nights in taverns.

But I couldn't think about that now. Ash was happy, and I wanted to be happy for her as well. "We must start sewing his clothing right away," I said.

"Yes." She reached for Shez, took him into her arms, and started humming.

I looked toward the bright horizon. "The afternoon is still early. I'll go to the market and pick out new cloth."

"Bring me some honeyed treats as well." Ash spun with Shez, making him giggle. "And hurry back."

I smiled at Shez's adorable laughter. "I will."

Akish was away for a few days, inspecting the borders with the military captain. It was the only way I felt comfortable leaving my sister at the palace.

I grabbed a scarf from my room and pulled it over my head as I crossed the courtyard. The scarf kept the heat of the sun off my face and offered me some anonymity. It was easier to make purchases when all of the merchants weren't simultaneously vying for my attention.

Upon reaching the market, I was soon caught up in the displays of beautiful cloths. I fingered the beaded scarves and soft feathered capes. I found a miniature bow and arrow set made for children. It would be awhile before Shez could play with it, but it was too charming to pass up, so I purchased it right away. I had nearly an armful of cloth when someone tapped me on the arm. I turned, fully expecting to be plied by another merchant who'd noticed my arms full of goods. But it was a young boy with a scroll in hand. He pressed it into my already laden hand and scurried away.

Something told me I shouldn't open it in public. My frenzy of shopping forgotten, I made a graceful exit from the current merchant and left the bustling market. I detoured onto a side road and stopped beneath a copal tree. When I opened the scroll, I gasped. It was a crude drawing of a tent on a seashore next to a large body of water. Two men stood together, one with a king's headdress and one with broad shoulders.

Levi had sent this to me. I knew it. I looked around the path beside me. There was no one in sight except for a bleating goat tied to a reed fence. I found a safe place for my purchases and hurried back to the market square, scroll clutched in hand, my eyes searching for a tall figure among the milling crowd. Would he dare come into the city? I wondered. I had to find out. I looked for the boy who'd delivered the scroll but found him nowhere.

Taking a deep breath, I slowed my step and walked in the direction of the temple. There was a small chance—no an impossible chance—but I had to know. I stopped in the grove of trees where we had met before.

The afternoon light filtered through the branches, making the earth glow in golden orange. Memories surfaced, twisting my heart and taking my breath away as I remembered Levi's proposal there. The proposal that eventually led to his banishment.

I stood still for a long time, listening to those memories and thinking of Levi. If I were to believe the picture on the scroll, he was with my grandfather in the land of Ablom.

Longing burst through me, and my eyes filled with tears as I stared at the image on the scroll. It looked as if Levi and Omer were walking along the seashore, deep in discussion. I longed to be on that shore, walking next to Levi, free from Akish.

The Lord had protected and guided Omer. Some might think giving up a kingdom was a sacrifice, but seeing this sketch made me understand that Omer had been greatly blessed.

The snap of a twig caught my attention. I looked up to see a hooded man standing in the shadows of the trees. My heart jolted. It had to be him.

I ran across the clearing and into Levi's arms. I cried and laughed.

"Come with me," he said into my hair. "I have a place for us. We can worship the Lord freely. We can raise our children in peace."

I clung to him, hardly believing his arms were around me. I didn't ever want to let him go again. "How did you get here?"

Levi slowly pulled back and cupped my face in his hands. "With great caution."

I stared at him. Something was wrong with his face. I reached up and lowered the hood that kept his features shadowed. A deep, jagged scar traveled from his forehead to beneath his chin. "This is your marking?"

He nodded, his gaze steady.

I touched his face, and he closed his eyes as I trailed my fingers along the raised skin. "You're risking your life coming here," I whispered.

"You're worth it." He grasped my fingers then leaned forward, and his lips touched mine.

My hands slid around his neck as I met his kiss.

A moment later, I finally pulled away, breathless. "I can't be the cause of your capture."

He leaned down again, and our foreheads touched. "I'd rather be here, in danger, than in Ablom without you."

I traced my fingers along his neck. "I know." I leaned into his embrace and listened to my heart. Did the Lord want me to go with Levi and live among Omer's people? Or did He want me to stay with my sister and protect her from the king? Could I be truly happy in Ablom knowing my sister was at the mercy of her husband? Could I truly be happy giving up my own chance at love with Levi? Either way, a part of my heart would be missing.

"Ash is a strong woman. She'll learn to manage her husband."

I nodded. It was what I hoped too. But hope and reality weren't always the same thing.

Levi took my hand and kissed my palm. I leaned against him and allowed him to stroke my hair and whisper sweet words of promise. "Let me tell you about a beautiful village on the shores of the sea. Where there is harmony among family members. Where a righteous man leads his family. Where women don't fear their husbands."

The time sped by too fast, and I knew I must hurry back to the palace.

"I can only risk one more day, Naiva," Levi said, his forest eyes holding mine. "Meet me here tomorrow at dusk. Your sister and nephew are welcome to come."

I blinked back tears. "She'd never come."

He kissed my forehead. "You must be strong. Tell your sister you've served her long enough. It's time you had some happiness as well. Akish is finished inspecting the west border and will be away for another two days making the circuit. That is how I dared to slip across the border."

I nodded. I literally had to pull myself away from him.

When I arrived at the palace after going back to retrieve my purchases, I was sure my sister thought my rose-colored cheeks came from the excitement of shopping in the market.

That evening, I held Shez a little tighter and a little closer. I paid attention to his every expression, every sound, and leaned in frequently to kiss his soft cheek.

Ash watched me with arched brows. "You act as if you've been away for weeks."

I have in my heart. "He's so easy to miss," I said, planting a firm kiss on his forehead. His skin felt hot. I placed a hand on his face. "Does he feel warm to you?" I asked my sister.

She put down the embroidery she was working on and touched Shez's cheek. "Yes," she said, fear in her voice.

"Perhaps he's overdressed." But even as I said it, I knew it wasn't so. He wore only a linen sheath.

His eyes seemed brighter than normal.

"Call Sara," Ash said in a sharp voice. Although the woman spent most of her time in the cooking room, she was the one servant Ash trusted completely.

I fled the room, my heart pounding as I dashed along the corridors. I found Sara waving a palm fan over a tray of steaming maize cakes.

"It's Shez. He's ill," I said.

Sara halted midmotion then grabbed a satchel that hung on the wall. After ordering a servant girl to fetch the healer, she hurried after me.

We reached Ash's room in time to see her strip off every bit of clothing from her son.

"What's wrong with him?" Ash burst out the moment she saw Sara.

Without hesitation, Sara scooped up Shez. She pressed her palm against his neck then peered into his eyes. "How much has he eaten today?"

Ash looked at me, but I had been gone part of the afternoon. "He's eaten very little, actually. Some days are like that, so I didn't worry."

Sara nodded then handed the baby back to Ash. She took out a swatch of linen from her satchel and gave it to me. "Soak this in water, and we'll wrap him in it. He won't like it."

I followed her instructions as she took out some dried orange leaves and broke them over a small bowl. She blended honey into the leaves, creating a thick paste. "Hold him steady," she instructed Ash.

* * *

Shez's fever broke in the early hours of the morning. I had never felt so much relief and had never known so much fear. Shez was a helpless baby, and he couldn't tell us what was wrong. He relied wholly on the adults in his life. It was a humbling experience. I could think of little else that might be worse than to lose my dear nephew.

Sara, Ash, and I gathered around Shez and watched him sleep. The steady rise of his chest seemed to be a miracle. The peace on his face was a blessing to us all. His body had cooled; he'd stopped fidgeting and whining.

Ash smiled at him, tears running down her face. Tears flooded my eyes as well but for a different reason from my sister's.

This afternoon when I went to the grove to meet Levi, I would have to bid him farewell. I couldn't leave behind a helpless child and my sister, who depended so much on me. The Lord would want me to be selfless and protect my family. I had to see that my nephew grew into a strong man and a righteous leader. I had to continue to teach my sister the truth until she would listen; if she'd but worship the true Lord, blessings would come into her life.

And most of all, I had to protect them all from the king.

My presence meant their legacy.

CHAPTER 30

11 Years Later

I STAND AT THE COPPER metal, gazing at my appearance. By some standards, I am a young woman, perhaps still eligible for marriage. By other standards, I am well past my zenith.

I have aged well. I have seen much sorrow, but childbirth has not touched my body. It is still firm, my waist narrow, my arms and legs strong.

My hair remains dark, thick, and full. I pull it back from my oval face and twist it into a bun at the nape of my neck. Today is my nephew's twelfth birth date. Today Shez will be ordained as crown prince of the land. If something happens to his father, Shez will have complete power to rule the kingdom. No one expects a boy of twelve to rule, but the ceremony makes the event possible.

Ash has four children now. Three boys and a daughter. She has sworn off birthing any more children, but she might change her mind yet. I smile as playful shouts and screams came from the garden. Sara watches them, as always, her ever-steady gaze taking in every mishap, every deed.

I smooth my tunic and touch the necklace that lies against my throat. The thin gold chain holds a gold ring set with turquoise stones—the ring Levi gave to me on the last day I saw him. I often think of him when I am alone. For that reason, I keep busy and surround myself with my nephews and niece.

The time has arrived to gather the children, inspect their clothing, then escort them into the throne room. An aunt has many duties. But first, I clasp my hands together and pray to the Lord, my God, and ask a blessing upon Levi and the life he leads, that he will be ever safe and protected. I pray for my sister and her young family. And finally, I pray for myself, that I might continue to endure and be a messenger for Him.

I blink back tears and pull on my robe. I've long since dismissed a personal servant, though my sister continually tries to change my mind. "You're the queen's sister. You deserve every bit of care," Ash often says to me.

But I always turn the offer down.

As I exit my room, Malia passes me in the hall. "Good afternoon, Naiva," she calls out in a cheerful voice. Her petite body is a force of energy, and it's no wonder Lib fell in love with her the moment he met her. They were married last month.

I sweep through the corridors, my luxurious robe trailing behind me. It's heavy with beading and much more elaborate than my everyday wear. As I enter the garden, I pause for just a moment to watch the children play. Nothing delights me more than to watch their carefree movements as they run through the garden. Even Shez is among them. My heart warms as he spins around his little sister Isabel.

Sara rises to her feet when she sees me and claps her hands together. "Gather together, children."

Shez spots me and hurries over. He places a dutiful kiss on my cheek, and I smile up at him. "Happy birth date," I say. He is just taller than me now, which always astounds me. How can my dear nephew, whom I used to cradle in my arms, almost be a man?

His gold-brown curls tumble about his face, and a light sheen of perspiration dots his nose. I am so proud of him I could nearly burst. There is incredible light and promise in those dark eyes of his. We've spent many mornings together discussing the things of the Lord. When he takes the throne, I am certain he will lead the people in righteousness and build synagogues throughout the land where we can worship the true God.

"Auntie," Shez says, still calling me by the nickname he used as a child. "Will you paint the events of tonight?"

"Of course," I say. Over the years, I've created paintings of the important events the royal family has participated in.

"Thank you," Shez replies. He bounds away and scoops up Isabel, making her squeal.

"No more of that," Sara says, but her tone is far from scolding. "Tonight you'll become a man, not a boy who teases his sister."

Shez laughs, and I can't help but smile. "No matter how old I am," he says, "I'll always tease her." To prove his point, he lifts her high in the air, making her scream with mixed delight and horror.

I suppress a laugh as Sara tugs Isabel back to the ground. "Follow your aunt into the great hall. The guests are assembled and waiting."

With a bit of scrimmaging, Shez is at my side and the other three trailing behind as we enter the palace.

A lump forms in my throat as we walk into the great hall. It seems as if hundreds of the court elite have gathered. They've all gathered here for Shez—the boy I am so proud of. King Akish and Queen Asherah rise as I lead in Shez. They both smile at their son, and it's as if they've been the perfect example of a loving family.

Shez, in all his grand youth, walks straight and tall toward his parents. I break off with the other siblings about halfway across the room, where we take our appropriate places.

The high priest of the Sun Temple, dressed in his best finery, stands to the right of the king. Isabel grasps my hand, craning her neck to see her brother receive a wide collar made out of silver. The king wears one of gold. I usher her in front of me so she has a good view.

Shez kneels before the high priest and bows his head, and the priest fits the silver collar. Then he leads us all in a chant, praising the sun god and honoring the king and queen. My mouth forms the words, but no sound escapes my lips. My heart is praising the true Lord for the blessing of seeing Shez grow into a man.

When the official ceremony ends, the people file into the banquet room. The tables have been laid with a grand display of food and drink— the best selections of meat, seasoned fish, steamed mushrooms, bean paste spread on tortillas, and endless wine.

Shez finds me in the crowd and shows me the heavy silver collar.

"Auntie," he says. "I can now officially rule over you."

I laugh at the joke between us. He unclasps it and holds it out.

"Don't let your father see you do this," I say.

He shrugs, not concerned in the least. He knows, as I do, his father is not around enough to pay much attention to children's antics. Perhaps that will change now.

The weight of the collar surprises me, and I realize it reflects the weight of his growing responsibility. I hand it back over. "You must put it on before your father notices."

Shez sighs good-naturedly and reclasps the collar around his neck.

Before we can say anything else, I'm quickly replaced by well-wishers. The banquet room has never seen such a crowd. Ash had to order extra platters for all of the invited guests.

The kingdom has celebrated Shez's birth from the very beginning, as the first son of the king and queen. His disposition and playfulness endears everyone to him. As I watch him accept the well-wishes, I think of the many nights I've spent on my knees praying that Akish will not influence his son for evil, that Shez will remain untouched by his father and untouched by the diabolical court life.

As I move away from my nephew toward my place at the banquet table, I catch the gaze of Akish. I quickly look away. He has changed much. Although he has ignored me for the most part over the years, my heart hammers in anxiety if we are ever too close. His visits to his wife are now purely for producing heirs—the only other time they spend together is when decorum calls for it. He employs a full harem now, thankfully on another property separate from the palace.

Ash gave up a long time ago on being the only woman in his life. She may be his queen, but whatever love had been between them has long since faded. She refuses to allow him concubines or other wives, but she cannot control his harlotry.

I sit between two women who are frequently at court. They're young and flirtatious with the men, making me feel even more ancient. And lonely. I eat lightly, not feeling hungry. Seeing my nephew enter the first stage of manhood and accept his role as crown prince of the land fills my heart until tears rise up. I know, though my sacrifices have been great, I've had a hand in creating who he is now.

Shez stands and gives a speech to an awe-filled room. Next to him, his parents look pleased. For a moment, I think Akish has tears in his eyes. He is looking at his son with renewed interest. Perhaps he is wondering, as I am, where all the years have gone.

As I pick at my food, I become absorbed in my own thoughts. It suddenly seems more and more possible that perhaps one day my duty here will be finished. Shez will become a strong leader, no longer in need of his aunt's guidance. He will stand up to his father in defense of truth. Our kingdom will change. Souls will be saved. And the Lord will reign supreme.

And then—it catches my breath just to think of it—and then I will travel to seek out Levi. I hope to find him still waiting for me. If not, I'll be pleased to meet his wife and children. I'll be honored to tell him how his love kept me hopeful all these years, knowing that true love is possible and that the Lord always watches over us and blesses us.

My thoughts blend together in a soft hum, and peace settles over me, confirming once again that I've made the right choice in staying with my sister's family. New hope enters my heart as I realize true love may yet fill my life.

CHAPTER 31

MY FAITH SUSTAINS ME THROUGH the small things and most definitely through the deepest sorrows and disappointments. Which is why, when my sister enters my room the morning following Shez's ordination, I am the calm one in the face of her panic.

"He's taken him!"

I sit up, alert at once. "Who?"

"Akish." The name is like poison on her lips. "He's taken Shez."

A dozen possibilities run through my mind, some more unpleasant than others—from hunting wild beasts to introducing Shez to the harem.

"Where?" I ask, hiding my annoyance at my sister's ever-present theatrics, though I love her as she is.

"To the west prison." She wrings her hands together, and tears drip down her cheeks. "In the borderland."

The west prison is near the west border. It's often used to house our enemies and is the site of torturing to warn anyone against making border crossings without permission.

I can see how Ash might be upset that Shez has been taken there to be shown the less-desirous methods of protecting the kingdom. But he's a young man now; both of us need to allow him to grow up. If Shez is to be king some day, he'll need to be strict in his punishments.

"We've sheltered him long enough, Ash." It pains me to say it, but I know it to be true. I want to protect him from everything, but if he is to be king, he must know how his father runs the kingdom.

Ash grips my hands, and I'm surprised at her intensity. "Shez isn't going there to visit. Akish has convicted him of stealing. Shez is the newest prisoner."

The warmth drains from my body, replaced by cold disbelief. "Are you sure?" I can't think—can't believe a father would truly do this. Maybe it's some part of an initiation, disturbing as it is.

Ash breaks into a sob, and I grasp her arms. "Tell me what happened!"

"Last night—" She begins then stops, emotion taking hold. "Last night Akish saw Shez in a new light. Not as a father sees a son and feels pride at all his accomplishments, but as a man sees another man—as a threat."

I cover my mouth with my hand, the shock intensifying. No prisoner has ever left the borderland alive.

"Akish accused Shez of being a traitor and of trying to steal the kingdom," she continues.

"How can a twelve-year-old boy be a traitor?"

Ash's voice grows quiet. "By accepting the role as crown prince. Akish said it was an outright show of defiance and rebelliousness. He claims Shez will now vie for his throne."

"That's madness," I say. "The ordination of the heir to the throne has happened throughout the history of our people."

"I know," Ash says, tears streaking her cheeks again. "But no one dares to question the king. I thought it would be different this morning and that the wine would wear off and Akish would forget his resolution. But before dawn, Akish signed the official law. Any boy or man who accepts the emblems of crown prince is in direct defiance of the current king."

I rise from the bed and pace the room. The glittering sun streaming in through my windows casts an ethereal glow about my room, making this news seem even more implausible.

"Shez could give back the silver collar," I say, mostly to myself.

Ash is on her feet. "I thought of that as well. I pleaded with Akish this morning. Begged him on my hands and knees."

The horror of the moment settles into my breast. "And Shez? What did he do?" I whisper.

"He didn't shed a tear. He didn't even complain." Her breath catches. "I think he was in shock. He never looked at me as they tied his hands behind his back and led him out." She sinks to the floor.

I cross to her and wrap my arms around her. "We'll get him back. This has been the most terrible mistake. The people can't put up with this—not even from their king. If we can't make Akish understand, we'll rescue Shez ourselves."

My sister shakes her head. "Akish will kill anyone who tries to free him." She leans against me, and her sobs shudder through her body.

If I am to rescue Shez, no one can know about it, not even his mother.

* * *

Ash and I are banned from court. I'm not exactly surprised that I am, but Ash is the rightful queen. To ban her from her own people only further proves the king's foolishness. I wonder if the Lord would condemn me to hell if I killed my brother-in-law. I wonder how the Lord can let such a vile man walk the earth. If He has all power, can He not strike down a mere human?

I pray morning, night, and every hour in between for Shez. I don't sleep, and I know Ash doesn't sleep. She insists on the children all staying in her room and keeping them close at all times in case her husband decides to turn on one of them.

The servants walk the halls in absolute silence. Everyone fears for their lives. If the king could throw his own son in prison—a twelve-year-old boy at that—nothing will stop him from making a new law to suit any action.

I plan to visit Shez, to see if a rescue is possible. I must also return before my absence is noticed.

The only person I can confide in is Lib. Yet even he is shaken by the king's actions. Even he's afraid this time. He agrees to travel with me, but we must leave and return in the same night. The journey will be fast and the danger high.

Then word comes—the worst possible news.

Lib finds us in the garden just as the sun is going down. My sister and I have taken refuge among the plants so we may speak in privacy. Lib bows his head as he speaks in whispered tones. "They are starving him. Have been for several days now. The end cannot be far."

"No!" my sister screeches, and she flings herself at Lib.

He lets her scratch and claw at him, her grief and rage aimed at him only because he is the messenger.

I rush to them and pull my sister from the attack, expecting her to fight against me. Instead, my sister turns on herself, clawing at her arms as if she can dull the pain inside her heart. I tell Lib to leave us, to find out any more news if he can.

"What have I done?" my sister asks me. Her arms are striped with deep claw marks from her own fingernails, fingernails that had once been shaped, stained, and etched with delicate gold designs. They are now broken and tattered—just as my sister's life has become.

I stare at her blood filling the cracks in the stone garden path.

"Naiva," she whispers, her dark eyes capturing mine. "How could I allow them to send my son to the borderland prison? He is everything to me. There's nothing—" Her voice breaks. "There's nothing left of my heart now; it's disappeared into my soul."

"Hush now," I say, though I doubt my sister still has a soul. I look away from her bloody arms as she stretches her hands out, reaching for me. I don't need to see her wild eyes, her unruly long hair soiled with ashes of grief, to know her pain. Nor do I need to see her lips twist with pleas of agony. Her grief and agony are mine too.

I pull her into my arms and hold on, trying to soak up her anguish in a small way, something I've done a hundred times over. My gaze goes unwillingly to the self-inflicted marks of grief in her arms, and I shudder. *He will be fine. He will live*, I want to promise her, but I know my words hold no power. If I could command as the Lord does, I would not be crouching next to my sister in the garden, like we're fugitives, on the day we discover her son is being starved to death by her own husband.

The torchlights begin to flicker out in the small courtyard near the garden we have hidden ourselves away in. The night is thick with darkness, nearly as thick as the silence in our palace of mourning.

My throat tightens as I think of my nephew and what he must feel right now, in a place we cannot reach to comfort him. He is only a child of twelve years. Fresh tears nearly break out when I envision his beautiful face. His eyes so much like his mother's, his lips and cheekbones like his father's, his contagious grin and his affection for me. All a memory now of a boy who was once heir to the throne.

Ash trembles inside my arms. Only then do I realize she is whispering again. "I have failed him. What mother lets her own son be tortured and starved by his father?"

I want to soothe her, but I can't. Every syllable she speaks is true. I wish for words of solace, yet they will not come. If I can only find a way to save her son, a way to change the king's mind . . . But I know he will not change his mind. He is fear itself. Neither my sister nor I dares approach him since he has banished us from court. There are the other children's lives to consider. There are our own.

I think back over the years—before my sister's countenance had dimmed and her golden-brown eyes had dulled, before she flinched at every sound and step, afraid of her own husband. The memories struggle to surface then fall back into nothingness. They seem a lifetime ago—no, two lifetimes ago. We were young. Ash was beautiful, talented, powerful . . . cunning. I wanted to be exactly like my older sister. I was her shadow. The dances, the jewels, the clothing, the games, the men . . . all dazzling.

But none of that matters now. We huddle together on a stone path in the middle of the royal gardens, afraid of life, afraid of death.

Her son, the crown prince, is as good as dead. And Ash has no one to blame but herself. She knew what her husband was when she married him.

I suppose I carry some blame as well, though I certainly warned her enough. Still, I wonder if I could have done more—interfered perhaps—or forced her against her will in the very beginning. But neither of us could have known or understood the consequences Ash's choice would have upon our kingdom. No one, except for perhaps the Lord Himself, foresaw the tragedy that our lives have become.

What's done is done. Neither of us can change it now. Our existence has dwindled to that of two grieving women, mourning the banishment of our beloved Shez. The bright sun in our lives has been extinguished like an oil lamp.

The anger and grief inside me build, and desperation rushes in. "I'll find a way to free your son. I'll take him somewhere where Akish can't find him."

"No. He'll catch you both," my sister says, her voice gaining strength. "And then he'll kill you as well." She turns her face toward mine, swollen from crying. "Don't leave me, Naiva. I couldn't bear this life without you. I have already lost too much." Her voice falters.

We have *all* lost too much, and we are afraid to fight any more.

"Naiva," my sister's voice breaks into my thoughts. "Do you think my son suffers in his last hours? Do you think the gods are there to comfort him?"

I flinch at her plural usage of *god*. Will she ever give up her idols? Each one of them has betrayed her. I cannot answer right away, for I cannot lie to my sister. I have never lied to her, even though I've been beaten, banished, and imprisoned for treason . . . all for telling my sister, the queen, the truth.

And no matter how hard it may be for her to hear the truth right now, it's all I have to offer.

"The Lord will comfort him," I whisper. "I have not stopped my prayers for one moment." On any other day, Ash might bristle at my mention of the God I worship, but tonight, she accepts my words.

"Do you think your God will allow my black soul into heaven?" she says.

I hesitate, and it's as if Ash knows why I cannot answer. She collapses against me, a wail building in her chest, turning into a high-pitched keening. The sound of a woman aching for her lost soul and a child with whom she will not be reunited in heaven.

I cling to her as tears finally break free onto my face, for I know the things my sister has done will be impossible for the Lord to forgive.

When we die, my sister and I will spend eternity apart. She, in hell. And when she arrives there, alone and afraid, my already fractured heart will at last break in two.

CHAPTER 32

DESPITE MY SISTER'S WARNINGS, I meet with Lib and plan to visit Shez.

I tell myself it's only to see him one last time before he dies. Even if I deliver food to Shez, I don't know if the guards will let him have it. I will not try anything foolish, like a rescue. Regardless, no one can know I am gone.

Lib and I leave on the eve of the Moon Festival. The servants are busy preparing, and if someone notices Lib's absence, they'll think he's on an errand. I haven't told my sister I'm leaving, and I hope no one comes to look for me. I wait in my room for the signal. When I hear the false call of a bird near my window, I sneak into the corridor and walk slowly to the cooking room, as if I am seeking a late-night treat.

The door connecting the cooking room to the garden has been left unlatched, and I slip through. I don't stop but continue walking until I reach the far garden wall. There are soldiers posted on the outside of the wall, and I must wait for the guard change.

Moments later, I join Lib on the other side. The lone soldier faces the opposite direction and doesn't even turn when I catch my foot and send a rock tumbling.

Lib grabs my arm, and we hurry away together.

"Did you pay him?" I whisper when we're out of hearing distance.

"No."

"Then how—"

"I threatened him," Lib says. "It works equally well. It turns out the guard accompanies the king to the harem from time to time, and his wife doesn't know about it."

I suppress a laugh, though it's nothing to laugh about.

We keep to the side roads and trees as much as possible. The moon provides plenty of light, but that's both good and bad. We aren't hard to spot, and I hope we can avoid any trouble.

The night is half over when we reach the west border. "I've only been here once before," Lib says. "To the left of the guard hut is the underground prison."

The hut is the only building in sight. No light comes from the inside, but the moon casts a silver glow on the thatch roof.

"Where are the guards?" I ask.

Lib stares at the landscape for a moment. "I don't see any movement. Maybe they're inside."

Or hidden, I think. But the terrain is open, and the trees are scarce. Nothing but flat land spreads to the left of the hut, where the prison holes are. To the right are a few scattered copal trees.

I concentrate on the trees, trying to make out any figures. "What should we do? We can't wait much longer."

"We'll knock on the door of the hut and ask permission to visit with the prisoner."

I nod, hoping we won't get an arrow in the chest in the process. We walk together toward the hut.

"Let me be the first to be seen," I whisper. "They won't feel threatened by a woman." I knock on the door, and my heart pounds, seemingly louder than the knocking.

When the door swings open, a man stands there, dagger in his hand. His size tells me he can easily overpower Lib. "Who are you?" he demands.

"We're here to visit the prisoner Shez. We have gifts for you and supplies for him."

The guard looks past my shoulder. Lib holds up the satchel with supplies. "Can I open it and show you the gifts?"

Another guard appears at the door, a sword in hand. "Drop the bag."

I take a step back, and Lib lets go of the bag.

The second guard waves his sword. "No deliveries for the boy."

It is as I expected, but I am determined. "Surely it would do no harm," I say.

They don't respond to my suggestion. The first guard grabs the satchel and opens the top.

"What's in it?" the second guard asks, keeping his eyes trained on us.

"Nothing the boy is allowed to have," the first guard says, dumping the contents on the ground.

"There's plenty of dried meat," I say. "Everything else is yours if you'll let him have the meat."

The second guard snorts. "We're under orders to keep food from the prisoner."

"You mean food that's delivered by others?" Lib asks.

"All food," the guard says.

I feel as if I've been punched in the stomach. A small bit of hope that Lib might have received wrong information has now died. Anger pushes its way up my throat, and I can't help but say, "You mean you're starving him?"

"We're following orders from the *king*," the first guard says, his voice defensive.

"He's just a boy!" I cry out. "He's done nothing." I grab the dried meat wrapped in a cloth and start running in the direction I assume the prison holes are. I hope I don't fall into one, but I'll take the risk if it means bringing food to my nephew.

"Shez!" I scream as I run. Seconds later, I'm sprawled on the ground.

One of the guards has grabbed me. I turn to claw at him, but the second guard joins him and pins me to the ground.

"Release her," Lib yells.

"Tie her up," one of the guards shouts over Lib's yells.

"No, she's the queen's sister." It's Lib.

The guards stop, still holding me captive, but they are finally listening to Lib.

"She merely wants to see how Shez is doing," Lib says.

"She was taking him food," one of the guards says. "Food is forbidden."

I moan. I can't let Shez starve. Surely it's a mistake. Surely Akish hasn't inflicted this torture on his own heir.

Lib's voice is closer as he says, "We'll return to the city with no further incident. Please release her."

"Let me see my nephew," I gasp. "Let me at least speak to him."

"We have strict orders, woman. No contact with the king's son for anyone," a voice says above me. "We aren't willing to risk our positions because you want to speak to a prisoner."

"We can bring silver or anything you want," I say. "Please give him the meat we brought."

Hands tighten around my arms. "And you don't think the king is counting down days until he can be sure his son is dead? Prolonging his death will only make it worse for everyone."

My heart nearly stops. I have never felt so cold, so stunned with disbelief. I can't imagine Shez's laughter silenced forever, his young body still in death. Something inside me changes. It's as if I've repressed every bit of anger and disappointment for many years, and now is the moment my mind will no longer hold off the madness.

Adrenaline pulses through me, and I feel the strength of ten men running through my veins. I twist out of the guards' grasp and scramble to my feet. I am running, free now, and calling for Shez. I will find him, and I'll rescue him. My own life does not matter. The king may do with me what he will, but I'll give my nephew a chance to escape.

My legs fly out from under me, and I slam into the ground again. This time, everything goes black.

CHAPTER 33

I AM BEING CARRIED TO the darkest abyss. The journey is bumpy, and my body is painfully jostled. The hot breathing of minions sounds above me—panting, as if in eager anticipation of delivering me to my final destination. I don't open my eyes yet, for I am not ready to see my punishment. I'll surely be tortured, if not physically then mentally.

My mind accepts this in a small way, but for the most part, I am ready to be nothing. The Lord has been good to me, but even He cannot stop an evil king. If I cannot save Shez, there is nothing for me anymore.

"You fool," a voice says above me. Loud and clear. Familiar.

Lib? I open my eyes and realize I am not being carried into the underworld but that Lib is taking me back to the palace.

"Good. You're awake." He sets me down carefully then stretches his arms and back. "I thought you'd wait until I carried you all the way home."

My knees give out, and I sink to the ground. "What are you doing? We can't leave Shez."

"I'm saving your life, Naiva," Lib says. He leans down, his eyes boring into mine, and I realize I can see the dark centers. The night has softened into approaching dawn. The sun is on its way. "We may not be able to help Shez, but I'll not be responsible for your death as well."

I twist away, disgusted that he's given up. "Go back to the palace, then. Leave me. I'll find a way to rescue my nephew."

Lib's laugh is bitter. "At first sight, the guards will slice your throat. Going back there is a sure execution. Then what will your sister do?"

I exhale, unable to comprehend leaving Shez in such a condition. Unable to comprehend how I will ever tell my sister her son really is being starved.

"We must hurry, or we'll surely be discovered," Lib says.

Tears fall onto my cheeks, and I cannot move.

"Naiva," Lib's voice is more gentle but still urgent. "I won't leave you behind. If you refuse to move, we'll both be punished."

I can't let Lib be punished on my behalf again. I grab his hand and hoist myself up. My head throbs fiercely, and I feel dizzy, but I move quickly with Lib, back to the palace, back to break my sister's heart.

* * *

Three days later, word comes. Shez is dead.

"He refused to eat," the king tells the court, false sorrow on his face. "I gave him the opportunity to recant his threat to the throne, but he would not. His final act of defiance to the kingdom was to starve himself. The queen is devastated and will not be receiving visitors until the period of mourning has passed."

I might have collapsed if I hadn't pressed myself against the wall for support. Ash cannot bear to hear her husband's proclamation, so I have come instead, standing in the hall, just outside the open court doors. The king has made no effort at privacy; he wants all the land to know his side of the story. Since my all-night escapade three days before, I've hardly eaten or slept, every moment spent in pleading to the Lord.

The Lord has not answered my prayers. The Lord has turned away His compassion and let a young boy with righteous promise waste away in a cold, dark prison. I am so angry at the king's words that I cannot speak when I return to Ash and her children. It's a miracle I can even walk the halls to her chamber—though I don't believe in miracles anymore.

I look into the innocent eyes of Isabel and her brothers, Nimrah and Jared the Younger. How can I tell them what their father did? I decide this is one thing I'll let Ash handle. What she tells them or how she tells them will be up to her. She crosses the room and falls into my arms.

We hold each other, both at a loss for words. The children gather around us, and we pull them against us. As I stand, enmeshed in the arms of those I love dearest in all the world, the Spirit whispers to me. I push it away. I do not want comfort. I want to be angry. I want to hate bitterly. I want to rant about the injustice of Shez's death and never forgive the Lord for His negligence.

But the Spirit whispers again, *He is safe now.*

I want to cry out, *I would have protected him! You didn't have to let him die!* Yet I have failed, and I know it. I have failed to protect my nephew from his evil father, and I have failed to listen for the Lord's answer to my prayers.

How can this be an answer? How can this be restitution for Shez's terrible imprisonment? Why was I not starved in prison but instead preserved at the loss of two other lives? What sets me apart from an innocent and beautiful boy?

His blood will cry out for vengeance, and all things will be made whole.

The words wash over me, and my tears are now ones of knowledge. I have yet to accept them completely in my heart, but my mind knows they are true.

Trust in me.

I do, I realize. I trust in the Lord, as I always have. I must allow Him to exact justice and dole out Akish's punishment, whether it is on earth or in the life hereafter.

I pull away from my sister and her children, and I look into their tear-filled eyes. "Your brother is in the arms of the Lord." I continue on before Ash can hush me—she's heard me speak of my God before, but she doesn't know what I've told her oldest son. "I do not worship the idols of the kingdom or the sun god. I worship the true God: the Lord, our Savior."

The children's eyes widen. I can see Isabel understands little of what I am saying, but by her brothers' reactions, she knows it's something forbidden.

"The Lord has told me Shez is safe now. He is in heaven, living with your grandmother." My tears are hot and fast. "We'll always miss him, always love him, but now we must do one last thing for him."

The children brush tears from their eyes and stare at me.

"We must select the things he loved so we can send them with his body to the sepulchre." I look at Ash. "We'll prepare his body for burial when it arrives."

CHAPTER 34

WITH THE DEATH OF SHEZ, everything changes. The atmosphere in the palace and throughout the land is somber. The court still pays its highest allegiance to King Akish, but it is only out of fear. Ash is reinstated at court, but she attends only when she must. All festivals are suspended, though there are banquets each night, a forced pleasure. Or maybe I hadn't noticed how much fear ruled everyone's hearts since I was so absorbed in my nephews and niece.

When the mourning period for Shez comes to an end, my sister arrives in my chamber. She is alone, and her eyes are bright with tears. "I have a plan."

We sit together on the cushions near the window.

"I'm sending Nimrah and Jared the Younger to the apprentice Hearthom to train as our brothers did." She takes a breath. "I know they're very young still, but I cannot have them around my husband." Her voice breaks, and I take her hands, squeezing them in comfort.

"Nimrah is nearly eleven," she says. "In a year's time, he'll be the crown prince. I do not want a second son murdered." Tears drip down her face as she stares at me, determined. "Jared is nine. He has seen too much in his young years." She wipes at her cheeks, and her voice trembles as she continues. "I need to ask one very last favor of you."

"What is it?" My stomach tightens. I'm now afraid.

"It's two favors, actually," she whispers. "I want you to leave me, to leave this palace, and find a place where you can live and worship as you please."

"Ash, I made my choice long ago—"

"I know you did. And now it's time to make another choice." She closes her eyes and exhales. Then in an ever-so-quiet voice she says, "I want you to take Isabel with you."

* * *

O Lord, my God, give me courage for what I am about to do, I pray, clasping Isabel's small hand in mine.

The night is black, the moon blocked by heavy clouds, and I stand in the courtyard of the palace, perhaps looking at my sister for the last time.

Ash puts on a brave smile for her daughter, a smile I know she cannot truly feel. Young Isabel thinks we're going on a grand journey, which we might be, but her little heart has yet to understand that she'll never see her parents again.

Even as I stall our farewell, I know we must make haste. Once Akish discovers our absence, the entire land will be turned upside down looking for his daughter. I'll be labeled a traitor again, worthy of fatal punishment.

I pull my hood up then Isabel's. I tie hers securely beneath her chin as her wide black eyes study me carefully. "Why is it so dark, Auntie?"

"Because it's the middle of the night," I whisper. "Hush now."

She makes a great show of clamping her lips together. I squeeze her hand. "Give your mother a kiss."

She dutifully rises up on her tiptoes and reaches for Ash. My sister bends down and holds her tight.

"I can't b-breathe," Isabel says.

Ash still clings to her for another moment then lets her go. I notice my sister's trembling chin and how she is trying not to break down in front of her daughter. "Go, my sweet girl. Go with Auntie and listen to everything she says." Ash kisses the top of her head and turns to me.

We embrace quickly, fiercely, both of us too emotional to speak. The decision has been made, and now we must carry it out. I'll leave Ash behind at her beautiful palace. She is carrying another child—a boy, she claims. Her sons will grow up at the apprentice's with a nursemaid, away from their father. Isabel will become as mine. My story to any I meet is that I am widowed.

I hope to reach the land of Ablom before I am caught.

Yes, I've decided to join Levi after all. I understand he might have a wife, and even if he doesn't, it's been many years since we were separated. I've certainly changed, and likely so has he. Regardless of what our relationship may or may not be, I want to live in freedom.

With a final look at my sister's tearful face, I grasp Isabel's hand and cross the courtyard. Tears blur my eyes—tears of missing my sister already, tears of grief over Shez, tears that I am taking a child from her mother.

* * *

The journey is longer and more tiring than I imagined, every step loaded with mixed emotions—every step wondering what Ash is doing at each moment. What she might be saying to Akish, what Akish might be ordering his guards to do.

I teach Isabel to pray to the Lord our first day on our journey. We stop often to kneel together, clasp our hands, bow our heads, and plead for guidance. At first, Isabel stumbles over the foreign, awkward words, but by the third day, she mimics me perfectly in her six-year-old voice.

We stay out of the way of others as much as possible. We travel mostly at night and keep to the tree line to enable us a quick disappearance. The farther we travel, the fear of being caught by the king's guards lessens and is replaced with worry about being waylaid by bandits.

On the fourth day of travel, we reach Ablom. I'm not expecting the size of the village that spreads out before us. There are dozens of huts arranged in neat rows. A market center opens up to a path leading to the sea. Small sea vessels dot the water that glows golden in the afternoon sun.

Isabel cries out, "Look! It's big water!"

"Yes," I say, my voice stuck in my throat. There are no statues in front of the reed doors, no carved edifices in the form of gods or goddesses. It's as if I can feel the presence of the Lord radiating from this community. Tears touch my eyes, and my heart swells with gratitude. The Lord has truly watched over Isabel and me and has delivered us safely to freedom.

"Come," I say. We join hands and walk toward the outlying huts.

Isabel skips along with my slower step. She laughs as a goat runs toward us, bleating.

A young boy chases it, calling out, "Stop!" He halts when he sees us, curiosity bright in his eyes.

Isabel says, "I Iello."

He raises his hand then scampers away.

"Where's he going?"

I laugh. "He's probably gone to tell his mother that he saw a beautiful girl walk past him."

Isabel giggles in her high, musical voice, so much like her mother's. "I don't think so, Auntie . . . I mean, *Mother*." She pushes out her lower lip. "Why must I call you *Mother*?"

"Because," I say, "I've explained to you that it's safer if people think you're my daughter."

"So the bad men won't get us?"

Hiding a smile, I say, "Yes." My heart is pounding. I am in the same village Levi lives in. I wonder if he has children; perhaps that was his little boy who ran past us. As we walk along the path, passing hut after hut, I wonder if each one might be his home.

A woman comes out of one of the huts as we walk by, and she shields her eyes against the setting sun's glow. She's dressed simply in a pale blue tunic, her hair wrapped in a colorful scarf. I gather my courage and walk up the path to her yard.

"We're looking for a friend," I say.

The woman looks from me to Isabel then meets my gaze again. "Where are you from?"

"The city of Heth." I don't know how news might travel, but I feel that I can trust the people in this village. After all, they are the people of the Lord, and Omer is their leader. "Do you know a man named Levi?"

Her brows lift slightly. "He's fishing."

My heart pounds at hearing the confirmation that he is indeed here, that he is relatively close, likely in one of the boats we saw earlier. I wonder at the woman's short answer and her seemingly sure knowledge of where he is. She looks as if she wants to ask more questions, but I quickly thank her and pull Isabel with me along the path.

At the next opening on the narrow road, I take a left turn and head toward the sea. Isabel and I reach the shore, and I'm surprised that it's quite empty. Several boats are on the water, but no one else is about. Smoke rises near the closest huts, and I realize the families are preparing their evening meals.

I find a large rock to sit on and watch as Isabel pads in her bare feet along the wet sand. She is fascinated with how the sea creeps closer then washes out, over and over. We wait for what seems like hours, though I know it could have only been a short time. As the sun begins its descent against the horizon, the boats head for the shore. I grip my hands together as I watch each fisherman unload his catch.

I look for anyone familiar, anything that might set Levi apart. It's been so long that I tell myself I may not recognize him.

Now there are only two boats left. The one closest to me contains two men. As the boat draws to shore, my mouth goes dry. Levi sits at the back, steering the boat. I'm sure it's him. His hair is longer, his skin tanner, but his form and even his mannerisms are all Levi. And the scar that runs along his face, the scar the king branded him with, is unmistakable.

I am about to stand when I hear someone shouting. Two children come running down the shoreline, splashing through the water. Levi and the other man wave at them.

His children, I think. I stay on the rock, unable to move. I wonder if it will be too painful to live in a village where I might see Levi often, might get to know his wife and children.

The fishermen climb out of the boat and pull it farther up onto shore. They unload the baskets just as the children reach them. The children clamor around both men, and I try to decipher if either of the children looks like Levi.

Then suddenly, the other fisherman is walking away, carrying a basket, accompanied by the children. Levi stays back, cleaning out the boat. My throat is nearly closed, and I can barely catch my breath, but I force myself to stand. Just as I do, Levi turns, as if sensing my presence.

His gaze slides from me to Isabel, who stands next to me. She grabs my hand, and Levi turns back to the boat.

"Is that him?" Isabel asks.

I nod, unable to speak. I force one foot in front of the other—forward.

Levi turns again, as if he has just realized that perhaps I am someone familiar. I keep walking toward him, and I see the recognition in his eyes.

He straightens, now staring at me. His gaze drifts to Isabel then back to my face. It's as if the world has gone silent, and the sounds of the churning sea and blowing wind can no longer be heard.

Isabel stops and tugs at my hand. She stoops and picks up a seashell. She says something about it, but the actual words don't reach my ears. Levi is walking toward us, and I can see only him. He is taller than I remember and his shoulders broader. But his forest-colored eyes are the same.

I wonder how he sees me. It has been many years. I'm not the young woman I once was. I'm well past my prime, and my skin has started to age. After many days of travel, I probably look as if I've arrived straight out of the jungle.

"Naiva?" Levi says. The sound of his voice nearly brings me to tears.

"Hello," I croak, but my throat cuts off everything else.

"My name is Isabel!" My niece holds out her hand.

Levi crouches to her level and takes her hand. "Nice to meet you, Isabel. I'm Levi."

"I know," Isabel says.

Levi smiles, and my heart turns. He's standing again, facing me. I can't stop staring at him.

"How many fish did you catch?" Isabel asks.

He looks down at her again. "Three baskets full. Do you want to see them?"

"Yes," Isabel says and runs toward the boat. Levi and I follow at a slower pace.

Levi casts me a sideways glance. "I wondered if I'd ever see you again."

"I have a lot to tell you," I manage to say, though my voice sounds strange to my ears. I wonder if I'm really here, walking beside Levi, or if this is a dream.

We reach the boat, and Levi answers Isabel's many questions. I have never heard her talk so much. It's as if she's been saving six years of questions for this moment.

"You're a bright girl, Isabel," Levi says.

She looks at me. "What is *bright*?"

"Smart," I say. "He means you're very smart."

She smiles at this. "I know."

"You should say *thank you* to Levi," I say to her. "It's a nice thing to say when someone tells you something nice first."

Her expression turns serious, and she bows her head. "Thank you."

He laughs. "Your mother is fortunate to have such a *smart* girl."

"She's . . ." Isabel lowers her voice, "not *really* my mother. We're just pretending so the bad men won't find us."

Levi looks at me, curiosity in his gaze.

"Isabel is Ash's daughter," I say. "She's your niece."

His brow arches. He bends down and takes Isabel's hand. "I'm your uncle, then."

She grins at him. "I know." Then she looks at me. "Can I get in the boat?"

"If Levi doesn't mind," I say, looking at him for confirmation.

"I don't mind." His eyes are on me, soaking me in—not as before, not with surprise but all-absorbing. "You aren't married?"

"No," I say. Isabel scrambles into the boat and climbs all over it as if it's the most amazing thing she's ever seen.

I feel the heat of Levi's gaze on me. And suddenly he is standing close, his hand brushing my wind-blown hair from my face.

"Have you come to live here?" he asks in a low voice.

"Yes," I whisper because I don't trust my own voice. "Isabel too. There is much that has happened."

He nods, still watching me. "I heard about Shez. I'm sorry."

Tears prick my eyes, and before I can blink them back, they cascade down my cheeks. I wipe at them swiftly.

"You've come a long way," Levi says. "But you'll be safe here. You and Isabel." He touches my arm as he says this, and it's all I can do to stop myself from melting against him.

I can't stand not knowing if he has a wife. I have to ask. "Are you married?"

He smiles, and fear shoots through my heart. I brace myself for an analog of his beautiful wife and many children.

"I never break a promise," he says. His hand moves from my arm to my waist. "I've been waiting for you, Naiva."

It takes a few seconds for his words to sink in. His hand slides to my back, and he pulls me close. Then he leans down, his other hand brushing my cheek.

Fresh tears fall—of gratitude, of love.

I wrap my arms around his neck, feeling the warmth of him saturate my skin. "You aren't married?"

"Of course not," he murmurs against my ear.

"It's been eleven years."

"Not long at all," he whispers. "I would have waited forever."

CHAPTER 35

TODAY IS MY WEDDING DAY. I have been in Ablom only a few days, but Levi sees no reason to wait. Neither do I.

"We will meet the king today?" Isabel asks for maybe the hundredth time this morning. "Then you will get married?"

"Yes," I say, brushing through her tangle of dark curls. We are staying in Levi's hut while he sleeps outside each night. Tonight, he will sleep within.

The morning sun warms the small bed chamber quickly, reminding me that I still have so much to do to prepare.

A village woman loaned me a tunic of fine linen, and I have remade it into something that will do for the wedding. But I still need to gather flowers to weave into a garland for a belt.

"Will the king come to the wedding?" Isabel asks.

I smile. "I'm not sure. He doesn't even know me."

"But he's our grandfather," she says.

"Your great-grandfather," I correct. "My grandfather. And we don't call him the king here." It was strange to think of a man I didn't know as *grandfather*. I look away from Isabel's bright eyes, thinking of the man whom my father and sister had once plotted against. What will he think of me? Certainly he knows I worship the Lord as he does, but is that and our family connection enough for him to receive me into his good graces?

Here, he is not king, at least from what Levi has told me, but he is a revered leader. Those in this village would defend Omer with their lives.

A whistle coming from outside pulls me from my thoughts, and I turn to the window. My breath catches at the sight of Levi standing there; I still can't believe he is real and I am here.

He grins when our eyes meet.

"How long have you been spying?" I ask, keeping my face straight.

Isabel pulls away from my hair combing and runs out of the room and out of the hut.

"Not long at all," he says, his eyes traveling to my feet.

I flush. I am wearing the same tunic I slept in. But he doesn't seem to mind my rumpled appearance.

"You could come into the hut; it's your place, after all," I say. "You don't need to sneak around and peer into windows."

Levi laughs, and just then he staggers back. Isabel has reached him and thrown her arms around his waist.

"Good morning," he says to his niece.

She starts to tell him about visiting Grandfather Omer and the flowers we're going to weave for the wedding, and while she talks, Levi continues to gaze at me through the window.

It's as if everything around me has disappeared and I can only see him. My rumpled tunic doesn't bother me anymore, and I walk to the window without a word, not wanting to interrupt Isabel's enthusiasm.

I lean out the window just as Levi leans in. He kisses me, and I close my eyes. For a moment, I can believe this is all my life is and will ever be. No evil king on the throne, no abused sister, no frightened children, just Levi and me stealing a kiss the morning of our wedding day.

When Levi pulls away, he says, "Are you ready?" He is still close enough that his breath touches my face.

"Not quite." I blink, clearing the haze from my mind.

"I'll wait out here until you are," he says in a quiet voice.

I nod. That is very wise. If he is feeling anything close to what I am, keeping the walls of the hut between us is a very good thing right now.

Isabel runs back into the hut, breathless with excitement. I cast another glance at Levi, and he gives me a wink then disappears, whistling again.

"Hurry," Isabel says, as if I need prodding from a child.

I finish combing her hair, and I dress in the finest robe I brought. My clothing is more luxurious than anything I've seen the women wear in the village, but I want to look my best when I meet Omer. After all, he is royalty.

Levi is waiting for us when we exit. He wraps my hand in his, and with his other hand, he takes Isabel's. I smile at him. It's as if we are already a little family.

Levi greets everyone as we pass through the village, and the ones I haven't met already, he quickly introduces to me. I receive plenty of knowing looks—everyone seems to know who I am and what my relation is to Omer.

The path of huts leads away from the coast and into the beginnings of jungle. Branches overhead provide plenty of shade as we walk. The birds chatter, and I wonder if they have any idea what an important moment this is for me. My heart pounds furiously, but I take great comfort in Levi's presence.

When he slows at a clearing in the trees, I expect to see a quaint palace, but instead, we've arrived at a collection of huts, not much bigger than Levi's.

Perhaps these are the guards' huts, I think. I am about to ask Levi when a man about my father's age steps out of the first one.

My knees lurch. He looks so much like my father, yet it is not he.

He seems to notice my gaping, and his expression goes soft. "I am Coriantumr."

When I still say nothing, Levi answers for me. "This is Jared's daughter, Naiva, and her niece, Isabel."

I stare at Coriantumr, his strong physique, his sculpted cheeks, his trimmed auburn beard. This is what my father would have looked like if he'd lived and if he hadn't given himself over to wine and darkness.

Thoughts of what might have been tumble through my mind, regret mixed with curiosity.

Coriantumr cautiously steps forward and takes my hand. Then he does the most extraordinary thing. He leans down and kisses my cheek. "Welcome to Ablom, my niece," he says.

Tears flood my eyes, and I suddenly notice others have come out of their huts. Have they all been waiting for me to arrive?

I am introduced to men, women, children . . . all aunts, uncles, cousins, whom I have never met. Their names blur together just as my tears blur my vision. And through it all, Levi keeps my hand in his. Isabel is delighted as children surround her. She's talking faster than I can follow, telling them things I should probably censor.

But for now, I can only marvel. All these people are here—living in exile—in small huts—because of the ambition of my father. How can they look at me with forgiveness . . . and love? Their gazes are open, pure, and welcoming.

And then a notable hush interrupts the introductions. A white-haired man walks through the gathering. I feel my legs weaken, and I grip Levi's hand tighter.

Omer is younger, yet older, than I had imagined. His gaze is alert, his thin lips turned up at the corners, and I can see my father's face shape in his.

But there is nothing of my father in this man's soul. It's as if the Spirit has enveloped me from head to toe, and I have come face to face with an angel.

Without a doubt, I know this is a man of God.

He stops a few steps in front of me, just gazing at me. His tunic is of rough linen, no better than what I've seen the villagers wear. He wears a leather band around one wrist and simple sandals on his feet. I try to speak, but nothing comes out, and then I realize I probably need permission to speak to him.

"Naiva," he says, his voice warm and deep. "At last you have joined us."

I blink, hot tears forming again. What does he mean, *at last*?

"When I heard about your arrival in Ablom," Omer says, "I offered a prayer of thanksgiving to the Lord God for answering our pleas."

Around me, heads nod in agreement. They have been praying for me? I can't comprehend it.

Isabel comes back to my side, staring at the man who is her great-grandfather. He bends over to touch Isabel's shoulder, and she grins up at him. "What a beautiful child. So much like her Auntie."

"You should see my real mother," Isabel says.

I worry about Omer's reaction, but he only smiles. "I hope to meet her someday." His tone is genuine, and I wonder what Asherah's reaction would be to meeting this man.

Omer continues, as if he doesn't notice my muteness. "We are grateful that Levi was the one to lure you here."

My relatives smile at me. *They are smiling!* Do they not know that my sister plotted against their father, that he is here in isolation because of my own father?

Yet they seem completely happy and content.

Take my daughter with you, Ash's words float through my mind. I wonder what Ash meant, what she knew . . .

"Your Highness," I whisper, not sure what I am going to say, only that I must somehow apologize and somehow explain.

Omer chuckles. "I have not been called that in many years. Around here, I am simply called Grandfather. Please, call me Grandfather."

I swallow against my swollen throat, and then I am able to form the words that mean more to me than I could have ever comprehended. "Grandfather, I am so very sorry."

The lightheartedness fades from Omer's eyes. "My child," he says as he steps forward and grasps both my hands. Levi has released my hand and is standing behind me.

"We know you were following your father's counsel," Omer says. "We forgive you, and you'll find no guile here."

I nod, my heart bursting. I do not deserve it. But I know he is sincere. As I look around at the people gathered to see me, I sense their hearts have long since healed.

"Come," he says, gently pulling my hands. "Let's visit for a few moments. Then I understand you have a wedding to prepare for." The sparkle in his eyes is back, framed by wrinkles of wisdom. I follow him to a circle of cut tree trunks, where we sit close to each other, and I tell him of my sister and her children.

I tell him of Shez and how I futilely tried to take him food. Omer's expression is grim as I speak. He does not ask about Akish, so perhaps we will discuss him another day.

My chest tightens as I tell him about my nephews, Nimrah and Jared the Younger, and how bright and kind they are—how Asherah has sent them to be apprentices.

Omer reaches over and places a hand on mine. "Someday, they will join us here."

I open my mouth to ask how he could possibly know that when I remember what he said to me when I met him. He'd been praying for me, just as he must now be praying for my nephews. Comfort washes over me, and I do not question him. I find that I want to believe what he is saying will come to pass.

"Levi has spoken to me about your marriage, but I wanted to meet you first," Omer says. "It would be my honor to marry the two of you under the commission of the Lord."

"Yes, I would be honored," I say without hesitation and realize I mean it more than I've meant anything in my life.

Levi joins us and places his hand on my shoulder.

"Thank you, Grandfather," I say, my voice trembling, "for welcoming me into your family."

"You've always been in our family; we have just been waiting for you to make the decision to come home." He kisses my cheek and clasps my hands. I squeeze back.

"Until this afternoon," I whisper.

Levi and I walk back toward the main village, hand in hand, Isabel running in front of us.

My heart knots and then expands as I think of marrying Levi in a few hours and the family who has greeted me so warmly.

My grandfather is right. I have truly come home.

ACKNOWLEDGMENTS

LEST MY READERS GROW WEARY of another Book of Mormon prophet novel, I decided to write something a little different, yet set in the same general era. Since writing an essay about the daughter of Jared for *Women of the Book of Mormon* (Covenant Communications, 2010), I've been intrigued with the idea of a woman whose wrong choices escalate into devastating consequences.

In the preplanning stages, I discussed this idea with my then-editor Eliza Nevin. It always means a lot to me to get an enthusiastic response, so I have to thank Eliza for that. I sent a proposal to managing editor Kathy Jenkins, and she encouraged me as well with two thumbs up. I appreciate the tremendous support my publisher, Covenant Communications, has given me over the past several years. When the project was put under contract, editor Samantha Van Walraven was assigned to the manuscript, and it has been a pleasure working with her in many aspects.

I'd like to especially thank my beta readers: Lu Ann Staheli, Julie Wright, and Loree Allison. It's a bit nerve-wracking waiting for that first critique to come back, and when it did, I was excited to receive such positive comments as well as much needed advice.

Also, members of my critique group offered great edits as always— many thanks to Sarah Eden, Rob Wells, Jeff Savage, Annette Lyon, Michele Holmes, and Lu Ann (again).

I must also thank those who are great supporters of my work and the time it takes to produce writing material versus other activities I neglect (like scrapbooking): my parents, Kent and Gayle Brown; my in-laws, Les and Jeanie Moore; and my husband, Chris, and our four children. (I'm not mentioning the cat since he can't read anyway.)

ABOUT THE AUTHOR

HEATHER B. MOORE IS A two-time Best of State and Whitney Award–winning author of the Out of Jerusalem series and *Abinadi*, *Alma*, *Alma the Younger*, and *Ammon*. She is also the author of the nonfiction work *Women of the Book of Mormon: Insights & Inspirations* and coauthor with Angela Eschler of *Christ's Gifts to Women*. Visit Heather's website for information on upcoming projects: www.hbmoore.com